C000124941

BURNING RIVER

JOSEPH H BASKIN

BURNING RIVER

Copyright © 2024 by Joseph H Baskin
(Defiance Press & Publishing, LLC)

First Edition: 2024

All rights reserved. No part of this publication may be reproduced, distributed, or transmitted in any form or by any means, including photocopying, recording, or other electronic or mechanical methods, without the prior written permission of the publisher, except in the case of brief quotations embodied in critical reviews and certain other noncommercial uses permitted by copyright law.

This book is a work of fiction. Names, characters, places, and incidents are either products of the author's imagination or are used fictitiously. Any resemblance to actual persons, living or dead, or locales is entirely coincidental.

ISBN-13: 978-1-963102-05-5 (Paperback)
ISBN-13: 978-1-963102-04-8 (eBook)
ISBN-13: 978-1-963102-06-2 (Hardcover)

Published by Defiance Press & Publishing, LLC

Bulk orders of this book may be obtained by contacting Defiance Press & Publishing, LLC. www.defiancepress.com.

Public Relations Dept. – Defiance Press & Publishing, LLC
281-581-9300
pr@defiancepress.com

Defiance Press & Publishing, LLC
281-581-9300
info@defiancepress.com

For my father – unconditional, unfailing encouragement

CHAPTER 1

Frank Wills's iPhone alarm went off at 6 a.m. He'd looked at the time every few minutes since five. Normally he got up at six whether he worked or not, but on interview days for a new job, so scared of oversleeping, consciousness always preceded the alarm. He got up and immediately set about making his bed. Hospital corners, tight as drums. If he had two quarters to rub together, he could bounce one off the covers to demonstrate his bed-making prowess. He walked the four paces or so to his tiny kitchen in this $550-a-month efficiency and started the coffee maker.

The other units in this shithole building had the unmistakable look of decrepit, run-down public housing. But Frank spent the first three days in his unit scrubbing every last inch of the 400 square feet and giving it as good a gleam as possible. Sparsely furnished, but everything in its place, spick and span. Coffee brewing, he stripped. Sweats, folded neatly, placed at the foot of his bed and his underwear stuffed into a laundry bag. He went into the tiny bathroom and started the hot water. No room for a tub in this joint, just barely enough space for standing and getting clean.

He shampooed his hair.

"Mr. Anderson, I know you've met a lot of candidates for this position, but I assure you none will have the experiences I've had. I led a Marine squadron in Iraq. Were you in the service?" He dunked his head under the anemic stream and rinsed out the shampoo.

"You were? Which branch? Then let him answer and you'll have to wing it. If Marines, you're golden; if Army or Navy, make a demeaning joke in good humor.

"If no, help him understand what it means to lead a Marine squadron. You see, Mr. Anderson, in the Marines we pride ourselves on our ability to act as a contained battle unit, even if there are only six or seven of us. To lead such a unit is to be flexible, prepared, adaptable, and, most importantly, effective. The way I will serve your firm."

He did a quick body wash, rinsed off, and stepped out. Wiping the mirror, he continued his rehearsal.

"I researched you online, and I know you do a lot of consulting for construction and urban planning, and I have a lot of ideas—innovations really."

A dollop of shaving cream in his palm, then another wipe down of the mirror and a close shave. Having performed this act in far worse conditions, he could almost do this in his sleep without a nick.

"I know I would be a real asset to your organization. Give me a chance to let me show you what I can do."

Toweled off, he grabbed his already laid-out clothes from the chair and dressed. He only had one good suit, but he wore it well. A light splash of cologne just in case someone got close enough to smell him but not enough to suggest he was an Iraqi going out on the town.

He stood at his counter drinking the coffee and looked out the one window in his place. Weak light came in. Late October, they'd yet to turn the clock back. But it had been unseasonably warm. Cleveland could be like that one minute, then drop fifty degrees and cold as hell the next. You had to enjoy whatever you got in this place.

After a lukewarm sip, he put it in the microwave. If coffee wasn't burning his throat going down, it wasn't worth it. He took it out of the microwave and walked to the window.

"Never thought I'd be stuck in this shithole city. So many stopovers in my life, and this is where everything comes to a screeching halt."

When his bitch wife kicked him out of the house, she offered to set him up in a decent place. Well, of course, she did. Her fucking parents were made of money. But there was no way he was going to accept anyone's handout, especially from those d-bags who'd forced the move to Northeast Ohio to be closer to them. He'd had better opportunities elsewhere, especially down south where his network of former Marines was stronger, but she'd threatened to leave him if they didn't move here.

"Ha!" The irony—she demanded a separation even after he capitulated to the move. And now he was forced to live down and out even though he'd served his country. Of course, she would have paid for at least a decent apartment with a couple of bedrooms so the kids could stay with him, but fuck her. If she wants me out, he reasoned, she'll have to wait until I can afford something nicer and then I'll take care of the kids every other weekend. Soon I'll be a huge goddamned success, and I'll buy a mansion.

The coffee finished, he rinsed the cup and put it in the rack. Nothing left to do but head out for the bus. He'd be early, but he subscribed to the notion if you're not five minutes early, you're late. He straightened his tie and grabbed his leather valise that contained his resume and a three-page detailed plan of his envisioned role with the company.

CHAPTER 2

Traveling via the Regional Transit Authority felt like a step backward. He'd had his own transportation up until three days ago when his car had thrown a rod. The mechanic chuckled as he gave Frank the news. Said it was divine retribution for revving the engine all the time and an engine rebuild would be more than the car was worth. Frank mirrored the guy's smiling face and told him to go fuck himself.

But this new job would be the start of him turning his life around. Here was a genuine opportunity for growth, not like the other jobs where they were content to keep him down.

He walked the short block from his apartment in Kamm's Corner to Lorain Avenue to catch the bus to Tremont. The firm's office was downtown, but the guy had suggested they meet in the trendy Tremont section to have a coffee and an informal chat. Whatever, Frank thought. I'll do it anywhere, anytime. They'll be lucky to have me, and I can make them see that no matter where and when.

There were only a handful of people waiting at the bus stop. Kamm's Corner boasted an ethnic mishmash like much of Cleveland herself—Irish, Italians, Hispanics, Blacks, Slavs of all sorts. Busy with stores, restaurants, and a farmer's market, it bustled with humanity. Frank liked it. He craved solitude but preferred to be alone surrounded by a lot of people. Rather than take one of the seats in the enclosure, he stood vigil in front of one support beam, as if at a parade ground, eyes scanning all the goings on. A part of him would remain on constant watch for unexpected trouble for the rest of his days—a consequence of two tours hunting IEDs.

In his head he continued peppering himself with interview questions. A battle is won before it's fought; the moment Frank shook the hand of his prospective employer the deed would be done. The bus pulled up, its front rack laden with bicycles. He waited while everyone else got on and settled himself in the middle preferring to continue his upright vigil. He stood facing front, eyes scanning all around. The smell of exhaust coupled with the need to balance himself against the swaying of the bus to him back to transports and Humvees. His smile faded as less pleasant associations intruded, but he performed the unconscious maneuver of sending them back down the memory hole and his contentment returned.

The ride was quiet. People's heads collectively entranced by their laps where their smartphones sat. Halfway downtown the bus stopped, and an elderly woman stood. She got up a little too early and pitched forward when the bus came to a complete stop, awkwardly hugging the bar next to the Black driver. Frank took a step forward but stopped when he saw the driver extend his hand to steady her.

"You okay, old girl?" he said with a grin.

"I'd be better if you'd get the lead out that foot of yours." She shook her head but was smiling just the same. As she descended the stairs, something blocked her exit.

"Excuse me, young men."

Two Black teens attempted to squeeze past her onto the bus before she descended to the street. They wore letterman jackets from St. Ignatius and big headphones situated above their ears.

"C'mon, now," the driver said. "Step down and get out of her way. I ain't leaving without you, show some respect."

The boys complied slowly with accompanying snide remarks and finger snaps.

They climbed back on bringing with them loud laughter. They looked past a watchful Frank, then chose seats right behind the driver, the ones designated for those in need. They seemed oblivious to their bus etiquette faux paus, or they just didn't give a shit.

Frank had seen thousands of these kids roll through in his days as an NCO. Their bullshit acts fell into one of two camps: those guys whose bluster gave way to embracing the system, embracing the authority and they became kick-ass soldiers, or they could never let go of their act and by extension, their fear and they dropped out. These two looked like the former. He could imagine their coach riding them pretty hard; it would explain their rambunctiousness when out from under his authoritarian thumb.

The bus pressed on with a whine of its diesel engine. Frank committed himself to keeping an eye on these two overgrown kids. They had the air of privates out on their first leave having just learned of the existence of prostitutes. Somewhere between trying out rap lyrics and making various wisecracks, they noticed Frank's watchful eye.

"Whatchu looking at?" one said.

Frank didn't answer but let his eyes linger on theirs for a moment before looking out the front window. His subtle smile remained.

"Yea, you better look away, you punk ass bitch."

They snapped fingers at that and carried on as before.

Nothing might have happened after that had circumstances gone another way. Just the random intersection of humans in a place and time, who then disperse, never to meet again. It wasn't as if Frank was really perturbed by them, just a minor offense to his sensibilities. Until then all they'd really done was act like the teenagers they were. No real harm done. But as much of life hinges on chance occurrences, their paths would be further intertwined by the next passenger who needed RTA's service that particular day.

CHAPTER 3

The bus came to a stop with a loud hiss of its brakes, and the driver opened the door. No one got off, but a woman slowly came aboard. She was a blond with her hair in a ponytail and a pretty floral dress. Apart from an oversized handbag she carried, she had what looked like at least ten pounds of kid bursting to escape the confines of her womb. She had a pleasant smile on her face as she scanned the bus looking for a seat. When no one made a move, Frank stepped forward to the young bucks from Ignatius.

"Hey, fellas, how about doing the right thing and give your seat up for the lady?"

They acted like they didn't hear him. The driver closed the door and started to move the bus along. Frank started to get a little irritated.

"C'mon, don't be assholes. You're young and strong – you can stand.

The one who'd mouthed off earlier slowly turned his head towards Frank while lowering his headphones over his ears. He gave a dismissive tongue click, turned his head away, and continued his rhythmic bouncing to the music. The other kid followed his ballsier friend's lead.

The woman walked past. An elderly Black man seated a couple of rows back stood up with a tip of his cap and offered his seat to her. She gratefully accepted. The man took a couple of steps towards the middle, grabbed a pole, and shook his head in commiseration with Frank.

"Kids today just don't got the same respect. A damned shame."

The woman made eye contact with Frank and flashed a grateful smile.

Frank balanced himself without the aid of something to hold onto, his blood still up. His mind raced through multiple confrontation scenarios with the two punks.

He waited until the leader looked his way (knowing curiosity always gets the best of us).

"What do you think of me reaching out to your coach to tell him how you behaved? Think he'd approve?"

The kid pushed his headphones atop his head with an irritated look. "The fuck you say?"

"I asked you what you think your coach would say if he knew how you behaved in public."

A dismissive wave. "Man, why don't you mind your own fucking' business. It ain't nothing to you."

The rest of the bus stayed quiet, the tension palpable. All sounds were muted apart from the whine of the engine and chuffing of the brakes. Frank knew he was being watched, and he also knew respect was a big thing among men. He went through a litany of responses for handling two overgrown adolescents with attitude problems; they ranged from doing nothing to violence. Before he could decide which direction to take, the bus reached West Thirtieth, and the boys stood and exited the bus.

The driver closed the door behind the two kids and shook his head.

"In my day we showed respect." The elderly Black man said.

Relief ran through Frank, down his spine all the way to his toes, and he despised himself for experiencing it, even though it wasn't on a conscious level. At this point, after all he'd seen and experienced, his visceral appetite, or even tolerance, for confrontation far exceeded his impulsive tendency to mix it up.

A well-preserved middle-aged woman responded to the elderly man. "Every generation has its rebels and miscreants. This generation ain't no different. If anything, it's our fault. We raised 'em."

Someone else spoke up. "At least that guy"—nodding towards Frank—"said something. The rest of us just sat here quietly."

There was a suspended moment as everyone waited for another comment, or a response from Frank. When nothing came all the gazes returned to their phone screens, and the bus plodded on to the tune of its engine, brakes, and transmission.

CHAPTER 4

When the Tremont stop approached Frank was grateful to get off the bus; he didn't relish the many eyes that followed him down the bus's stairs. Such a small confrontation, not even physical, and yet he felt all the telltale signs of adrenaline's rush and subsequent recession. He was spent and knew he had to rejuvenate.

He stood for a minute in the sun's morning rays like a snake on a rock, eyes closed, head tilted upwards. Deep breaths in and out. Then he walked over to the coffee shop—not a Starbucks, but local chic, thus every bit as expensive. He stood outside wavering on whether he should pull the trigger or not. Five bucks for a coffee was more than he could afford at the moment and, curse it, the prospective employer was likely to buy him one in about an hour, so he should just wait. But he wasn't sure he would be at his best. He'd be waiting for the caffeine and wouldn't be able to tolerate a change in plans, like what if the guy said, let's go for a walk or suggested they go Dutch; then he'd still have to spend the money and he'd be waiting for the caffeine's boost. No, chalk it up as an investment in himself and go for it.

Armed with his triple venti latte, he walked into Lincoln Park, the centerpiece to Tremont's trendy shops and eateries, and looked for a bench on which he could sip his coffee and recompose himself. It was turning out to be a glorious day. Already in the mid-sixties, the temperature promised to rise. There was a southerly wind bringing warmth and good smells. He sat on a bench, threw his Ray-Bans on, and leaned back. His telephone ringing shook him from his sun worship. The volume was set high to make sure he didn't oversleep this morning. It startled him, causing him to spill some of his coffee on his shirt.

"Fuck!" He put the phone down and stood up to clean himself while the phone continued its shrill reminder someone wanted his attention. He hated that fucking phone. Brought nothing but bad tidings. He looked at who was calling: Laurie. Speak of the devil...

"Yes, Laurie. What do you want to take from me now?" His anger at the coffee on his shirt, the lost caffeine, her intrusion on his meditation all compounded and came through in his tone. He sat back down and waited for her response.

She sighed. "Do you always have to have your claws out?"

"Ha. Look who's talking."

"Okay, whatever. I just wanted to remind you that John Paul has his birthday coming up this weekend, and he was really hoping you could be there."

He put the coffee on the ground and stood up again. "Where's there? You still having it at your parents' house?"

"Yes. That hasn't changed."

"How about your new beau, he going to be there?"

She stayed silent.

"Laurie? Your new boyfriend going to be there, too?"

"I don't know what you're talking about."

"C'mon, can't you even be honest?" Frank said.

"Have you been spying on me? Stalking me at the house?"

"Don't flatter yourself. Word gets around when you act like a whore."

More silence, then, "You know what, this was a mistake. Be better if you don't come."

"You've been trying to shut me out of their life anyway. Don't kid yourself. Fuckin' bitch."

He thought she'd hung up, but then he heard her take a deep breath. "Frank, I don't want our anger at each other to affect our son. You mean the world to John Paul. Please put aside your intense hatred of me and come for his sake. Forget about the rest. Just be there for him."

He massaged his temples, guilt temporarily pushing the rage aside. "I just don't know if I'll need to work that day, is all. You know I have an interview today for a new job. It's a lot of pressure."

"Well, I hope you get it and can still make it for John Paul," she said.

"You don't give a shit. Don't pretend now like you do."

"Okay, Frank, we're done." And she hung up.

His fury dissipated as quickly as it had flared up; he gave a moment's thought to whipping his phone at the nearest tree but controlled himself and did shallow laps around the bench, cursing. He appeared like a madman to anyone watching. He looked at his phone, thought once, twice, three times about calling her right back. But that would be just like him, wouldn't it? Yeah, just like ol' Frank to lose his temper with Laurie and then have to come crawling back with apologies. But it *was* her fault. The whole thing was on her. She was the one who ended things, violated her vows. For better or worse, didn't that mean standing by your partner when he goes through hard times? Loses a job or two (or three— but hey, who's counting?) and keeps on trying. Didn't he deserve that? Not in Laurie's eyes, or her cunty parents for that matter with their two acres and ponies and FUCK 'EM—he chucked the phone after all, but at the last second held onto it long enough for it to skip harmlessly across the grass.

Frank looked down at his white shirt, the one he'd ironed himself last night. He saw the unmistakable trail of spilled coffee and shook his head at his misfortune. He buttoned the suit jacket and that covered it up some. Well, nothing to do about it now. Had to adapt. He smiled wryly and addressed the employer sitting across from his mind's eye in the coffee shop.

"Yeah, you know how it is, sir, you buy yourself a fresh cup of coffee with a nice white shirt and wouldn't you know some of that latte is inevitably going to end up on you? Murphy's Law, right?"

CHAPTER 5

He slowly walked over and snatched the phone from the ground as if it was its fault it ended up there. Rather than take a seat in the same bench, he moved to one in the shade. Frank opened Safari and rolled through his favorites. One was freshly bookmarked. It was an article detailing a trend where men decided to shun the traditional coupling with a woman and venture out on their own.

He could see how it was an attractive stance. He'd had his own share of rejections by women, none as jarring as the recent separation from his wife, of course. More and more, of late, Frank resented being on the receiving end of punishment for generations of predeceasing men whose bill for indiscretions and domination was now coming due. Lots of support for women's rights, but no discussion of the men who had to be stepped over to right past wrongs. Didn't seem fair to him that he should be punished for the sins of others. If he perpetrated a wrong on someone, he'd be the first person to say he deserved retribution. These days at work you had to be mindful of not only things you've done, but also by someone who looked like you. A real crock of shit, if you asked Frank.

Telling women to collectively fuck off was seductive, though he didn't think he could swear off the sex. But the website didn't advocate celibacy. It suggested maintaining a businesslike relationship with a woman where goods are exchanged in one-off deals rather than coupling for life. Made sense. Men didn't do well in monogamous relationships anyway, and who needed the hassle of an affair. Immersed in these musings he only peripherally noted the presence of others. The sounds of a group pulled his attention from his phone.

Three Black teens were huddling in the gazebo at the center of the park's walkways. Their banter was loud, but they were staying to themselves. From where Frank sat, they were maybe thirty feet to his right. No reason to get upset, he told himself, but the resonance of his earlier encounter made him uneasy. He could feel sweat beading up on his forehead even in this shaded seat. He readied himself to move. Maybe return to the coffee shop. He felt sure they'd let him sit and wait. After all, he'd already bought a drink from them and was surely to get a pastry of sorts when his interview started. He stood.

From the periphery on his left, he saw a woman, and he spun his head in that direction. For a second it looked like Laurie. His breath stopped short until he correctly identified it wasn't her, then castigated himself for hoping it was, knowing it couldn't be. His heart hammered in his chest. What the fuck is the matter with you? She just called you from home, you know that.

Too many stimuli. The downside to having too much time before the big interview.

Time is a funny thing. There's no way of knowing the synchronicity of events; humans don't have the benefit of a bird's eye view. It is, however, worth noting the amount of time it took for Frank to do his double take, mistaking a stranger for his wife; that moment in time delayed him long enough to be in prime position to witness an event from which he couldn't, wouldn't walk. That millisecond difference changed Frank Wills's life forever.

CHAPTER 6

He turned back to the right to head to the coffee shop when he got a better look at the boys. They wore loose jeans and hoodies; two had big chains around their necks. They smoked cigarettes and laughed easily, no cares in this world. Harmless enough. But just then a Black woman in her twenties walked by them. She was dressed in a tight-fitting clothes that highlighted her God-given curves. Even the way she walked suggested she wasn't looking to get anywhere specific, but to advertise her sensuality and confidence. It was a hell of a thing to behold.

Frank saw all this in slo-mo, watching as she walked, picturing her like a seal swimming in the vicinity of Killer Whales. Hoping she would pass by without their noticing, but knowing, in that deep place where intuition lives and doesn't require proof, they were going to see her, and it was going to be trouble.

Sure enough, they spotted her and started following behind with catcalls.

"Hey, baby, why don't you come over here for a second."

"C'mon, baby, let's see you shake that thang over here."

She looked over her shoulder then stopped, one hand on her hip, an irritated look on her face. "What kind of shit is that? Yelling at a woman. Shouldn't you be in school? I don't think your mamas wouldn't want you acting like this."

Frank groaned. It was only going to urge them on more.

Sure enough, they moved towards her like a pack of wolves, one straight on and the other two fanning out to flank her like a sheep that wandered too far from its flock. She stood her ground, God bless her, straightened up and tightened her grip on her handbag.

The one who took the beeline towards her stopped right in front of her. Frank had been mistaken. He wasn't smoking a cigarette. From this close, and Frank stood maybe fifteen feet away leaning against a tree, he could see it was a blunt. After a hit on that, he tried to smooth talk her.

"Hey, I'm sorry about my friends, they're just a little exuberant."

She stood face to face with him, not backing down.

"Exuberant. Now aren't you just the scholarly boy."

"I ain't a boy, I'm a man; you can see that. And I can see you very much a woman." He pronounced it woo-man.

"Alright, play time's over, kids," she said and made to walk away, but the other two stepped in her path. She shook her head and made to walk around, and they blocked her again.

And maybe that would have been all they did, it's hard to say. Maybe they were just giving her a hard time, that there was no intention of causing her real harm. Just slow her down, give her a pain in the ass on this beautiful morning, but then be on their way. But Frank couldn't take that chance.

"Hey, fellas, why don't you leave the lady alone and go about your business."

They turned to him. Another country heard from. Only the leader didn't look at Frank. He kept his eyes on the woman but spoke to Frank.

"Who asked your opinion, old man?"

Frank lowered his voice, smiled, and walked slowly, hands spread.

"C'mon, man, there's no reason for there to be any conflict. You had a little fun with her, now just let her be. You can see she's dressed up to go somewhere, and you're holding her up. It's a beautiful day. What say you just let her be, huh?"

He held out his hand to the woman as an invitation to walk with him. She paused for a second and shook her head.

"Ah, no, my well-meaning white knight in shining suit. I don't need your help. Your old self can just move along."

The boys practically went nuts at that. They gave each other congratulatory hand slaps and finger snaps, whooped it up more.

"Looks like you just got told to fuck off, old man, so-fuck-off," Leader said.

Frank could feel his face turn red, but he backed away. If she didn't want his help, so be it. He didn't need the headache. But he forgot his plan to go to the coffee shop and instead found himself back on the shaded bench where he could watch as she told them off again and walked on. They let her go this time and when she passed Frank, she shook her head at him in a schoolmarm sort of way. Human behavior puzzled the shit out of Frank.

The teens returned to their perches on the gazebo like so many birds. The blunts came back out and the sweet, acrid smell reached him on the light morning breeze. Hard as he tried not to constantly check the time on his phone, he couldn't help it. Like a mosquito bite you know will be worse if you keep scratching it. He still had a half hour to kill, and he was getting antsy. Frank decided to walk around the park, get some light exercise, clear his head. Always better to be moving, he knew.

On his loop around he marveled at the hustle and bustle. Being on the work merry-go-round was a pain in the ass, but not as toxic to him as getting off. Problem was he'd gotten off (or more accurately had been kicked off) many times since leaving the service. He was grateful for the job interview. Time in between jobs filled him with the dreaded feeling of being on the outs of life. That was the only way to describe it. Being on the outside in the cold of an endless desert looking in on a club from which he'd be forever excluded.

His loop brought him closer to the gazebo; his thoughts returned to the punks hanging out there. Being honest with himself, he realized, he'd itched to teach them a lesson. Young kids have always been disrespectful. They needed their elders to teach them, to guide, and sometimes kick some ass to get them in line. He didn't mind doing it; far from it, he felt like to just pass on by and ignore it was to shirk a sacred generational responsibility. Nobody was doing the youngins any favors by letting them get their way all the time.

As if karma sensed his musings, another woman walked by the gazebo and elicited the same display as before. This one was middle-aged and white. Perhaps the youths sensed her timidity because they were less playful, less overtly sexual, and more menacing. Frank drew close enough to hear them badgering her.

"Hey, lady, give us a dollar for the value menu at Mickie D's."

"C'mon, it's just a buck. Do us a solid."

Frank stalked over there, straight at them, chest out, and put himself in between them and the woman.

"Uh, look who's back. Suit man with the coffee stains. Don't you work, man?"

Speaking to the woman, Frank said, "Have a nice day."

She didn't require further explanation; she hustled away.

Leader stepped out like he was going to try and stop her, and Frank positioned himself in front and they bumped lightly, enough for Leader to re-focus his attention. He forgot the lady, flicked his roach into the bushes, and puffed up his own chest.

"Alright, old man, looks like you fixin' for a fight. Ima bout to give you one."

"C'mon, man, relax," Frank said. He stood taller than two of them and the biggest, standing back a little, had a paunch and didn't look like much of a fighter. Even so, he had enough self-reflection to recognize he'd left the itch to fight several thousand miles eastward after too many violent encounters. He did his best to smile. "There's no reason to fight. I'm more of a lover than a fighter. You really need a dollar; I can hook you up."

"Man, fuck you," the chubby one said. The three surrounded Frank.

"Well, lover, you a faggot, ain't'cha?" Leader said. "You think we hustlin' out here. That's what you wanted, ain't it? Man, we really gonna fuck you up." He punctuated the last with a jab of his finger into Frank's chest.

Reflexively Frank grabbed the offending hand, twisted it quickly and had Leader in a subdued position, his head pushed down by Frank's left hand while he kept pressure on the arm and shoulder. Adrenaline took over and the apprehension vanished.

"What the fuck, man, you let him go before we fuck you up." They circled around him, bobbing up and down on the balls of their feet, Frank keeping leader's body between him and the two.

He leaned over and spoke in leader's ear as he carefully kept his distance from the other two. "What's your name?"

A grunt, then—"Gregory."

"Okay, Gregory, just calm down. I'm going to let you go. You gonna be cool?"

"Fuck you." Gregory spat.

Frank twisted harder and Gregory shrieked.

"You ain't as tough as you think, are you? You gonna be cool?" he asked again.

"Yes, godammit, yes."

Frank let go and backed away.

"What the hell are you doing?"

They all looked to the left. A middle aged Black postal worker walked towards them.

"You leave those kids alone."

Gregory took this as a cue and shouted loudly: "This fucking white boy came up to us and began yelling at us for just being here. He a racist."

Other people heard this clarion call and began moving over.

Frank looked around. The postal worker stepped between the boys and Frank.

"You bugging these kids? Why don't you pick on someone your own age?"

"I was doing nothing of the sort, sir. These 'boys' were harassing women passing by, and I wasn't going to let them."

"Let them? What are you, their master?"

Frank shook his head. "This wasn't a racial thing. Why does everything get reduced to that? They were acting like bone-headed teenagers, and I stepped in to teach them a lesson, that's all. Nothing racial."

More people crowded around and now there were about twenty people, mixed white and Black, encircling the five of them. Frank opposite the postal work flanked by the three teens.

"Why you think they need you teaching them a lesson? Who appointed you?"

Frank's hackles were now fully up; he smirked. "I guess they wouldn't need it if they had fathers at home who taught them how to behave like men."

Now shouts began raining down on him from the crowd, the loudest from the whites.

"You privileged piece of shit."

"Somebody needs to teach this white supremacist a lesson."

The postal worker shook his head angrily.

"I should teach *you* a lesson, but you won't learn. Just get the fuck out of here right now before I kick your ass."

For a moment Frank stood his ground, oblivious to the growing crowd around him cutting off any egress. His insides fumed at the way the situation spiraled out of control, his intentions refashioned into something hateful. But his sensibility prevailed; he knew nothing good could come out of a situation like this.

Just as he relaxed and made to retreat a punch came from the crowd and blasted across his face. Fists went flying, bodies, too. There was a scrum around him, and he was being pressed from all sides. Frank let his martial art instincts take over, parrying most thrusts, throwing a choice few of his own.

He didn't recognize the faces in front of him, but they were contorted in anger. No, rage and disgust, a look he'd also seen before some seven thousand miles away. In a strange pause that would etch forever on his memory he saw two scenes, one on top of the other like overlaid cartoon transparencies. Instead of Iraqis he now saw a riot of his own countrymen, but the look of pure venom on their faces was identical. He dropped to the ground in the fetal position.

He heard approaching sirens, felt the flashing of lights through his squeezed lids and was grateful.

CHAPTER 7

The air was easier to breathe, and he chanced a peek. People were scrambling and running away from the many police arriving on the scene. Frank exhaled. He'd been hurt far worse before. He stood, straightening his suit. It was fucking useless. There were more wrinkles than if he'd walked through the rain, slept in the damn thing. Making matters worse were the grass stains on the pants. That brought him back to coming home in summer evenings as a kid and his mother yelling at him for ruining another pair of pants.

Rough hands grabbed his upper arm.

"Sir, you need to come with me," a CPD officer said.

He pulled Frank to the street where the police vehicles had blocked off an intersection.

"Am I under arrest?"

No answer. Just tension on the upper arm.

"Hey, I'm a veteran. How about talking to me?"

The officer held him for about five minutes. Frank's insides stewed, but he knew calm would be the only thing to get him through something like this, so he breathed deeply and did his best to model placidity in the face of authority. Finally, the officer brought him to a sergeant with the recognizable stripes on his delts.

"What's your name?" the Cleveland Police sergeant asked.

"Frank Wills, sir."

"Well, Frank, you're going to have to explain this at the station. Give a full statement."

"Am I under arrest?"

The sergeant was a big man, sweating in the morning sun. He took off his hat, wiped his brow. "This is a big mess, and I'm not sure how things are going to shake out. Right now, we've got a dozen witnesses who said you were picking on a threesome of kids." He consulted a little notebook, seemed to confirm something, closed it, and looked back at Frank. "Had one of them in some sort of wrestling hold, spinning him around. Those were the exact words of several witnesses."

Frank looked at the badge. "Sergeant Boardman, I'm a Marine veteran—"

"And we thank you for your service."

"I appreciate that," Frank continued, "but what I was trying to say was it wouldn't be in my nature to spontaneously pick on three innocent kids. I don't have a record of anything of that sort. In fact, I have no criminal record whatsoever. Doesn't it seem unlikely I would choose today to lead a life of wanton violence? Dressed in a suit? In broad daylight? Maybe there's more to the story."

The sergeant looked around. There were a few people still milling about, hovering at makeshift borders manned by uniformed officers holding back the onlookers. Occasional curses and shouts reached their ears with great clarity. Boardman shook his head.

"I gotta take you in. No way around that with the crowd here and the way things are today. I'm sorry, but I gotta do it."

"Oh, c'mon. Listen, I have an interview with a prospective employer in"—he checked his phone which, thank the Lord, survived the pummeling—"fifteen minutes. How about this, if I'm not under arrest, I leave you my license, as collateral, this way you can be sure I will come by the station house, give a full statement or whatever. Just, please, let me go to this interview. I really need this job."

The sergeant shook his head and held out his hand. "If you don't show up by noon, I promise you I will have you picked up and I will ask the prosecutor to press all kinds of charges, first offense or not."

"I understand, sergeant, and I give you my word as a US Marine, I will be there."

Boardman's gaze went over Frank's head to something behind him.

A black box truck pulled up to where they stood. It shined like patent leather and had no markings, no windows in the back or sides. Two men disembarked and approached.

They dressed in jumpsuits of jet black like they wanted to blend into their vehicle. Their outfits looked like something a furniture mover would wear. They wore identical aviator sunglasses and ski hats. Walked right up to Boardman.

"Is this Frank Wills?"

"Yeah, I'm Frank Wills."

The men ignored him, waited patiently in front of Boardman.

"Is this Frank Wills?" Asked again, same monotone, no irony or anger.

The sergeant simply nodded his head, a perplexed look firmly in place now.

"We'll take him from here."

The other pulled Frank's arms behind his back and cuffed him faster than seemed possible.

"What the fuck?" Frank looked pleadingly at the sergeant. "What the hell is going on here?"

Boardman shrugged.

"What agency are you guys with?" he asked, almost in a daze.

The one on the left flashed a badge. Boardman squinted, but the badge was removed from sight seconds after being preferred.

"I'm sorry, sir, I saw something that said 'Justice,' but you didn't give me enough time to properly inspect your credentials." The sergeant adjusted the duty belt around his impressive waist, stood straighter.

The one who flashed his badge shot a glance at his comrade who understood the meaning perfectly—he led Frank away from the scene towards the rear of the van.

Frank looked pleadingly at Boardman who stepped forward, but found his progress halted by the man in black.

"Boardman, stand your fucking ground and don't move. There are things at stake here so far above your pay grade it would be like you trying to read newspaper print on the moon. Step back and let us do our jobs."

Seeing the withered look on Boardman's face, Frank started to panic.

"You can't do this, who are you and what do you want with me? Is this America? What's with this Gestapo bullshit?!" He struggled in his cuffs and would surely have escalated further—Marines don't easily let themselves be taken in without a fight—had it not been for a well-placed blow to the head from a sap.

The move was swifter than the sergeant had ever seen and he marveled at the economical way the two men stashed Frank's unconscious body in the truck. They boarded their truck without haste and left the scene with a flash of the sun's reflection off the sleek black vehicle.

CHAPTER 8

At its deepest Lake Erie reaches down 210 feet, but mostly it languishes at a pedestrian 60. The least of the Great Lakes, it could never be mistaken for the mighty Superior. Gordon Lightfoot didn't warble about Erie never giving up its dead when the skies of November turn gloomy. Years of toxic dumping when ignorance and expedience reigned only further damaged its reputation.

Unknown to most, though, Erie covers a secret held some two thousand feet below its surface. Spreading for three miles, a salt mine provides ample stores of the necessary element for melting ice and snow; it is a marvel of mining efficiency and resourcefulness. But standing at the water's edge, one would never guess at the riches beneath.

So it was that a crestfallen Dave Logan sat on the sand at Edgewater Park in his fifteenth summer and watched the water gently lap the shoreline. At fourteen, he'd broken through on the surfing circuit, a burgeoning promise of glory and fame. Then his parents divorced, and his mother forced a move from San Diego to Cleveland to be closer to her family.

And they called this a body of water. The locals splashed moronically around, no fear of getting slammed by a raging rush of white, let alone having to watch out for the occasional dorsal fin. Closing his eyes, he could see the endless Pacific; this was a cruel cosmic joke.

One day, on a whim, he'd brought his surfboard. If only to maintain the ritual. Not caring how stupid he looked, he even planted it firmly in the sand and stood by its side, like a forlorn sentinel to an abandoned castle. Chest out he practically dared anyone to offer a snide comment on his vigil.

An older guy with a raging farmer's tan and a paunch came up to him and struck up a friendly conversation. Dave shared his contempt for the pathetic lake hoping for a confrontation and maybe a small release of anger. But the guy laughed off the insults and shared his own surfing experience. Then he touted the possibilities of this little lake. Here, he boasted, you have to really earn it. He went on to explain that the peak months for surfing Lake Erie were the winter months when the waves kicked up.

"You want to be a surfer and a man, come here in the winter, and I'll show you how it's done."

Dave took him up on that challenge and it blossomed into a passion. Now fifteen years later, Dave stood in his wetsuit on that same shoreline, his board on the sand waiting expectantly. Never could he have envisioned even tolerating Cleveland winters, much less looking forward to them. He found the surfing here uniquely challenging. You had to wait patiently for a good wave, and when it came it was short lived, so you had to really maximize. A flight medic, he worked monthly clips, allowing him time to take off for the Pacific. And while he loved surfing out west, he was eternally grateful to this humble little lake and the lessons it taught him.

Today was a beautiful December Lake Erie day. Gray, cloudy and threatening. The waves topped five feet, maybe six. Angry, pugnacious water. No room for error, only total concentration. Perfect.

Dave stood alone on the beach. Another bonus to winter surfing— no crowds whatsoever.

A few stretches of his hammies, a brief run in place, knees kicking high, to limber up the wetsuit and get warm. Once in the water he would be fine—the intense concentration gave him a Zen protection from the cold. Afterwards was another story, but he kept supplies in his truck to warm up quickly.

Dave picked up the board and waded into the surf. He took a deep breath, got onto his belly, and paddled into the fray. The wind whistled past him, the bass of the surf pounding from behind. He heard something then, of a different pitch. Almost like a scream.

He scanned the gray horizon, ears straining. He saw only churning water—nothing out of the ordinary. Pleasure craft were all stored away, and nobody but those insane Polar Bears would dare venture out into these just above freezing waters, and they traveled in easily identified groups of middle-aged pudgy men. Dave resumed his paddling, then when the moment seemed right, he gripped the board tightly readying himself for the jump to his feet. He caught the swell at the right time and hopped up.

Just as the wave crested, he heard another shriek, louder this time and unmistakable. His concentration broken, the balance went with it, and Dave went ass over teakettle into the surf. He spun around a couple of times before he found his feet and pushed himself upright. When he surfaced and cleared his vision, he saw someone thrashing in the water. The sight was so bizarre for a moment he thought he must be hallucinating. The figure looked to be a man, about his age, dressed in what might have been a yellow jumpsuit, like the kind a mechanic wears, but now it looked in tatters. The man was near the shoreline but kept diving back into the waves. Dave grabbed his surfboard either to rescue the man or to knock him unconscious if need be. Sometimes the drowning person could be as violent as someone on PCP. Come to think of it, this guy probably was on PCP.

Yeah, this guy looked like he could be tweaking. Maybe he'd had enough of the drug life, decided to swim out into the lake until fatigue took over.

Drawing closer Dave called out, "Hey buddy, I'm a medic. I can help you."

But Dave's presence didn't register with the guy. Every time he got his feet under him he would frantically spin around as if looking for something, then dive back into the wave only to come up again sputtering.

Unsure how to approach, Dave called out again. "I'm a medic. I want to help."

Finally, the man stopped his thrashing. He was about six feet away, and his eyes were wild and shot with red.

"You seen Seth?" There was desperation in his voice.

"I'm sorry, man, haven't seen anyone besides you."

Another bout of wild spinning while scanning the water.

"Whoa, man. You gotta stop and let me help. It's real cold out here."

As if to underscore the point, the man's legs buckled at the next wave.

Dave thrust forward and caught him as he collapsed.

"Shit, man, you're heavier than you look. What's your name?"

Head down, the man groaned. "What happened to Seth?" Then he pulled away violently and turned to head back out to the lake. In his sudden movement he caught Dave in the face with the back of his hand and a long nail sliced Dave's cheek. For a moment, anger flashed, and he considered giving this yellow man up for lost.

But Dave knew, whatever intoxicant caused this guy to act so erratically, it would wear off and, in its place, would be a docile, probably likable fellow. Someone would miss him. Shit. So Dave wiped away the blood and cautiously followed behind until the man tired himself out and again collapsed.

The next wave hit them both hard. Dave could feel the just above freezing water assaulting him, its bite cutting through the neoprene suit. He couldn't imagine what it felt like to this shabbily dressed madman.

When yellow man again tried to gain his feet, Dave stepped in and grabbed an extended arm. He pulled the arm around his shoulders and lumbered, knees high, to the shoreline. Yellow man's legs collapsed again, and his head wobbled like he was ready to pass out.

Dave had no choice, but to ease the man to his knees on the cold, wet sand where he regained a little stability.

"Hey, stay with me. Look at me. Look at me. Okay, good. Now, tell me your name."

His yellow frayed outfit hung loosely, the skin showing through looked red and raw.

"Frank," the yellow man croaked.

"Okay, excellent. Frank. No time to give up, Frank. C'mon, let me help you before hypothermic shock sets in. In fact, I'm impressed it hasn't already. You must be strong as hell."

Frank was already shivering mightily. A bad sign, Dave knew, but worse when it stopped.

Dave's truck stood parked up the hill in the lot. His cell phone was there, too.

The man looked up with sad eyes. Up close, they didn't have the look of someone intoxicated.

"Where the hell am I?" he asked.

"Edgewater Park, Frank. Let me get you out of here and to my truck.

I got a portable heater, blankets, and hot water."

Dave reached out a hand, but the guy didn't respond, had his head down, sitting like a martial artist, on his knees. He finally reached out a weak hand.

"Okay, buddy, I got you, I got you." Dave helped him to his feet, draped an arm over his shoulder and grabbed at the man's waist. They started walking up the beach towards the hill on top of which sat the parking lot. The wind howled and pelted them with sleet. It was slow going with Frank stumbling along the way. Dave could feel the man's breath quickening. In short order Frank would be in complete shock.

"Where is Seth? Where is Seth, do you know?" Frank moaned.

"Sorry, buddy, I didn't see anyone else. But you have to work with me here, I'll get you safe, but don't fight me, okay?"

Suddenly Frank stopped and grabbed Dave in a death grip, looked into his eyes. "What year is this?" That sapped the remainder of his strength and he stopped talking.

Dave pulled his grip tighter and double timed it. Like doing an Iron Man dragging a two-hundred-pound sack. They were halfway up the hill when Frank's feet gave out altogether and he slid down Dave's body to the sloped ground. Dave's lungs and legs burned. But he knew he had no choice. He deep squatted, took the nearly unconscious man's arm, ducked his head underneath the torso and lifted him into the classic fireman's carry, something ironically, Dave hadn't performed until that moment. Standing and shifting the body he looked up agonizingly at the twenty-degree angle, took a deep breath, and growled his way to the top.

Reaching the tailgate of his Durango, he set Frank down and put his own head between his knees to catch his breath, then went to the driver's side, opened it, and pulled out his cell phone.

After calling EMS, he turned the engine on, cranked up the heat and lifted the tailgate. He had a whole ecosystem in there to combat the intense cold that followed being on the lake in December. The most unpleasant aspect to subzero surfing to be sure. He turned on the portable heater. He lifted Frank up into the rear and set him next to the heater; it was like moving an impossibly heavy rag doll.

Dave felt for a pulse and got that panicky feeling where he wasn't sure if he was feeling something or not. That usually meant not.

"Oh, shit. C'mon, man, stay with me." He had some basic first aid in the truck, but no AED. He grabbed at blankets to try and keep the guy warm. Frank's skin had the gray look that portended death. Dave heard the sirens in the distance. He kneeled over and checked for any breath or chest movement, then again felt for a pulse. Nothing. Out of habit he said aloud, "Starting chest compressions."

The EMS's growing wail filled his ears as he pumped on the chest; he hoped the cold weather would preserve brain function until the paddles could hopefully shock Frank's heart back to life.

CHAPTER 9

The opening crack of consciousness came with pain. His head hurt like a mother. His eyes felt heavy. As awareness grew so did the smells. Funny how powerful odors can elicit memory. His recollection of being in Burning River would be hazy, like a vivid dream experienced in flashes of emotions rather than images. But for the rest of his life, certain smells would bring back the trauma. A potent combination of urine and mildew. Normally one acclimates to the smell, the sensation fading. Frank's first clue that this place was different than any other he'd experienced was the smells never faded, never muted. He did not grow accustomed; the noxiousness never subsided.

He sat up, put his hands down, and felt the vinyl-covered mattress, thin, yet lumpy. Slowly rising, he looked at the platform on which the mattress perched. Like a hollow cut out of a concrete wall, its ledge knee-high. He found out its exact dimension by completing his stand and banging his head painfully on the hollow's upper limit. He experienced a fresh batch of head-pounding pain.

"Fuck." He rubbed his head as he ducked and stood aside the hollow.

At first, he thought his eyes hadn't fully recovered from the blow to the head by the black clad man (he remembered that well, along with the indignity of being taken into custody). The room wasn't much bigger than a broom closet. On one end was a metal toilet, sans seat, attached to a metal sink with three buttons and an upturned spigot. The water in the toilet looked clear, but there was such a reek coming from it he imagined it could never clear the generations of excreta there deposited.

Over the sink hung a piece of metal intended to serve as a mirror, but at best it reflected a funhouse image. He paced the room and came up with eight feet by four of floor space and estimated the height at higher than seven feet. Closed door on one end and blacked-out window at the other.

The only other feature was a makeshift shelving system behind the sleeping hollow. On one shelf stood several rolls of toilet paper. At least his jailers weren't cruel enough to leave him without the barest amenities of a civilized society.

He walked to the door and pushed. Locked. That figured but was worth the try. There was a small circular window near the top and a rectangular chute near the bottom, like a mail slot. The only light source was a weak bulb high over the sink that cast a weak and disorienting orange glow over everything.

Sitting back down (careful to avoid the top of the hollow), he patted the mat. On one end they'd left two blankets and the flattest pillow you've ever seen. The blankets were not the comforters your grandmother would leave for you near the Murphy bed. They were like a cross between a quilt and a tarp you'd use to protect a car. These could not be turned into anything resembling a rope or noose. He guessed these folks, whoever they might be, weren't interested in anyone deciding to check out on their own. Lastly, he looked at his own clothing.

They'd taken his clothing and all his belongings. He wore a jumpsuit, not unlike those mover-looking bastards had. The color was something light, he knew that, but the orange made it difficult to discern specifics. He had on Crocs instead of his loafers. No socks. He unbuttoned the jumpsuit down to his navel and could see they'd even replaced his underwear. Jockeys. He'd been wearing boxers since he could remember. That explained at least some of the tightness he felt in his nuts.

The cobwebs receded from his head and in their place came brief confusion followed by quickly developing indignation and rage. He stood and walked to the door, looked out the window. His eyes slowly adjusted to the darkness outside, and all he could see was a blank wall opposite him, maybe four feet away. He began banging on the door with his fists and feet. Though he could feel pain welling up in his toes, he didn't hear a sound.

"Hey, what the fuck is this place! Why do you have me locked up!"

His yelling didn't ring in his ears as it normally had done. Instead, he experienced a quiet he'd never before appreciated. Oppressive silence. Like the place wasn't only soundproof but could consume acoustics wholesale.

"You can't keep me here! It's against the law!" More bangs—hands, feet, then a desperate head butt followed by intense pain.

"Godammit. That was fucking stupid, Frank." He rubbed his forehead and sat back down.

"Okay. You need to be smarter than this. Obviously, you aren't in control here and you'll do nothing, but figuratively and literally bang your head against the wall and end up in the same place. So, fucking relax." He made arm movements signifying bringing his energy down while slowing his breathing down. After a few minutes of that, he stood carefully, grabbed the blankets and pillow, made his bed as best he could. Couldn't fold the damn blankets under the mattress, but seeing as how they weren't real blankets, and it wasn't much of a mattress, he gave that up. He lay back down on top of the blankets, folded the pillow under his head, and closed his eyes. He must have fallen asleep because the sound of metal grating jarred him awake.

Someone was monkeying with the chute on his door. He couldn't see anyone in the window. The chute opened suddenly, and a package was dropped unceremoniously on the ground with a hollow plop. Frank scrambled to get to the door, banged his head again on the hollow's ceiling, but propelled himself to the door just as the chute got relocked.

"Hey, hey, what the fuck is going on here?! Answer me!" He squinted hard, left eye pressed on the window struggling to see anything. Just that blank wall opposite. Not even a hint that someone had walked by. He pounded again, now oblivious to the pain he felt in his fists. Spent, his head low, he cursed. One croc inadvertently kicked at the package just dropped through the chute.

He bent over and picked it up. A cellophane-wrapped flimsy cardboard container, like Delta might serve you thirty thousand feet over Nebraska on your way to LA. He sat down on the bed and ripped it open. There was an eight-ounce carton of milk, a squeeze packet of peanut butter, a single slice of bread, and a clementine. He reflected for a moment. He didn't know how long he'd slept because there was no way to keep time in this place. Yet he found he wasn't terribly hungry. Certainly, the proffered repast didn't tantalize. He grabbed the milk, let the container drop to the floor, and opened the carton, tilted it back.

It took a millisecond to know something was wrong. He spat the milk out and looked for the date on the edge. Light too weak on the bed. Standing on the toilet he got as close to the light as he could and squinted at the date, turning the carton this way and that to tease it out.

He couldn't see the month and day, but the year read either 2007 or 2017.

"Jesus." Stepping back on the floor he spilled the carton's long-standing contents nto the toilet. It fell in nauseating chunks. He regarded the two buttons over the sink, one larger. He pressed the larger one and the toilet flushed in a roar worthy of an airplane's loo. The second button unleashed a weak stream of water that arced over the sink, just reaching the midway point. Bending down he drank some. It was lukewarm and tasted metallic; he hoped there wasn't something more sinister in these pipes. He lay back down, one arm over his eyes.

During the next days, he fell into a pattern of push-ups, sit-ups, and dips off of the edge of the bed. He did these as much for routine as to get the blood moving. Because he didn't have access to the outside, he couldn't tell when it was day or night. He thought he'd fallen into a pattern of sleeping mostly at night, but he could have been wrong. Three times a day there would be a delivery of the packages through the chute. Each time he would hear the rattle of the chute's lock he would spring up.

"Hey, you can't keep me here like this! I know my rights; you have to present me to a judge or something! Hey, I'm talking to you."

But he couldn't actually see anyone or anything. When he tried to look through the chute after the package dropped, he just saw the blank wall opposite his cell. Not even the hint of a shadow. His episodes of yelling and banging on the door dissipated quickly as there was no satisfaction in it whatsoever.

The variability of the chute's lock being open made it difficult to guess when it would happen, and it was over so quickly it left him little time to react. One time, after waking up and exercising, he sat with his back to the wall adjacent to the door and waited. When he heard the jangling, he sprang into action, kneeling before the chute and thrusting his hands through. He couldn't get a good view of who delivered the food, but this time he thought he caught a glimpse of a uniform. Groping blindly, he tried to catch hold of something. All he got was a whack across his wrists from something wooden, right on the bones. The intense pain from that experience learned him good not to try it again.

The packages all contained pretty much the same fare. Sometimes there were crackers with peanut butter, a small box of corn flakes, and occasionally a box of orange juice in lieu of a clementine. Hunger hadn't returned, but Frank knew he had to eat something. At this point he'd resolved not to give these bastards satisfaction. He wasn't going to buy it in this place, wherever and whatever it might be.

CHAPTER 10

After some time, he couldn't be sure how many days had passed as the idea of day had taken on a different meaning, something unusual occurred. Anything different stood out in bas relief to the monotony to which he'd grown accustomed. Instead of the metallic shaking, he heard a loud click while still lying on his bed at the end of a long sleep. In his somnolence, the sound registered in his dream before he consciously appreciated its meaning.

Pulling the charging handle back on his Marine issued M27. Locking and loading, muzzle pointed southward, but poised—always ready. Second nature, like buttoning a shirt or tying a shoe. Driving in a Humvee down dusty roads in the hot desert heat. On either side of him shops and vendors. Ramadi's market district. Well, the rebuilt, ad hoc market district with the occasional stores still intact, but makeshift stalls wherever room is available.

The vehicle is a common site to these folks, but an annoyance, like the ever-present bugs. Frank stands atop the vehicle just behind the .50 caliber Ma Deuce and its tucked-in gunner. He poses like George

Washington crossing the Delaware, eyes peeled for any sight of trouble. An IED, or a suicidal, pissed-off Iraqi. The rolling sound of the Humvee is soothing, its armor comforting.

He sees himself as an arm of liberation, never accepting the naysayers' accusations of oil conquest or indigenous subjugation.

They roll down the road, Frank nodding his head in approval of the crowds coming out to repopulate the *souk*. The lead vehicle begins slowing, and Frank focuses forward and sees a man dressed in a traditional *thawb* and *kefiyyah*. He looks like he's just crossing the street, reason enough for the Marines to be cautious, but then stops right in the middle and is shouting, gesticulating wildly. Not a welcome sign for the Americans. Frank gives the signal to stop vehicles. He bends down and bangs on the right-side door.

"Alibaba! Get out here."

Their translator disembarks the vehicle. Just so happens he grew up outside of Detroit, but that doesn't mean anything when nicknames are being handed out.

"Tread lightly, Ali, he looks pissed."

A half salute and Ali steps to the front of the convoy. Frank's Humvee is second so he can just about hear the man shouting above the general din in the street coupled with the idling V8s.

Ali listens to the man's rants and occasionally shouts back some translation.

"He's had it with the lawlessness."

Loud guttural shouts, the man's face red and sweaty.

"He had a prosperous clothing store with his two sons, and now they're dead because of ISIS."

The man keeps up his shouting, looking from the Americans to the Iraqis, scanning from one side of the street to the other, hands then going into his flowing robes.

"He comes back to his store to find it destroyed and then it becomes looters rule, no respect for elders, no respect for tradition. You Americans have done too little to keep real peace; he has lost the will to live."

The man brings his hands from his robes and there is a grenade there and he pulls the pin but holds the lever and shakes his explosive fist around. Like birds fleeing a predator, the people on the street scatter in every direction away from the man. Frank's insides go cold.

"Weapons down; lower your weapons!" He tries to keep his voice calm while being as firm as possible. He slowly descends his vehicle while speaking to Ali.

"Tell this man that we support him. We hate what happened to his sons and the lack of respect. Tell him *I* respect the hell out of him and his courage."

Ali speaks while retreating behind the front vehicle. Frank gives the signal for the Humvees to slowly reverse giving them breathing space.

"Don't shoot. He's a dead man with that grenade. But we are not letting this guy die." He addresses his guys, his band of brothers. "You all understand; he-doesn't-die. This is a good guy who's at his breaking point; this is not a terrorist."

The man continues his waving while Frank slowly approaches, his own hands up, gun swinging free from his shoulder.

"Sergeant, don't go any closer," one of his guys implores.

Frank is within ten feet of the guy, speaking softly.

"Hey, I'm on your side, I am not letting you die. You're a good man—godammit, Ali, translate—" Ali hastily catches up, and Frank continues in his most soothing tone, "We are here to help. Please let us help."

A single shot rings out, but it doesn't come from behind Frank, and the front of the man's robes grow crimson, he falls to his knees, still gripping the grenade. In that millisecond before he collapses, his eyes meet Frank's and there is a connection, a communication of sorts. There is gratitude for Frank's gesture of kindness and a hint of relief to be released from the chaos and sadness he's had to endure.

Frank turns and leaps underneath the Humvee as the man expires and his grip goes slack. An explosion in his mind, in his dream, in his oh-so vivid memory like it just happened.

CHAPTER 11

lothes felt wet and sticky, throat dry. The dream receded quickly, but his conscious mind nagged at him that something was different. There had been a loud click. It wasn't just his dream. The door now sported a crack of light where it met the frame. Frank tentatively sat up, stood, his habitual motion now taking him well clear of the hollow's ceiling. He walked in slo-mo to the door and gave it a gentle nudge. It opened. He didn't cry when his mother died, but he nearly did when this door opened all the way. He looked left, then retreated. Crouched down and rolled into the hallway, sprang up ready for anything. But anything turned out to be nothing. As in, nobody, nothing. Just a dead-ending short hallway to the left and a long one to the right.

The color of putty spanned from the floor to the walls to the ceiling. Not even another cell in sight, which seemed strange, but then Frank realized his whole frame of reference was warped by the near sensory deprivation chamber masquerading as the cell he'd inhabited for who knew how long. Only a little more light in the hallway, but he could not spot a source. It was as if the surfaces themselves were luminescent.

He continued his deliberate tiptoeing down the hall for reasons he couldn't verbalize. Not wanting to wake whatever entity existed there to sound an alarm.

But why would an alarm be sounded? he reasoned. Clearly, they (whoever they were) wanted the door open because it was they who opened it. But perhaps they opened it to lure him into a trap. Should he stay in the cell? Was he missing a rare opportunity if he didn't act? He tried to shake free from circular thinking, but found that only intensified it. One foot in front of the other, that was the ticket.

The unchanging tones of the monochromatic hallway compounded his fuzzy head. Not enough protein in the food, he told himself. The fucked-up sleep wake cycle. All these elements of psychological torture he'd peripherally learned about during his time in the service. Reading about it was quite different from experiencing it. The combination worked to disorient; he would testify to that.

Much like a ship traveling the ocean, looking on horizons of endless waves, a sailor doesn't appreciate shoreline immediately and questions the sight. Frank thought he saw a T in the distance. Drawing nearer it resolved itself, and he could clearly see a choice, to left or right. At the same time as that realization hit, an odor wafted over to him. So different than the usual diet of noxious fumes, this one was pleasant— barbecue: meat cooking, sauce blackening on ribs. When he got to the T, the smell intensified to his left. On the right however, a light shone, brighter and nurturing in its intensity. Similar to the sun's warming rays. Drawn to that light, he turned his back on the smell despite his stomach's grumbling and made his way right.

The walls, floor, and ceiling were a stunning white. A clean sheet billowing in the wind from its perch on a clothesline white. He reached out to stroke the walls, his hands glowing pink like when you put a hand in front of a flashlight. But like the previous hallways, he saw no evidence of the source.

His footfalls felt softer somehow, and his energy improved. With renewed spirit he made his way forward until he saw a dogleg to the left. He slowed up and peeked around the bend. Nothing but more hallway. Proceeding with less caution, he came finally to a single elevator. Like any other, he supposed, only there were no buttons on the outside and nothing above to indicate where the car currently stood.

He tried to jimmy the crack in the middle, but there was no give. Frank stepped back for a moment of reflection. Feeling something like a mouse in a maze, he accepted this was a dead end. Turned and headed back when he heard the doors slide open behind him. No ding, no ceremony, just an almost inaudible movement of gears. His cynical mind told him the doors would close just as he got there, but his deeper limbic brain registered fear and assured him the elevator would welcome him – as it did.

The hairs on his neck stood up. As bright as the vestibule in front the open elevator shone, that was how pitch black the interior looked. In fact, under normal circumstances light shines into darkness creating some areas of shadow. Not so here. It was as if the elevator brooked no illumination into its confines. Turning back didn't dawn on him even as his heart thundered behind his sternum.

One leg acting as counterweight to his leaning torso, he attempted to peek in while keeping a foot in the light. No use. Nothing to see. He marveled at the way the light bisected his form from top to bottom at the entrance. Straining to see did nothing; there was no light inside to perceive no matter how big his pupils became. Sliding a hand along the inside front walls, straining to find the usual buttons on an elevators front wall, he felt only smooth metal. He stepped all the way in and turned back to the vestibule. He knew he'd only taken a step inside, but the vestibule looked at least ten feet away. Anger replaced fear and he welcomed it as a change towards something more active.

"I've had enough of these optical illusions. You can find yourself another fucking guinea pig."

He made to leave the elevators when the doors closed, leaving him in the dark amid a blackness he'd never before experienced. Pressing down on him from all sides with enough pressure to force him to kneel. No sound, not even that of his own breath came to his ears. Had he not had the sensation of his knees on the ground, he would have no sense whatsoever.

Frank stood unsteadily. Without his sight, his balance faltered, and he felt queasy. He widened his gait some and the nausea subsided. He walked ahead slowly, feeling for the door. Even a couple of steps left him feeling lightheaded, and he stopped to collect himself. Head between his knees, drawing shallow breaths, he heard a click just a moment before the elevator car descended like an anvil in a Bugs Bunny cartoon and rendered Frank weightless.

CHAPTER 12

The car came to a soundless halt as quickly as it had launched its descent. Frank was left crumpled on the ground as the opened doors revealed another vestibule, similar to the one he'd just left. Frank looked up into that light like he might have done at the moment of birth had he the cognizance to do so. He shielded his eyes, reached out to it slowly. With trepidation and on wobbly legs, he stood and made his way slowly out. Frank turned back to the elevator and spoke shakily.

"Thanks for the ride. You could use some decor and an announcer. You know, bottom floor coming up, watch your ass, that kind of thing." The doors closed.

Just off the vestibule a dogleg to the right, opposite the arrangement upstairs.

"I suppose architectural consistency is antithetical to fucking with minds." His voice still trembled. He looked back at the closed elevator and understood the unspoken mandate to move forward.

"Alright, here we go." His equilibrium improved with each step. The coloring in this hallway was the same putty as around his cell. The bright, shining light he'd felt upstairs, so nurturing and re-energizing, gone. He felt its absence in his core.

At the end of the hallway there again was a T. Peering both ways he saw a long corridor and doors at each end.

"Eeny, meeny, miney, moe…" His finger pointed to the right, and he walked.

The door at the end didn't have a knob. He gave it a gentle nudge and it gave.

"Let's see what's behind door number one, shall we."

Before he stepped in, he heard a gut-wrenching sound. It was one he heard before, but never like this.

Laurie could never tolerate it when their kids cried. She could always be relied on to cave into their tantrums if they pitched enough of a fit. The more tears, the more theatrics and yelling, the quicker she relented. Not Frank, though. He understood, if you give in you only reinforce the behavior and worsen it for the next time. He learned to compartmentalize the shrieks, the tearful entreaties; he put himself in a faraway place and observed the behavior from a distance.

The cacophony overwhelming his current senses was every pitch of a baby's cries from the earliest mewlings of a newborn to the full-throated screams of a three-year-old. And the sound rose and fell like crashing waves, one atop the other, with no interruption. He couldn't compartmentalize this; it acted like a blade cutting through even the toughest Zen armor.

He made to turn back, but the door closed, and he couldn't get any finger hold. Grappling with the edge he only succeeded in breaking a fingernail.

"Fuck." He put the damaged fingertip in his mouth, turned and backed up to the door.

The hallway gently sloped upwards like a tunnel from a locker room.

Slowly, licking his minor wound, he made his way to the mouth of the shaft. It deposited him in a circular room, quite spacious. Despite the intensified sound of crying, whose source he still didn't see, the sight that filled his eyes was as welcome as any he'd remembered. The room was teeming with people, their forms hazy as if seen through the shimmer of heat emanating from blacktop.

"Oh, thank God." He made a beeline for the first person, back to him. Drawing nearer, he saw it was a woman in a jumpsuit like his own, only in forest green.

"Hey, could you tell me what is going on here?" He shouted above the din.

The form turned around. It was a woman, young, maybe in her twenties, long stringy blond hair. She appeared unkempt and the most striking aspect of her appearance were twin wet spots over her breasts.

"You got the stuff?" she asked, a desperate plea in her voice.

"Uh, what?" He couldn't keep his eyes off her breasts, the crying seeming to bring more wetness to the general area. She didn't even notice, just raised her voice.

"You got it? 'Cause I need it badly." She began clawing at his jumpsuit. Others heard her and turned to him. A ripple ran through the crowd of forms as they turned like a chorus line to face him. All women, he now saw, and each one sporting the same twin wet spots over the chests of their jumpsuits. They began crowding in on him, and he flashed back to the scene just prior to his arrest and panic set in.

Hands reaching out, grabbing at his retreating body. A barrage of entreaties from all around him. There was nothing sexual in these shouted requests; they were more like need for water from a person starving of thirst.

"Give it to me!"

"I need it badly!"

Above it all the incessant rise and fall of the crying, the source unseen.

"I want it first! I'm jonesing bad!"

"Stop being stingy! You know what I need!"

Frank spun around and fled down the tunnel towards the door. Moving felt like it did in dreams, painfully slow, unable to generate the kind of momentum that could lead to escape. His dread intensified as he approached the door, fearing the fickleness he'd already come to appreciate from this place. He wasn't sure what these women might do to him if they could trap him in this narrow tunnel, but he could easily envision them ripping him apart like a pack of hyenas, searching him for whatever they believed he harbored on his person. The desperation conveyed in their eyes convinced him of that.

He hit the door hard with his shoulder and heard a click, the door rebounding back open a crack. Grabbing at the lifeline, he jammed his fingers in it, pain be damned, and ripped the door open. There might have been hands reaching out to him from behind or it could just have been his imagination because nobody was behind. The door had slammed behind him and with its closure the oppressive silence returned like he'd put on ear protection at the gun range.

Running down the hall that seemed longer than when he first traversed it, arms pumping away, he came at last to the T and did the Looney Tunes skiddoo on his right foot before thrusting himself to the left.

Out of breath about halfway back to the vestibule, he slowed and looked over his shoulder. Nothing but the putty walls, ceiling, floor. He stopped, breathing heavy, and squinted as best he could to lengthen his vision. Still nothing. He couldn't even see the T any longer.

"Oh, Jesus. What the fuck was that, and what the fuck is this place?"

Hunched over, hands on his knees, laughter bubbled up uninvited and uncontrolled. The nature of distances was all out of whack here.

"Normally, when you haven't been somewhere, the way there feels longer than the way back 'cause you got some familiarity." He looked up and around. "Everything's opposite, ain't it. You really got this placed wired for sound."

More laughter as his heart rate came down and his breath normalized. Standing straight he looked in the distance at the T that he knew beckoned him. Could he stand to return to his cell without checking out door number two? What was waiting for him back in that lonely cell? Nothing that couldn't wait just a little while longer. He walked towards the T and when it again materialized, he slowed down and stayed to the left inching forward. He approached the angle where the wall would no longer obstruct his view and stopped, ears perked to detect any sound. Steeling himself, he moved a little forward and peered around the bend.

CHAPTER 13

Empty.

Just to be on the safe side, he double-timed it backwards towards the second door keeping his eyes firmly on the door that stood between him and those demented, grabbing women. Satisfied nothing stalked him, he turned and approached the second door. This one had a curious handle: like something you'd see on a refrigerator or freezer.

He gently tugged at it and felt the grip of a vacuum seal. Both hands and a little more force led to some give, but no success. One foot on the wall, both hands and a grunt later, he felt the seal give way and the door opened inward. A blast of cold air – welcome after all his running and sweating – hit him.

Through the door another tunnel, this one leading steeply down-wards. At its end weak light made an anemic attempt to illuminate the passageway. The tunnel's ceiling cut off any view of what might lie at the end of the slope. Turning sideways he inched down like you might on a mountainside.

"Getting real cold." He hugged his chest, feeling himself shivering.

"Or maybe you're just scared shitless again, Kemosabe."

At the bottom he realized he'd seen another optical illusion. He didn't reach an opening, per se, but a low ceiling. He crouched down and inspected. There was a low circular tunnel on the ground, two feet in diameter, maybe six feet long, he couldn't be sure. In this light he couldn't tell what stood at the end of the tunnel. He would have to do the span on his stomach or back, wriggling until he got to the other side.

Frank stood back up. "Christ. I am not taking that bait, man. There's no fucking way I'm putting myself through that." He'd never considered himself a claustrophobic, but he couldn't stand the sensation of being in dimensions like a coffin. Even when he knew it was temporary; like this one time touring a cave in Israel and they told him, hey, it will just be a minute and I promise you on the other side is pussy, oxygen, life—it didn't matter. It was a no go.

He turned to make his way up the slope back to the door and exit. And wouldn't you know it, putting his foot up the slope, he couldn't find purchase; seemed that a slick of ice had formed just after his descent. He lunged upward and slid helplessly back down to the bottom. After two more futile attempts he lay on the ground, out of breath, hands up in surrender.

"Okay, okay, you win. Looks like I'm crawling through the coffin tunnel of death."

He got into a crouch, one hand on the low ceiling of the tunnel and tried to survey the terrain. Going back to habits. Tried and true, that's the way.

Problem was, everything was colored in the same tone and badly lit. In fact, if he kept his gaze for just a few seconds it all came out of focus. No bas relief. He tried again, really focused, and only succeeded in falling on his ass.

"Shit." Frank righted himself and turned back to the slope upwards towards the door where he entered. He gripped the wall and jammed a foot as sturdily as he could muster. Rocking back and forth like a kid psyching himself up for a water slide, he drew a deep breath and launched upwards, scrabbling with both feet and hands.

Sliding back down on his ass didn't bring the same shame as the first time, but it came close. Sitting, facing the coffin tunnel once again with little recourse.

"Oh, fuck it."

He reappraised the situation, crouched at the aperture. Go forward on stomach, he decided. Won't have to look at the cursed ceiling pressing down on him. He looked behind and thought he might have three feet in which to try for some sort of running start. Need to get as close to the other side as possible with some momentum. He backed up to the wall, one hand caressing it while he willed his mind to seeing himself through to the other side.

"And what's on the other side, Frank, genius, that you're so keen on getting to? Huh?!"

He shook his head free of the doubt, giving in to the fact that he seemed to have no choice. "Shit, gotta stop thinking. Doing, that's the key. Doing. Okay, here we go."

Pushing with his legs he gave a powerful thrust and slid headfirst like it was the game-winning run. The momentum took him well into the tunnel, but not to the edge.

"Christ."

It was painfully close in here, both his shoulders nearly rubbing the walls. He couldn't but look ahead and try to use his outstretched arms like seal flippers; hard to get any purchase. His breathing intensified, sounding like hurricane winds in his ears. He willed his heart and lungs to slow down, offering himself reassuring words and images. The edge seemed tantalizingly close. If he tilted his head this way and that, he could make it out. Inching himself forward, he made painstakingly slow progress ---

Something on his leg. Grabbing at his ankle. He kicked his feet, couldn't tell if this was genuine or his fucking mind playing tricks on him. Or this place. He desperately tried to angle his head to see, but it wasn't physically possible. Stuck in here with his arms pinned above his head, useless.

His goddamned breathing, now so fucking loud, coupled with his heart hammering in his chest, drowned out other sounds. Perspiration ran into his eyes and stung. Despite all this Frank willed himself to draw perfectly still for one second and succeeded for a moment—quiet. Nothing.

Then he felt something against his leg. Unmistakable.

"Fuck you!!!"

Driven by rage and sheer panic, those zombie ladies on his mind, he heaved himself forward like a demented caterpillar until at last his fingertips found the bottom edge of the tunnel. Ripping a couple of nails, he got enough of a purchase to wriggle clear of the hole.

Chest heaving, hands up in defensive position ready to kick whatever the fuck emerged from the tunnel, he sat there. Nothing emerged. Slowly, slowly the adrenaline receded and with it some of his sanity.

His panic abated; he wiped his brow on his sleeves. It looked like he'd dipped his arms in a bucket of water. Hands on his knees, breathing deeply, he realized the only thing left to do was contend with whatever this obstacle course was guarding so assiduously. And was the tunnel meant to keep others out, or prevent what was inside from getting out?

CHAPTER 14

The slope upwards, identical to its slippery brother on the other side, was clear and easy to climb. Frank did so slowly, keeping his eyes front. At the crest it opened to a sunken circular area, maybe half the size of the women's area.

There were little groups of figures huddling together. They all wore the same jumpsuits; these looked like they might have been white at one point, but now were varying degrees of discoloration, from off yellow, to some that were heavily streaked with black.

The overall atmosphere in here didn't have the dangerous feel of his last stop. He didn't know how he knew, but he felt it. He stood fully on the crest and descended the other side easily to the floor. The ground felt uneven, like a field in late winter, early spring on the cusp of a thaw. The temperature felt a shade over freezing. Welcome after the exertion, but he could feel his body temperature falling rapidly. Frank walked up to the first group of four sitting in a circle. They were men, ranging in age from young to old and those who regarded him did so with benignity—or resignation.

"You gotta lighter by any chance?" one asked, his jumpsuit filthy.

Frank was so startled by the placid way it was asked he almost didn't respond. He quickly said, "I don't. I'm sorry."

The response was an almost imperceptible shrug.

In the middle of the circle was the makings of a fire pit, and there were some pieces of wood smoldering, but it offered no heat or light. Beside it was some frozen meat, or what might have been meat—it was hard to tell. It was obvious, though, it'd gone bad; some parts looked positively gray. Still he could see these guys had ripped off pieces from it. He could only imagine the hunger that drove them to consume it.

"Fellas, I was wondering if you could tell me where we are?"

No one answered. They kept their eyes fixed on the would-be fire in front of them, shivering. Each one appeared to be cachectic to some degree. Every once in a while, someone from the group would prod the wood, grab a couple of sticks and rub them fruitlessly together. Frank moved on and found other groups in a similar state. He saw no place where they specifically slept but could see some metal toilets in one corner of the area.

"So, I'm guessing I'm not going to get much in the way of food or answers here, so I'll just be moseying along." He clapped his hands together like Clark Griswold and started back for the door, then stopped, his body going colder than the room.

The huddled groups sat in a depression, ringed by rising slopes. Identical rising slopes. From this vantage point he saw nothing distinguishable. He didn't even see his footprints anywhere.

None of the huddled men in their dirty white jumpsuits so much as flinched as he sprinted around their perimeter looking for some indication of where he came in. Finally, he ran up the hill and stood on the crest looking down. The light (no source he could espy) reflected oddly off the bottoms of the slopes on the other side, and he saw nothing to indicate which one hid the coffin tunnel. To make things worse, like spokes on a wheel or the playing pieces of Trivial Pursuit, each slice was cut off from the others by a wall. He saw no other option; he had to explore each area individually and systematically to avoid repeating the same area. Not an easy task given their uniformity.

He ran down the slope.

"Don't anybody get up or anything. Don't worry about me, I'll be fine."

Nobody stirred. Far as he could tell, they never took their eyes off of the pathetic fire pits in front of them.

The sweat of exertion and panic combined with the cold to make him shiver. On the third hill he crested, he saw something different than the last two. It looked like ground, but higher than the other two sides, and he suspected this optical illusion kept any of the more intrepid dirty white jumpsuit men from venturing out of their frozen prison.

Sure enough it wasn't a true ground, and he slid through until he came to the opening of the coffin tunnel.

"I never thought I'd be happy to see you again."

A glance behind to make sure he'd not been followed (he hadn't), and he didn't hesitate for a moment—he launched himself back into the tunnel. This time he slid easily to the other side without a problem. Like it didn't care if he was leaving. He wondered briefly if the slope would still be too slick to traverse, but he sensed this place would have trapped him on the other side rather than here. And sure enough, he was able to climb back up without a problem, pushed open the heavy door and gratefully stepped back in the warmth, shutting the door behind him.

He stood with his back against the door. A mighty shiver rolled through him, starting from the top of his head all the way to the home going piggies on both feet. He might have lost some urine, but he didn't care.

"I think I've had enough exploration for one day. I get it, it could always be worse. Enjoy what you got. Make the most of your situation. Holy shit."

Frank walked more confidently now, convinced this little adventure was over. In fact, he knew the elevator would be waiting for him, its vast darkness opened to ferry him back to his single cell and shitty meals. It wasn't looking to surprise him now.

The ride up wasn't as nauseating. The doors opened back up to the vestibule from his floor. They all looked the same, but he felt sure this was where he came on. Sadly, the bright light he'd enjoyed previously was gone, the putty luminescence in its place. He returned to his cell and found the door open. Much to his surprise, his spirits were lifted when he saw the package of food being pushed out of the way as he opened the door. He munched on his food with delight, enjoyed a satisfactory evacuation, then lay down gratefully and thought of what he'd seen. He dozed off to a sound and dreamless sleep.

CHAPTER 15

When he awakened, the door was locked again.

He stretched, made his bed, and began his exercises. His mind felt clearer. He reviewed his recent excursion from the safety of his cell.

"I have to wonder about the food they're giving me. Seems plausible they lace it with some sort of hallucinogen. Probably didn't see half what I thought I did. The whole thing was just a fevered dream."

Another set of push-ups. He felt slimmer, for sure, but he didn't feel stronger despite the consistency of his calisthenics.

The lock on his chute clicked and another package dropped to the floor.

He picked it up, looked it over, yelled out the window.

"Don't you have anything different? More fucking crackers and peanut butter?! How much peanut butter can one man consume?!"

The door, window, and wall across remained impassive.

Turning away he did his short pace to the opposite wall and heard the unmistakable sound of the door's lock being released. He looked at the container in his hands.

"I haven't eaten you. You can't have me tweakin' just yet."

To confirm, he pushed on the door. It opened easily and soundlessly on its greased hinges. Such a heavy door and yet almost weightless to the touch. Yet another of the paradoxes in this place. He returned to his bed, sat, and opened the food package. A tangerine, cheese crackers, the ever-present tube of peanut butter, and, miracle of miracles, chocolate milk.

Daring to hope, he inspected the carton for a date, but, alas, smudged. A hopeful sniff after opening it.

"Shit." It didn't smell like the cow had been milked in 1991, but it didn't smell good. He couldn't take the risk and replaced it in the package.

"Fucking bastards!" Frank shouted. Peeling the fruit, he regarded the open door.

"Practically daring me, ain't ya? What other strange and mysterious shit you got planned for me out there?"

The tangerine was on the dry side, but edible. He spoke through a mouthful to the door. "You know I can't sit here with that fucking door open. I've gotta go back out there."

He thought of taking the crackers with him, but the jumpsuit had no pockets, and he didn't think he was quite ready to make use of his human pocketbook, especially for perishable food items.

A deep draw from the lukewarm and metallic tasting water, a quick whizz, and he felt ready to go back out there. He stepped out and made his way down the dimly lit hallway, no sound but his own breathing. When he stopped for a moment and held his breath, there was such an absence of sound unpleasant ringing welled up in his ears. Finally, he came to the T.

When he approached, he once again picked up tantalizing smells from the left. No bright light on the right this time.

Seemed he was meant to go left.

"Well, here goes nothing."

With each step the smell grew; it didn't smell so much like charred meat, but how a diner smells in the morning with eggs and bacon cooking. His mouth watered; his stomach grumbled.

"What are you complaining about, you got your daily staple of peanut butter."

In the distance a change in his field of vision. In this place of deranged optics, he couldn't be sure what he saw, but he knew with each step he drew closer to whatever it was. Another downwards slope revealed itself to him and he understood why he saw a change in the coloration of the walls and floor from afar. A final breath to steel himself at the edge, and he descended the gentle slope, pupils open to the their max while his brain deciphered the sight at the tunnel's widened end.

CHAPTER 16

When historians write of war, they usually focus on the politics leading to conflict, the major battles waged, the deals made in the aftermath. The truly intrepid will delve into the mind-numbing tragedy of the collateral damage including the ubiquitous refugee. But nothing written can compare with the sight of an ingathering of the displaced, the hungry, and the traumatized. In Iraq he'd seen a colossal warehouse converted for such a purpose. Inside you could barely navigate all the people, the areas set up to feed and provide shelter to a horde far greater than the edifice could hope to possibly accommodate.

It was the first thing he thought of when he contemplated the scene in front of him.

Like the interior of a scaled-down Superdome or basketball arena. The light didn't hit his eyes until he crossed over the threshold from the tunnel into the open area. The ceiling looked like the night sky projected by a planetarium. Plainly not the real open sky, but a damn reasonable facsimile replete with the moon, the source of white light. He knew it to be a poor facsimile to the sun or even the real moon, but since he'd acclimated to the dimness of his cell, this produced a positively brilliant glow.

A round space of grand proportions, the single most dominant aspect of which was a tall chain link fence encircling an inner portion of the area. Inside the fence were tents in concentric circles. From where he stood outside the mouth of the tunnel, he couldn't see past the array of tents, but he could see a trail of smoke ascending above them from the center. Overall, it looked like a scene you might see from the prairie in the 1880s if you came across a tribe of Lakota. The ground looked fairly clean, the tents organized.

Then there was the situation outside the fence. Trash, strewn about. No tents here, but random pieces of debris set on the grimy ground. Like something from New York City in the 1980s where the homeless congregated.

More important than that were the many figures he saw in various activities outside the fence, each one in a similar jumpsuit to his. Whereas his remained yellow, theirs bore the scars of wear and tear. Many looked torn and haggard, the yellow dulled and blackened with dirt.

He walked cautiously towards a group of three, two lying on the ground, the third with his back to the wall. They each bore the look of the resigned.

"Hey, how you doing?"

No response from any.

Frank crouched in front of the seated fellow. He looked to be in his fifties, or he might have been younger, but had some rough mileage on his wheels. He looked gaunt and emaciated. His nose bore the hallmarks of someone repeatedly bashing it in and his pitted cheeks spoke of few meals and a history of cigarette smoking. On one side of his jaw, he sported a bulge like he had chew or something in there.

Frank waved a hand in front of his glazed eyes.

"Hello? Anybody there."

No answer.

Frank left them and did a quick tour of the area outside the fence heading counterclockwise. The whole area had an omega shape to it; the only other exit he could see was a tunnel whose opening was inside the fence. There were toilets, the doors to the stalls hanging off a single hinge if on at all. No place to shower from the looks of it.

Beginning to despair he'd ever encounter another functional human in this place, somebody spoke to him.

"They won't respond. See his right cheek? He's got mash in there. Feeling no pain."

Frank rose. Before him stood a healthy looking older Black man in a spanking-clean cream jumpsuit, a fanny pack, beard, and a knit cap on his head.

"You can call me Pastor," he said and extended a hand.

Ignoring the hand, Frank said, "Who the hell are you, and what the hell am I doing here?"

"A man who gets to the point. I can see why they brought you here."

Frank stepped in aggressively and grabbed the upper elbow of Pastor's arm and pushed him against the fence. "Who's the *they*, who the fuck are you, and what the fuck is this place?"

"There's no reason to get worked up; ain't going to do you no good." There was no aggression in his demeanor. "I can give you some help if you relax."

Frank let go of the man's arm and stalked away. He walked back the other way ignoring Pastor as he stomped past, deftly avoiding some of the men haphazardly lying around in varying degrees of consciousness. The combo of body odor and urine was powerful enough to cut through the food bouquet. He went back the way he came, past the tunnel leading back to his solitary cell and scoped out the other side. Pretty much a mirror image, though, of course, the human debris varied…but not by much.

One way in (already used) and one way out (no access unless he scaled the fence; that didn't look like too hard a chore). He leaned against the fence studying the goings on in there. Somebody on the inside spotted him at the fence and gleefully yelled.

"Lookit the new banana! All fresh and unspoiled. Hey, Pastor, bring him over here for a match, he looks fit as a fiddle." Three guys in crimson jumpsuits stood around, all of them appearing well fed. The guy yelling had a baggy outfit; the other two wore tight fitting jumpsuits. They moved towards the fence as if they had all the time in the world.

Frank began climbing the fence aggressively.

"Thataboy, jerkoff, come get some."

"Look at this fucking asshole, all balls, no brains."

Nearing the top Frank felt a forceful tug on his ankle. He tried to kick free, but it was surprisingly strong.

"Come back down, hear. Do you no good to get killed so quickly."

Pastor's face exuded calm, his voice not much above a whisper. Frank heard and froze near the top of the fence. The three crimson guys continued their taunts but made no move to come closer. Slowly he descended back to the ground. His wind was short, energy spent. He looked pleadingly at Pastor.

"What the fuck is this place?" he finally asked.

"Hey, c'mon with me away from the fence. Those guys will be trouble."

Without looking back, he gently brought Frank away towards the wall and sat him down.

"Take it easy, young man. This is a lot to take in." A hand on Frank's shoulder.

"I don't want to take it easy." He jerked free of the reassuring hand. Pastor took no offense.

Frank grew angry again. "Where the hell am I and why am I here?" He grabbed at the front of Pastor's clothing and pulled him in. "If you know something, you tell me now."

Ice water and compassion in his veins, Pastor eased free of Frank's grip.

"Just so you know, I'm not part of management. So there are things I know and things I don't. I'm happy to share with you what I can, but some of it will be hard for you to understand right now."

They squatted at the wall.

"What's your name, son?"

"Frank."

"Well, Frank, you're looking at the intake pod for the jail." He made a sweeping gesture. "You can see there are two parts. Inside the fence there is food provided to the group, shelter (he pointed at the tents), and protection. Out here is the opposite—no food, no shelter."

As if to underscore his point he stood, walked over to a prostrate form, and lifted it into a more comfortable position.

"Why would anyone be out here?" Frank asked, just as another thought occurred to him. "How does one get inside the fence? I didn't see any entrances."

"There's only two ways to get inside. One is to scale the fence. But you gotta know before you go—there are a finite number of outfits designated for the interior of the pod. To stay inside the fence, you have to climb it, get inside, and take one of the outfits by force. That is how you get to stay."

"What does that mean? You gotta kill the person who is wearing it?"

"That would be the most extreme. You could simply beat him into submission and take it. But it has to be taken by force. Otherwise ---"

Someone behind them groaned. Pastor crouched down besides the man, pulled something from his fanny pack, and put it inside the man's mouth. The man's face went from screwed in agony to a flash of gratitude and repose.

Frank prompted. "What happens if I just jump the fence and blend in?"

"Well, if you're not there with a red jumpsuit, the men in black come and get you."

Frank started laughing. "Men in black? This must be an elaborate nightmare. Or maybe I'm in a coma in a hospital somewhere."

"I wish it was. But this is happening, my friend. I'm sorry to have to break it to you. If it makes you feel better, I'm a prisoner just like you."

"A prisoner of what? Who are our jailers?"

A shrug.

"You rest for a moment. You've been eating sub-nutritional food for some time, I'm guessing." Pastor stood and continued his ministrations to the scattered figures who lay around like so much debris and refuse.

"What the fuck? How did these men just give up?" Frank asked.

Pastor turned to Frank, furrowing his brow.

"How long would you estimate you've been here?"

No immediate answer, Pastor continued, "Not so easy to determine, is it. And you just got here. Some of these guys have been here long enough to understand real despair. You put some more time under your belt, and we'll revisit that question—if you're even still curious. I suspect you'll get it soon enough."

"Hey, you said there are two ways to get inside."

Pastor stopped and looked over. "You can agree to participate in the nightly fights. It's the one way to break up the monotony. Everyone looks forward to them. If you can knockout Boxing Betsy, you're king."

"Boxing Betsy?"

"That's what he's called. He does some pretty gruesome things when he knocks a guy out."

He pulled Frank up and guided him to a specific area of the fence.

"See there?" He pointed at a spot through the tents. From this vantage point they could see to the middle and a fire roaring there, a big man seated in front on a lawn chair.

"Jesus. He's a big fucker, ain't he. They get guys willing to fight him?"

"It's sport, you understand. Guys out here get to a point of desperation where they simply don't care if they live or die. And everyone who fights gets enough mash to zone out afterwards."

They stood at the fence for a moment looking at the fire, fellows in crimson milling about.

"Why doesn't anyone escape?"

Pastor looked at him and paused. "Now that's a different bag of worms, isn't it, Frank?"

They stood facing one another for a moment. It still felt surreal to Frank. And even having been isolated, craving human contact, he couldn't believe how exhausted he was by what Pastor told him.

"I'm going to go back to my cell. I still think this is one big fucking nightmare, and I'll wake up soon enough."

He walked away. Pastor called after him. "Just so you know, nothing changes over there. You can stay in your cell as long as you want, eating that bird food they bring you, but nothing will change."

Without turning back, he replied in a voice not loud enough to carry, "Thanks for pointing out the obvious."

CHAPTER 17

After three sleep/wake cycles, push-ups and sit-ups nearing a thousand, Frank (and especially his stomach) decided it was time to go back and do more recon.

He arrived again down the tunnel when the ceiling advertised nighttime. Well, he had a one-in-two chance. Some of the figures outside the fence could be found in the same places with little change. No sign of Pastor this time. He parked himself between two zoned-out men with the best view of the fire inside the fence. The three of them, Frank and his two flankers, looked like cheese sandwiched between two stale, gray slices of bread.

Not a lot of activity inside the fence. Pastor's words came back to him. His only means of getting inside the fence would be to scale it and beat someone into submission. He looked up to the top.

"Not as easy as it looks."

Frank looked to his left.

The graying man smiled wanly, his missing teeth making him look like a jack-o'-lantern. He seemed oblivious to the odd contortion of his body: his torso and legs lay on the ground, but his head was unnaturally propped up on the wall so he could see forward. "I know the look on your face," he said.

"You do, do you?" Frank noticed muscle wasting, but this guy was probably fierce in his heyday.

As if reading Frank's mind, he said, "Was on my face not too long ago. That look I see on yours."

"What happened?"

"I tried two different times. Almost made it the second time; that beating nearly killed me. See, if you don't succeed, the fellow's crew, the one you target, they come after you to dissuade further attacks. Like a pack mentality in there. Anyways, I probably should have let them kill me rather than go on living like this."

"Why don't you go back to your cell?"

The guy didn't answer, just grunted. Then he pointed.

"Check out the fit of those jumpsuits. See, if it's baggy it means he defeated someone bigger than him. If it's tight, the opposite. Not a lot of those tight ones because they don't last. So if you're really interested in staying, you gotta take on someone bigger so people know not to fuck with you."

"Can you choose the same person repeatedly?"

"Sure. That happens. Someone weakens with repeated attacks; everyone sees it, continues to focus on him till he falls. But you gotta be careful, because again these crews can be funny. Some see a weakening comrade and come to his aid with greater force, and some see him as a liability, and they just let him sink or swim on his own. You gotta choose carefully," he said gravely.

"You know anything about the guys inside?" Frank asked.

Another grunt. "I can tell you they're all jackers."

"Jackers?"

"Armed robbers on the outside. Guys who take what they want with force and no mask. They don't give a shit who can identify them because they fear no man. That's what makes them so dangerous."

"Who is the top cheese?"

"Chucho. The boss. He's a fierce one."

"Where does this Chucho come from?"

No answer.

Frank took his eyes off the fence and looked at his new best friend. The mans' eyes were closed, though his chest still rose and fell.

"Thanks for the information. You rest now." He patted the man's shoulder, stood, and walked to the fence. Gripped it tight to get a feel and even started to climb, then jumped back to the ground, rubbed his hands together.

"You going to make a try?"

Frank didn't have to turn to recognize Pastor's deep voice. Something about the air of religious authority brought out the adolescent in Frank.

"I don't do violence for violence's sake," he said, dimly aware he was cutting his nose off to spite his face.

"Too bad. You ain't gonna last long with that attitude," Pastor said.

"What the fuck does that mean? I'm not a criminal. My mind doesn't work like these lowlifes. I shouldn't even be here."

"Yet here you are. They brought you here for a purpose. You can fight that purpose, or you can embrace it. But there's only one way through."

"I didn't do anything to warrant this type of jailing. This is bullshit."

"Didn't you?" Pastor asked.

Frank just stared at him, then waved him off. "Go fuck yourself, Father." And he stomped off.

"I'm not a priest," Pastor called after him.

"Whatever," Frank said under his breath.

CHAPTER 18

Each time he ate the proffered food in their shitty packages he felt worse. It was starch hell. When hunger settled in, it was unpleasant, but an equilibrium emerged, and he found he could think more clearly. When he indulged in just a nibble, carb craving overtook his whole consciousness with an intensity he wouldn't have believed possible. And no matter how much he indulged he never felt satiated.

He'd been lying back in his cell, trying to come up with a plan. The chute opened with a clink and a package dropped to the ground. Restless. Fucking restless and trapped.

He snapped out of bed and stumbled a bit, lightheaded, got his legs under him and checked the contents (more fucking crackers and peanut butter); he chucked it to the other side to rest among several other opened and unopened brethren.

"Have to clear my mind, have to dig deep." Pacing seemed to help. They'd locked the door since he came back so there wasn't much space for it, but it felt like action all the same.

"Fickle motherfuckers!" He shouted at the ceiling, but of course the cri de coeur, emasculated by the oppressive acoustics, lacked any catharsis.

"You want me to be your bitch, don't you. To march to the beat of your fucking drum. But that ain't me. Yeah, I was in the military, but I was a Marine, godammit, and that means independence, pride, and courage." A pound to the chest with each proclamation of Frank's virtues.

Already worn out, he sat down hard on the mattress, hands on his head, pulling at his hair.

"What the hell is going on?"

He lay back down and focused his intellect, ignored his emotions. It was a daily exercise when he was a combat sergeant, and he needed to get back in the habit.

"Sometimes you went days without sleeping, eating MREs when you could get your hands on them. This isn't pleasant, but it isn't the end of the world. You need to think."

Back to a sitting position.

"Two options as I see it. Either A, you figure out how to get inside the fence and stay there. Or B, you try again to escape." His breathing sped up unconsciously, and he realized just how much he longed to avoid even the elevator, let alone whatever ghouls this place still had in store for him. But deep resentment welled up and refueled the furnace of his anger. He stood up. Began speaking but realized it would be sheer stupidity to announce his intentions and clasped a hand over his mouth.

Bottom line, he thought, I don't deserve to be here; I'm not going to do what they say I should. I'd rather take my chances on my own.

It was at least four more restless sleep/wake cycles before he again heard the distinct click of the door opening. By then he had an impressive six pack, but only partly for the right reasons. His body fat had dropped, but so had his muscle tone. His strength was diminished; he could feel it.

Propping the door open with a makeshift door stop (several empty package husks pressed together and slept on), he collected the food he'd saved, those items he thought would provide him at least some of the energy he'd need. He folded his sleeves around the packages as he had practiced.

One last look at his cell and out he went. The light in the hallway remained brighter than in his cell, but muted all the same. At the T, his stomach gurgled.

"Keep quiet."

A turn to the right, away from the enticing smells. Despite having traversed this section previously he couldn't gauge the distance. He decided to whistle for company and did so, off key, to the tune of Stairway to Heaven. The vestibule appeared just as he came to the Jimmy Page guitar solo. Elevator doors stood closed and impassive. He stood facing them.

"Open sesame."

Nothing happened.

"That was a joke. I didn't really think that would do the trick."

Tired, he settled down on his ass, back against the wall facing the elevators, arms on his knees. He lifted them in supplication.

"Oh, Lords of the elevator, open thy bounty that I might partake in thee and get the flying fuck out of here."

Still no action. He unfolded his sleeves, a package of crackers dropping from one side and a tangerine from the other. Munching on them he eyeballed the elevator doors. He'd been to Vegas once; everyone should go at least once. It wasn't to his liking. He enjoyed the flash of it all, but the slot machines offended his sensibilities. Variable timing for payoffs put him in mind of a rat pressing a lever for the chance at cocaine. You fuck with dopamine in the brain, and you can manipulate a person to do just about anything. He didn't understand the logic of letting someone else dictate when you walk away. And it was this that came to mind watching this jerk-off elevator hold him hostage. He willed it to open; some time passed.

Noiselessly and without fanfare the doors opened. Not believing his fortune, he stood up slowly, his knees creaking. He squinted, straining to see inside the elevator, but it remained impervious to light's penetration. Slow steps towards the velvety blackness inside and then a hesitation. He didn't want to move but felt compelled to push forward. Like a gentle hand to the small of his back, so much so he actually turned around to confirm nothing stood behind him.

Standing at the edge of the elevator's abyss, his eyes adjusted slowly, and he struggled to make out any details. Two spots glimmered briefly, about eye height, then vanished. Like the need to periodically use peripheral vision for stars because direct sight fails, he adjusted his head position, moved his eyes. But it remained impenetrable. He would have to give in and submit his fate to the capriciousness of the elevator's whim.

Frank drew a deep breath and stepped over the threshold. Once he broke the plane of the door's entrance, the scene inside resolved like a camera's aperture coming into focus. Sets of glimmering rubies at eye level popped out of the blackness. Then arms extended towards him, and panic kicked up and he made to retreat. A painful slowness to his movement as if the darkness were matter, thick and impassable.

He awoke with a start, his heart racing, shirt soaked through. Still sitting on the floor, the elevator doors firmly closed.

"Jesus." He looked all around, but the walls remained stoic, held their secrets. After a moment he understood. "Alright, I get it. I'm going back." Standing uneasily, tangerine peel falling to the floor, he collected himself and walked back to his cell to regroup.

CHAPTER 19

I t took one cycle for Frank to abandon any pride at having to return to the land of Pastor. He *was* the only source of decent information. A left at the T and the hallway gently sloped downwards.

"All roads lead downtown," popped into his mind. At the bottom of the tunnel he crossed the threshold, once again experiencing that dramatic change in scenery.

"Fuck," he said. It was again faux night.

Rather than risk any confrontations, he slinked off to the side and crouched to give his eyes time to acclimate.

"The prodigal son returns."

Hand shielding against the night's light he looked up at Pastor.

"Everything's got religious connotations, don't it," Frank said. His spirits buoyed, despite himself, and he realized he was glad to see this man.

"Occupational hazard." He offered a helpful hand to stand.

Frank took it and stood.

They strolled, Pastor's hands folded behind his back as if this was simply a walk in the park. The activity outside the fence once again resembled the streets of Europe during the bubonic plague. Figures lay about in various states of unconsciousness and desperation. The two men weaved their way around the scattered forms.

"How did your thinking time go?" Pastor asked.

Figuring he'd take a page from the people he'd met here who deflected questions with those of their own, he said, "How come you're here? You don't seem like an armed robber."

"I'm not. I have a different status."

"Which is?"

"I have passage to different areas in order to provide spiritual succor to those in need."

"You're Christian?"

"I am," Pastor said.

"You look like a Muslim with that kufi," Frank said.

"It's a covering elders wear. A sign of respect in here. How you know about the kufi?"

"I spent some time in Iraq." He didn't say more, and Pastor didn't press. Frank appreciated that. He asked, "Why haven't you used your free passage to get out of here?"

"Look, Frank, everyone has their reasons for being here, their personal journeys. Mine is my own. Let's talk about you."

"Okay. I wandered upon other areas of this place, too."

"Did you?" Pastor said, a curious note in his voice.

"I did. There's an elevator on the other side and it took me down to another level. There were two different rooms. In one there were intense cries and lots of women with wet fronts who looked like they would attack me. The other was real cold and there were only men. They kept trying to light fires, but couldn't and they just huddled, shivering in the cold."

The older Black man fingered his beard thoughtfully. "Looks like you came across the drug addicts and arsonists. See those women are here because they'd forsaken their children for illicit drugs. The crying stimulates their breasts to produce milk; that's why you saw the wet tops. The arsonists are doomed to eternal coldness without the provisions to make a proper fire."

Frank stopped, a smile plastered on his face, and put a hand on Pastor's arm.

"What the fuck are you saying? That this place carries out some sort of divine retribution?"

The Pastor countered with an enigmatic smile of his own and a wave of his hand.

Their walk ended where the fence forced them to stop. A wall extended into the fenced in area, the opening to the other exit, the one Frank couldn't access.

"Where does it lead?" he asked.

A shrug from Pastor. "Many things, like your encounter with those other pods, can't be explained. They have to be experienced. One last piece of advice."

Pastor stopped and put his hands on Frank's shoulders.

"Don't take too much time. Already I can see you wasting away. Happens when you eat just what they give you. The only real protein you gonna get is inside that fence. The longer you wait, the weaker you gonna get."

Normally Frank didn't do well with men putting their hands on him, especially when it was done in an affectionate way. He restrained the impulse to throw the hands off.

"You're telling me I'm trapped in here without any due process and my only option is to join the rabble by becoming a jacker?"

Pastor nodded. "You still thinking about your rights and all that?"

"Of course I am. I was arrested on bullshit and taken by some guys in these kind of jumpsuits, but in black. Looked like movers."

"What? You were brought here by couriers?"

"That what you call them?"

"Couriers, but mostly people just call them the men in black."

"Why the look on your face, huh?" Frank asked, not liking the puzzlement on the Pastor's usually serene visage.

"Just unusual for someone to remember being brought here by them."

"How did you get here?"

Now Pastor's smile returned. "That's for a different day. For now, you need to think about your priorities. Usually they don't open the cells until guys are calmer and understand they won't be getting the type of satisfaction they're used to. You need to adapt to a new situation. Energy spent lamenting the 'injustice' of it all won't get you anything, but weaker."

A moment's reflection, silence between the two. Then Frank offered a hand. "I'll wish you a good night."

Pastor shook it but held for a beat. "Why not just spend the night here? If you want you can always go back in the morning, but at least you'll see the regular activity. I'll get you a mat."

He weighed his options, but he didn't really have to wrangle—being around someone with whom he could converse outweighed any other option. But he made it seem as if it was a struggle. "Fine," Frank said at last. "I can do that."

"Good. I'll be right back with a mat."

Frank strolled some and stumbled on the same guy he'd talked to previously. Same position, too, head propped up against the wall, body on the ground. Looked dead, but there was a shallow rhythm to his breathing indicating lingering life. Frank sat beside him.

Pastor brought over a dirty something that might have once been a yoga mat.

"I see you've met Tommy. Good. He knows about the way things work. He can fill you in."

"Already did," Tommy said, eyes still closed.

"Signs of life." Frank smiled.

"You're in good hands. See you in the morning," Pastor said and walked away.

Frank stretched out his mat and lay down, arms crossed behind his head.

"You know, this 'sky' or whatever it is is quite pretty if you don't think about anything else."

"Where you from, Soldier?" Tommy asked, unmoved from his position, eyes still closed.

"How do you know I'm a soldier."

"Overheard you talkin' to the Pastor. Said you was in Iraq. I just assumed."

"I'm from out west but moved to Cleveland for my wife's family."

"And now you're in here, man. This is your home."

Frank sat up. "Yea, but I don't belong here. That's the fucked-up thing; I didn't do anything."

Tommy opened one eye. "Oh, you're serious. Because you know, everybody says the same goddamned thing, right? Nobody thinks they belong here."

"Well, I'm here to tell you I didn't break the law. I stepped in the way of some punks assaulting women, and it got out of control. But no prosecutor would pursue charges, I can promise you that."

A deep breath, but still no change in position for the grizzled man. "You think you're in the county jail? Look around you—this ain't inside any jurisdiction I know of. I mean, this place makes its own rules. And it ain't bound by any laws I ever heard of. I mean, it ain't like the

ACLU is coming around the bend at any moment."

"So what the fuck is this place?"

"What you think?" Tommy asked after a moment.

"I don't know. I just assume it's a kind of rendition. You know, an extrajudicial location the military or CIA take unfriendlies to sweat them out."

"Man, you were in the service, you fought in combat, and you know about rendition. You trying to tell me you were a boy scout in combat? Because I'd venture a guess that the reason you're here has more to do with your record in the service than whatever you did just before they picked you up."

"I sleep just fine at night; my conscious is clear," Frank said, some plaintiveness in his voice.

Tommy's seemingly sole working eye opened again for a sarcastic glance at Frank. "What did Mr. Shakespeare say about too much protest?"

Frank lay back down. "Fuck you, man."

"I'm not trying to insult you, soldier boy. This place don't tolerate passivity. It only rewards aggression. If you choose to defy her, she'll make you pay. You gotta harden yourself, man. It's the only way you'll survive. And surviving is the only thing worth doing in this place. I've said my piece." The eye closed.

Frank closed his own and breathed deeply. He didn't think he'd fall asleep, and maybe he only lingered in half sleep, but he dreamed of his wife in better times. When they'd camped out for a week in Zion National Park. They were in love then, their whole lives in front of them. When he woke briefly between sleep cycles there were tears in his eyes; he wiped them away and shifted his body on the mat.

CHAPTER 20

Frank woke to Pastor kneeling beside him.

"Rise and shine."

He rubbed the sleep from his eyes and looked around. The ceiling reflected a clear blue sky replete with scattered white clouds for good measure. No sun, but the light provided by the simulated daytime was ample.

Outside the fence there was little difference among the detritus. But inside the fence he could see activity. A column of smoke rose from the middle, and the smell of cooking wafted down tantalizingly. Men were emerging from their tents, stretching and making their way to the middle.

Tommy was up, leaning against the fence, his nose and lips pressed through. He was taller than Frank had estimated and had broad shoulders, but his muscles and sinew had a slack look to them.

Frank joined him at the fence.

Eyes closed, Tommy spoke, his lips minimally opening. "I can't do this anymore. I've come to the end." No melodrama, just matter of fact.

"What does that mean? We've only just begun, you and I."

Tommy's response was a single harsh laugh. "I'm never going to get out of here. I'm okay with that. I had a good run; I did some fun things." He turned to look at Frank. "You know, I partied in Soho with Philip Seymour Hoffman."

"Really?" Frank asked.

Tommy shrugged. "He might have been there. There was a buzz about someone famous coming in, but the place was so packed we couldn't see. A ripple ran through the crowd and that was thrilling. I like to think I partied in some high falutin' places before the man caught up with me."

They looked through the fence. Tommy pointed at two guys with their backs to them, sitting before the fire in lawn chairs.

"Chucho Fuerza. He's the man inside. Got every crew under his thumb. He's a fearsome sonofabitch. You wouldn't think he is 'cause he keeps his pet brute nearby for protection, but you don't know who's protecting who."

"That's the fighter, right?"

"Yeah. Boxing Betsy."

"Pastor says he's cruel."

"That would be one way of saying it."

"Whatta ya mean?" Frank asked.

Tommy backed away from the fence and spoke in hushed tones. "When Betsy knocks you out, he takes your ass. You dig?"

It took a second, but Frank dug, and said, "Jesus. I guess that's extra incentive to give it all you got once you're in the ring."

"I can tell you it's extra humiliation and intense pain. If you're lucky, you're unconscious and you only feel pain afterwards. Betsy don't like those as much. He appreciates if you're conscious enough to moan. From pain or pleasure, don't matter cause Betsy ain't picky."

They went back to looking through the fence.

"That's why I'm done," Tommy said. "I can't win in the ring, I can't overpower anyone in the shape I'm in, and I'm not going to get stronger. Time for me to move on to the next phase."

"What the hell's the next phase?"

Tommy put his hand out and shook Frank's hand.

"You seem like a good fellow, soldier boy. I'm sorry to leave you. As far as the next phase, it's something you'll have to experience for yourself. But for me, the time is right. Good luck and God bless." He let go of Frank's hand and began climbing the fence.

Pastor joined Frank at the fence as Tommy jumped down on the other side. He gave the two a last wink and then slinked off between the tents.

Frank gripped the chain links tightly.

They watched Tommy weave his way through tents doing a good job of staying low. It looked like his target was a smaller guy wearing a baggy jumpsuit. Coming around the last cover tent Tommy crouched behind it, waiting. He didn't realize he was being tracked by a couple of other guys.

"We gotta warn him; he's going to get creamed," Frank said.

Pastor said nothing.

From where Frank stood it looked like Tommy had to cover at least ten feet of open space if he was going to reach his target.

"Doesn't the baggy mean he jacked a guy bigger than him?" Frank asked.

A simple nod of the head.

"C'mon, Tommy boy, you can do it," Pastor said.

Tommy launched at his quarry with impressive spring and more power than Frank would have predicted given his emaciated appearance. He'd nearly covered the whole distance before the target turned to face him. A glimmer of hope, but then the guy parried the tackle using a stiff arm on Tommy's head like a well-practiced halfback. Once he had Tommy on the ground, he pummeled him with brutal fists to the torso. Whatever adrenaline coursed through Tommy's veins, gave him the brief appearance of ferocity, was spent. The two other guys who'd been stalking Tommy held up and watched with amusement.

From the fence they couldn't make out all the words, but there was a triumphant and mocking tone that drifted towards them.

Pastor pulled on Frank's arm and led him to a different position where the view took in not only Tommy, but the tunnel inside the fence leading out. Tommy lay crumpled on the ground, all fight gone from his body.

"I can't stand here and watch him die," Frank said, gripping the fence tightly. "I'm going to go in there and at least try to pull him out."

"Can't be done," Pastor said and held Frank's arm at the elbow.

"Why, why can't I at least try?"

"Not the way it works," Pastor said, then nodded towards the mouth of the tunnel. "Watch from there. It won't be long now. See, if no one is claiming Tommy he will be in the area with the wrong color. That's a no-no."

A moment later, three guys emerged from the tunnel. They were dressed in black jumpsuits, black boots, and flak jackets. On their heads they wore visored helmets like riot cops, and in their right hands they carried batons. The marched in single file, left hand on the shoulder of the man directly in front, legs marching in unison. There was a sinewy look to the procession as if they weren't three men at all, but one entity moving with singular purpose.

"Shit, man." Pastor wiped his mouth. "They only gave him three. That's a slap in his face. If he weren't so weak, they'd need a whole squadron."

The three double-timed it to where Tommy lay.

The crowd scattered in the face of the black clad men's approach. Almost without breaking stride they hefted Tommy's unconscious body in their arms, turned heel, and marched back into the tunnel. The whole thing had taken no more than twenty seconds to complete. And just like that Tommy was gone. The rest of the crowd went about what they had been doing as if nothing had happened.

Pastor led Frank away from the fence. Settling down to sit, the older man unzipped his fanny pack and pulled out a piece of dried meat, offered it to Frank.

"Homemade jerky. It's good and it's protein. Take it, take it."

Frank accepted it. He felt unsteady. Seeing violence, brief thought it was, brought back a flood of emotions. He felt like he was falling, the ground beneath his feet not steady enough.

Pastor pulled out a jerky for himself and tore off a piece with his teeth.

"Shame about Tommy. I knew him for a minute. Not a great way to go."

"You don't seem that upset." Frank observed.

"Not my first rodeo. Let me tell you, I seen that happen more times than I want to admit. 'Sides, I happen to know Tommy's backstory. On the outside, he worked for an exterminator company. He'd come into your house and spray for roaches while scoping the joint. If you was elderly, he'd come back later that night to rob and terrorize you. So, while it's hard to watch, it wasn't exactly a miscarriage of justice. He got what he had coming."

Anger welled up in Frank. "How do you know what he did? You some kind of judge?"

Pastor shrugged. "In my position I'm privy to information."

"That mean you know why I'm here?"

Another shrug. Maybe it was the indifference of the gesture or the subtle indication he wouldn't get a satisfactory answer, but at the sight of it, Frank's blood rose up. He tossed the remainder of his jerky angrily at Pastor and stood.

"Fuck you and your mysterious bullshit." He walked away.

"Don't linger too long here, Frank. You'll end up just like Tommy."

Grumbling as he made his way back to the tunnel and his cell, he caught a glimpse through the tents to the fire. He recognized the guy who'd dealt with Tommy. It wasn't possible to hear what they were saying, but the scenes they acted out were deeply familiar to Frank. After combat excursions, the more strenuous, the more fraught with danger, the greater the decompressing afterwards. It was always filled with reliving the exploits and reveling in surviving, sharing that feeling with anyone and everyone who could understand. He couldn't make out the exact words, but he knew the banter well.

They were bragging to each other of their exploits. Probably exaggerating their own contributions, retelling tales of their own prowess and successes.

Frank turned disgustedly from the fence and stalked up the tunnel.

He'd always hated the bullshit talk following skirmishes. The bravado and testosterone-filled chest puffing. Disgusted with the brutality necessary to survive skirmishes, his afterglow involved self-loathing and the bitter feel of adrenaline's aftertaste.

Frank stopped short in the tunnel. He made a decision and felt the clearheaded relief of certitude. A pirouette and back down into the pod.

Without hesitation he stalked up to the fence and clambered to the top, vaulting himself over like a gymnast and landing gently on the other side. The light inside the fence was better, the air clearer, as if it contained more oxygen. Instead of urine and garbage, it smelled like a spring morning after a rain. He regulated his respiration, taking in deep belly breaths, loosening his limbs, and willing his body to a state of relaxation.

He made a direct assault on the center. His field vision had always been preternatural; he took in the surrounding area making millisecond calculations and adjustments. Zeroed in on the baggy-suited fucker who took out Tommy while his peripheral vision sized up threats.

When they saw him approaching, understood the look on his face, their laughter ceased.

They recognized a serious threat. They were scared.

His vision narrowed to the field of battle. Three men hung closely around his target, their crimson jumpsuits more bright red in this light. They fanned out to flank him. He didn't break stride and each one moved into his path to protect their guy.

Maintaining his laser focus on his target, he felled the first guy with a head fake upwards followed by a heel kick to the side of the knee. The second guy threw a punch that Frank dodged, then delivered fast kidney punches and a leg sweep putting number two on the ground. Three was a head taller than Frank with a long skinny neck and a prominent Adam's apple. A simple feint downwards, as if to take out his knees (the fallen comrade still clutching his in agony), left the neck wide open. Frank jabbed at the prominence, and the big guy fell gasping for air.

Now just Frank and his bunny rabbit. They squared off for a moment, the guy looking left and right for any other help. When it was obvious nothing more was coming from the crowd that had gathered to watch, he lunged at Frank.

It was a desperate move; prepared for a greater challenge it disappointed Frank.

He sidestepped the assault, parried the arms and fists coming at him and deftly grabbed the man from behind in a Graciesque hold, jamming the head and neck against the shoulder, cutting off the carotids.

His quarry subdued, he slowly displayed his prize to all watching, making sure to make eye contact. The intensity of his stare contrasted with the ease in which he maintained his dominance over his opponent. When the man in his grip went limp, Frank let go unceremoniously and the body crumpled at his feet.

Still keeping his eyes on the crowd, he violently stripped his defeated foe's suit. Slowly and calmly, he removed his own yellow clothing, and put on the crimson one. It hung a little loosely on him.

CHAPTER 21

Chucho Fuerza hated loudmouths. They were usually a disgrace to whatever cause they trumpeted in their brash voices and showed no insight into the difference between their noise and value. Beware the quiet ones, his father had taught him. The loudest will always give away their weaknesses.

Trudeau, the man now lying in a heap with only his underwear to cover his shame, had been like that. He'd taken his own opponent out after three others had weakened the larger man, and then he acted as if he'd done it one his own. Rah, rah, afterwards, pounding his chest. No respect and no self-awareness.

To watch him now get trounced by this new man didn't sadden Chucho. But this man, the *soldado* he'd heard talked about by Pastor, took out four men like they were nothing. And he didn't say a word. His eyes told it all. They bore the look of someone who understands; this man had seen violence and understood its toll. This was someone to watch out for.

CHAPTER 22

The crowd dispersed with little fanfare.

Frank stood in his new crimson jumpsuit, defeated foe at his feet.

The other combatants rose slowly, one limping noticeably, and took a hold of their fallen buddy. They shot wary glances at Frank, but moved with deference, purposefully showing their intentions clearly so as not to re-draw his ire. The dressed their man in Frank's discarded yellow outfit and dragged him quietly away.

Once they were out of sight, Frank allowed himself to relax and take a closer look at his surroundings. The center area had a soft ground like the white sand on the Gulf Coast. Arrayed around a large fire pit were huge logs and an occasional lawn chair. They stood empty at the moment. He looked down at his hands and waited for the internal backlash. The emotional waves of shame that followed his violent out-bursts. But they didn't come. He felt good—justified even.

He walked on the soft sand, enjoying the feel of it after the hard surface everywhere else and took a seat in a lawn chair. It was a brief moment of repose before somebody spoke to him.

"Not so fast, hombre. Those are for chiefs."

Frank stood up and looked eye to eye with a Hispanic about his age. Next to him was a behemoth of a Black man with a Neanderthal-looking forehead and a prominent jaw.

"My name is Chucho, and this is Betsy."

Frank shook the first man's hand, then watched his hand get positively lost in the second man's mitt.

"That was an impressive display, my frien'. Welcome. Let me show you 'round because it can be confusing to be new here."

Betsy trailed behind the two as Chucho acted the tour guide.

"You can see our fire here, just embers right now, but tonight, will be a big, roaring flame." He gestured in grand sweeping motions with his arms. "Thanks to you, amigo."

"I see you are a man of few words, but you also look puzzled. So let me tell you. The Gods of Burning River require a daily tribute of violence in order for us to get fed. When we have a day of quiet, we do not eat. *Entiendes?*"

When Frank didn't answer, Chucho stopped and put a hand on his chest.

"You do speak English, right?"

"I do."

"Then maybe you think my English is no good for you?" Unmistakable menace in the question.

"No, your English is just fine. I'm a little tired, that's all. Taking it all in. I mean no disrespect."

The look of aggression vanished, and a broad smile took its place. Chucho sported a bald head and had prominent laugh lines and dimples that exploded on his face when he grinned.

He clapped Frank on the back. "We are going to be fast amigos, you and me. I like a man of action who is quiet."

They left the sandy area and Frank could see, when viewed from the inside, the pattern of tents looked like a stone's ripple of concentric circles in a pond. They passed by the open mouths of several tents. Modest space, just enough for two people to lie down, no more.

Chucho stopped in front of one and pointed.

"This is my. I am only one with no bunkie. Everyone else has."

"Including Betsy?" Frank said.

Chucho laughed. "He has different partners depend on night. Come, I show you your tent."

They stopped at another and Chucho unzipped its door. A man lie lay on one side, his back to them when Chucho poked his head in.

"Oh, I think you meet already your tent partner." Then he laughed.

Frank placed his head where Chucho's just vacated. The man lying there turned his head to see who it was, and Frank stared at the prominent Adam's apple he'd just violated.

"Hey, man, sorry about that. It wasn't personal," Frank said.

The man grunted, lunged forward for what Frank thought was a foray into another fight, but he only grabbed at the zipper with his long arms and closed the door.

Chucho stepped away, gestured for Frank to follow. "Never personal. He not pissed, just embarrassed." He laughed and unleashed his big grin. "You took down Big Lou with two fingers."

"Anyways, you rest now, we get food soon and you'll eat *mucho*. You can use it. Skin and bones." He slapped Frank's back, leaned his head way back and howled. He looked around dramatically though no one was paying them any attention. "We have a new wolf," Chucho yelled and walked back to the center.

Frank, exhausted and wired, didn't think he could rest for a minute. He sniffed at his jumpsuit. Smoke and vague odor of cologne. That surprised him. He considered going back to the tent and trying to work things out with his new roommate but thought better of it. Instead he did some recon of the space inside the fence.

The tents looked pretty much uniform—an army of olive two- person dwellings. Whenever he came across someone sitting outside their tent, conversing with a neighbor, they regarded him with weariness and respect. Word must have gotten around. Or the baggy fit sufficed as advertisement.

He crossed past the central area with its sand and fire pit, two guys in lime green working on erecting a large spit. Finally after traversing the other side of the space he found what he sought. An enclosure like you might see at a state park. He stepped in. Concrete floor, sinks, and individual stalls. Then a sight nearly brought tears to his eyes: shower stalls. Each one had buttons and a primitive spigot. He pushed one and a decent spray emerged for a few seconds and then stopped. Without hesitation he began taking off his jumpsuit and would have been enjoying a much-needed hosing down when noise behind him made him stop.

A Hispanic man stood in the doorway, his arms folded across his chest, two of his crew just behind him.

"C'mon newbie, show us what you got. 'Cause we're always on the make for new ass."

A big sigh and Frank pulled his jumpsuit back on.

"Fellas, can't a man just enjoy a shower without catching shit?" He immediately regretted it.

"How you like this whiny bitch?" Putting his voice up an octave the leader continued. "Can't you just leave me alone. All I want is to wank my willy in private."

They laughed it up.

Frank kept quiet, slid himself sideways out the door with his hands in surrender position.

The two lackeys stepped back to let him leave, taking their cue from their leader.

"Yea, you better watch yourself, *cabron*. I got my eyes on you."

He felt his face burning but decided against another fight. He made to return to his tent and realized he couldn't distinguish one from the other. He found a quiet place near the fence and sat. He might have dozed for a few minutes. Someone passing by jolted him from his kip. His new roommate, the tall fellow he'd felled with the finger thrust to the throat, jogged by.

Frank stood up and gave chase.

"Hey, hey," Frank called out and took an angle to cut him off.

"Whatchu want?" The tall guy slowed but didn't stop. His glower remained.

"I'm really sorry about before. I had to do what I had to do; you can understand that."

A grudging look of understanding.

"Lou, right? Hey, man, I can't find our tent. Can you show me where it is?"

"Sure." Lou lightened up and slowed his pace. "I just never been hit like that. It really fucking hurt."

"Sorry again." He followed the taller man through the tents.

"Where'd you learn that move?"

"The corps."

"You were a Marine?" Lou asked, respect in his voice.

"I was."

A smile. "I was in the Army. For a time," Lou said and slowed to a stop in front of a tent.

He unzipped it, held the flap open, and stood aside. "Here we are."

Frank smiled and stuck his head in. He felt a sharp shove from be-hind and went sprawling to the tent's floor. In a second Lou was on top of him raining blows on Frank's head and torso. Like a demented boxer working a heavy bag, Lou grunted and spit while punching.

"Pieceofshit-motherfucker-cocksucker-you-took-out-my-guy-Chauncey."

They tussled in that small space, threatening to bring it down from within. At first Frank just curled up like an armadillo trying to absorb the punches in his bigger muscles. When Lou tired enough, Frank maneuvered the larger man into scissored legs and a brutal arm bar.

Lou wailed; Frank knew this wasn't feigned pain.

"Are you gonna stop trying to fight me!"

"FUCK YOU!" Lou half screamed, half cried.

More tension on the arm and Lou's desire to fight vanished.

"Okay, okay, okay, uncleuncleuncle. Please stop! Mercyyyyyyyyy!"

He let go of the arm but kept the pincer tension on Lou's torso.

"I need a friend here, Lou. We both were in the service— that means we speak the same language. I don't want to fight you anymore. Can we be friends?"

"Yes." A whisper.

"I can't hear you."

"That's because you crushed my windpipe and almost pulled my arm out of its socket."

Frank gently pushed Lou away with his legs. Each sat and nursed his wounds in that overheated tight space.

"Jesus, this place is fucked up," Frank finally said.

Lou held his arm. "I'll be your friend on one condition."

"What is that?"

"You teach me some of these moves."

Frank stood and stepped just outside the tent's door flap and extended a hand. Lou flinched at first, but then accepted the help up.

CHAPTER 23

"It's good to have someone to talk to," Frank said.

"I'll bet. Nothing but rejects on the outside."

"What do you know about this place?"

"Not much more than you, I'd wager. Maybe Chucho has some inside info. I don't."

They crossed to the center and the fire pit. Lou took a seat at one of the logs.

"No lawn chair?" Frank asked.

"Not unless you want to get jumped by Betsy. Those are only for Chucho's crew."

Frank sat down. "Tell me about the politics of this place."

"You gotta be with a crew." He turned to Frank. "I had a crew; you took it out." Lou jabbed Frank in the side, leaned in and spoke. "That's why I took it so hard."

Some guys in lime green uniforms appeared in front of them and began building a lattice work of logs in the pit, drawing the fire higher.

"See, in here, man, you gotta have a tight crew. It's every person for themselves, and the place wants conflict. I mean, creates conflict, like it needs it."

A couple of lime guys left and returned each returned with a side of a hog over their shoulder. They reconstructed the huge pig on the spit as it'd lived prior to being gutted and halved.

Lou continued: "Chucho keeps a lid on things, but just barely. He's tough in his way, but he'd be nothing if he didn't have Betsy by his side. Everyone's afraid of that big motherfucker. He has no conscience. Almost like a shark who attacks without emotion. Except he don't bite you with a mouthful of jagged teeth, he attacks with a big, black cock."

Frank chuckled until he saw Lou's face was dead serious.

The lime jumpsuits opened some canisters and big paint brushes. Dipping the brushes, they coated every exposed surface with a barbecue sauce whose smell was so enticing, Frank was tempted to eat the meat raw.

Other men started coming to the center. Some nodded at Lou, others ignored him. They collected in little groups including the three who threatened Frank in the shower. The leader of that particular clique winked salaciously at Frank.

"I tried to get a shower earlier and almost got raped by that piece of shit." He indicated with a nod of his head.

"Rodrigo," Lou said. ""He gets protection from Chucho 'cause they're both Rican. That kind of connection helps here. "

"Over there are the Aryan Brotherhood guys. Only one of them, the big guy with the bald head, is a believer. His name is Anderson. The rest are hangers on; they'll talk a big racist game, but their hearts are not in it like his. To your left are the Ricans, like I said. Big contingent here owing to Chucho's position. The brothers aren't here yet, but they represent pretty heavy, too. Scraggins is their leader."

Frank listened raptly to Lou's impromptu orientation. He knew well the psychological dynamics of groups in congregated living.

"You ever in combat, Lou?"

A head shake, a mild blush.

"Hey, man, nothing to be ashamed of. Combat might make for good stories when you're drunk in a bar, but it takes years off your life," Frank said.

"Anyway, " Frank continued, "you remember life in the barracks?"

"Of course. Guys tend to hang out with the familiar."

"Right. Well in combat, the divisions exist, but they go in a different direction based on how you handle yourself in a fight. You cross a lot of ethnic barriers when the shit goes down." Frank lowered his voice. "Who here is good in a fight?"

Lou didn't answer right away. The lime guys put the hog over the fire and started its cooking. They alternated between working the spit and adding layers of sauce to the meat.

"I gotta think on that."

There was a decent crowd already assembled. Then a stir rippled through, and Chucho and his crew walked up. He acted like a politician pressing the flesh, making little remarks to each guy he passed and flashing that huge smile of his.

Chucho walked right up to Frank.

"Hey, it's our new amigo. And it looks like you worked things out with Big Lou. That's great. Welcome. You gonna have the best meal tonight, I can tell you. I still remember my first bite of meat after that *mierda* they give you. Oh, like the first time you pop your cherry, you see." He laughed, enjoying himself. "Okay, have good time."

Chucho continued past the two of them and pressed more flesh. He stood in front of the fire and held his hands up for quiet.

"Welcome, gentlemen. Tonight we thank our newest member, Frank, for the offering we gonna enjoy. Warden send compliments. Really like what he did. They say, never we see such a display. That is why we got *el grande puerco*." He pointed magnanimously to the slowly rotating hog. "So, have good time and eat, eat, eat!"

Frank watched it all in a daze. The ceiling's colors went through the blues to the indigos and then black. Like a summer night on the beach. The lime guys roasted the hell out of the pig, cut it up and divvied out portions on sticks.

All ate with gusto, the quiet a testimony to hunger. After a time one of the Black guys stood up and limped over to the meat, cut himself a big chunk.

"Hey Scraggins," Lou called out, "You gonna ever tell us how you got your gimp?"

"Fuck you, Lou."

"Naw, c'mon, man. Tells us, we're all curious." Lou sat up and began rhythmic clapping, and everyone around the fire joined in and shouted out encouragement.

"Ya'll want a story?" Scraggins said good naturedly.

A chorus of yays.

He held up his hands. "Alright, alright. I got ya."

After biting off a hunk of meat and chewing he began in a loud voice:

"So I'm fucking my neighbor's wife." The crowd whooped it up. "Now, now, before you go passing judgment you should know my neighbor stopped fucking his wife long before I came along. See, she gained some weight and that turned him off. But me, I've always been partial to the bigger girls. Prolly cause my own mama was a heavy woman. Don't matter. I found her gorgeous, flirted some time over the fence, you know, girl, you fine. How come your old man don't keep you inside all the time making sweet love. That kind of shit. And because I meant it, she only put me off for a little while then suggested I come over. Ima give her the name Wanda, just so you can put a name to the face you got in your head. But Wanda warn't her name, you know that.

"Now they had one of those old houses, the ones with three floors including an attic. That's where she liked to fuck. In the goddamned attic where it was hotter than hell. I mean it, it was like hell in heaven. Or heaven in hell, I can't say. Even in the winter it roasted up there cause all the heat rises, you know. So we're going at it this one night, and it was always at night cause her husband worked third shift in a factory. We hear him pull up in his old beater. You could hear that fucking thing down the block cause the cheap bastard wouldn't fix his muffler if Jesus came down from a cloud and told this motherfucker his shit was just too damn loud.

"We was glad for that warning, but there was nowhere to go, see. Only one set of stairs and it would take me right to him. She says, get on the roof. I say, girl, you crazy, it's like ten below out there, and I'm butt-ass naked. Begging and I mean fucking pleadin' with me, so I give in, and I open the window, one of those tight-ass jobs where you got to squeeze through. Well, squeezing through warn't that bad cause I'd been sweating. I always worked up a good sweat when fucking Wanda, and I know she appreciated it 'cause it meant I'd earned my time with her.

"Anyways, I squeeze through and now I'm on the roof. But it ain't one of those gently sloping jobs, but a steep-ass roof with them shingles that are slick as fuck when they've got some ice on them. Which these did.

"So my ass, and I mean my literal bare ass, starts sliding down and I'm panicking. I turn my body so I on my front, but fellas, you can imagine that didn't improve my sichayshun much.

Now I'm at the edge and I can feel my legs slipping over the sides and I can't do nothing about it.

But that was not even the beginning of my troubles. I got nothing

I can do to keep myself from sliding except to hang from the gutters.

"So there my black ass is. Hanging from the goddamned gutters when the nails give out slowly and now it drops me about four feet and stops. I tell you, brothers, I almost lost my hold right there, but somehow, I hung on.

"I should prolly tell you this house, this grand old house with its hot fucking attic, slippery-ass roof shingles, and crappy gutters that can't hold shit, was one of those multi-generational dwellings. Wanda's aging mama lived there with them. On the second floor, as it was. A large woman herself and I didn't know her in her younger days, but by now she got a touch of the senile and didn't hear so good and she one of those older ladies who say whatever shit come to her mind. She mostly stayed in her room. Anyways, like I was saying, the gutter give out and drop me a few feet lower and the momentum push me towards a window. Wasn't enough to break the glass, but I humped that window pretty damn good.

"Who you think was standing at that window at that goddamned moment when I tried to jam my cock through the glass? You gotta it. Big, ol', deaf, senile mama. For a moment we were frozen like that—me hanging right at her window, my shit just hanging out inches from her face divided by a double pane. And she just looks at me and I'm sure she about to let out with a great scream. Instead she say, I mean I hear this clear through the glass, she say, damn boy, ain't your parents got sense? Why didn't they circumcise you when you was born?"

The laughter echoed all around. Scraggins, a gifted raconteur, let the audience enjoy that moment before continuing.

"Big Mama walks away from the window just as I hear another snap and the gutter gives way completely. I don't know how many feet it was to the ground, but when you cold and you hit cold concrete it ain't like any pain I'd ever felt. Shot through me from the bottoms of my feet to the top of my head.

"The fall broke both my ankles."

"So that's why you limp?" Someone shouted.

"Don't be interruptin', I ain't finished yet. I sure as shit limped back into my own damn house. First thing I did was get some drawers on. Then I called my brother, and he took me to the hospital. I got myself two casts and some crutches. Sho enough, next morning my neighbor comes a knockin'.

"I open the door and he don't got a gun, so that was good. He say, 'can I come in?' I say, of course. We been neighbors going on ten years and we always been what you would call friendly. We sit down together. He say, 'sorry about yo legs, man. And I don't care you was bonin' my wife; she deserve some good lovin'. But I can't abide what you done to my gutters, what with winter and all.'

"Right there I cut him a check and we shook hands as friends."

Scraggins gave a half bow, both middle fingers aimed at his audience and sat down.

"So how come you still limp, ya bastard!" Lou shouted.

"Shit, that?" Scraggins called back. "I had bad asthma when I was a kid and I used to get steroids. They fucked up my hip."

"If you got steroids, how come you not built?"

"They ain't them kind of steroids,you ignorant cracka," Scraggins said.

Some finger pointing and laughing at Lou. Then Chucho spoke up.

"Why did you tell us the whole story about you fuckin' your neighbor's wife and falling from the roof?"

Scraggins stood, spread his arms wide to embrace the audience, and shouted, "'Cause it's a great fucking story, am I right?!"

Everyone cheered.

It was a most excellent meal. There was a surfeit of meat; by the time Frank felt satiated he could see a little bump in his abdomen like a snake that swallowed a goat. Somebody passed around a flask and it came to Lou. He took a deep pull, shook his head like a dog and yelled out.

"Have some of this, Marine. It'll put hair on your chest."

Frank did as he was told. It went down like fire and sent out emissaries of good will to all his nerve endings. He felt no pain. For a moment he forgot where he was. A second swig and he passed it to his right.

He repositioned himself on the ground, only his head propped up by the log.

"This is for you, Tommy," he shouted and looked upward at the ceiling's mimicry of a country night's sky, resplendent with an array of recognizable constellations.

At some point Lou hit him on the leg to indicate they were going back. His first attempt at standing failed; he got dizzy and fell back down with a laugh. Standing again with some help, he weaved after Lou, held the tent open so the tall man could go first (still aware enough and a little snakebit to take the chance of preceding Lou inside again), and then passed out just before his body hit the mat.

CHAPTER 24

Down a narrow alleyway, the sounds of screaming, dishes breaking. The heat unbearable, sweat running down his back, stinging his eyes. At the front of his roving combat crew, just six of them, but he trusts them with his life. The camaraderie, the blind loyalty, binds them with ties tangible enough to be felt. They give him confidence.

Dicey to be in the straits. The buildings here are taller than usual, windows scattered throughout, any one of them ideal for a sniper or even a knucklehead with a potted plant. But he is compelled to chase down the sound. In his ear, the crackling of the radio sounding off with various updates and warnings.

He comes to a doorway and puts his fist up; the others hold their positions behind him, the spacing exquisite. The handle pushes easily and he opens just a crack, strains to hear sounds within.

A fight. High- pitched squawks alternating with baritone growls, the guttural symphony of Arabic. He pushes the door open and sees what he always sees, what he wants to see. She is in distress, already bearing the bruises, a rainbow of colors decorating her face. He steps in, but his path is blocked. The man is obstructing, preventing the full entrance into the room, pushes him back against the door. His guys forcing themselves into the room on the other side of the door driving him into his assailant.

She continues her screams; her visceral entreaties give purpose to his efforts, but he can't pass, can't free his arms to join the battle or even defend himself. And then the blows come, the fists pummeling and penetrating through the Kevlar driving deep into his vital abdominal organs…

Frank woke up with the intense pain of fists to his body. The dream images dissolved rapidly into the inside of his tent, still dark outside. And an imposing figure slapping him around.

"Jesus, Lou, I thought we were past this."

"I ain't your Lou, motherfucker."

Sneaking peaks between his arms held up in protection, he identified the perpetrator.

A shot straight to the plexus knocked the wind out. Once Frank's torso was suitably tenderized, Betsy grabbed him by the feet and dragged him out of the tent. It was still night.

"Hey, Frank, how you doin'?" A now familiar voice said.

Uncurling himself, he got on all fours and puked, worked to force air into his lungs.

He turned finally to look at Chucho, his face unlined and serious.

"Listen, Frank, I like you. That's why I go to the trouble of letting you know; I am law here. You prolly has your own ideas of how things should run, but here I make decision."

"I don't have a problem with that," Frank croaked.

"*Bueno*." The face broke into the affable, well-lined grin. "Then we get along great. I gotta lay things out clear, you know, right away, so no misunderstanding. Alright, you go back to bed now. Sleep good."

He hugged his knees and watched Chucho stroll away, pet golem trailing just behind.

Lou materialized and sat down next to Frank.

"You should feel special. Chucho doesn't just beat up anyone preemptively. That's

reserved only for those he thinks will be a problem."

"It wasn't Chucho who laid the beating."

"Same thing. You okay? Let's get you back inside, sleep it off."

"Where were you?" Frank asked.

Lou shrugged. "I serve at the pleasure of the chairman. When he says scram, I does it."

"Thanks, Lou. All the same, I'll just stay here for a moment."

Lou went inside the tent; Frank looked at his emesis with disgust. After a couple of minutes he crawled in, the pain receded to a dull ache, and he fell back asleep.

CHAPTER 25

The fire roasted ham felt better going down. Now it didn't sit well. Or maybe it was the cumulative effect of being a punching bag too many times. Whatever the case, Frank rose slowly in the morning light, and grimaced. He had the tent to himself. Some tentative stretching and a few push-ups to get the blood going.

He stepped outside. It was a pleasant day. Sky of blue. He wondered if and how it would ever rain in this place. He made his way to the center. There were groups of guys sitting around. Lou sat on a log holding a bowl.

He held it up. "Grab some oatmeal. Breakfast of champions."

Frank sat down next to him. "I'll pass. My stomach is a little uneasy." After a minute of thought he said,: "How come you're not with the white guys?"

Lou spooned his runny oats into his mouth. "Was a time I was, but I just kind of drifted into my own thing. I did a turn for Chucho back when, and he allowed me to be just with my crew. We were a tight quartet."

Frank turned and felt a sharp pain in his ribs. "Shit." He leaned in close. "Hey, Pastor told me you guys have mash here. I wonder how I could score some."

"You don't want that shit, take my word for it. Makes you weak and complacent and those are things you can't afford here. But the plant it comes from has two parts, the leaf and the stalk. We brew a drink from the stalk and it's a stimulant. Now that shit, you want. It will make you Superman."

"How do you score that?"

"Everything in here runs on a currency dictated by the captain of the pod. Right now that's Chucho. If you do things he likes, you get credits with him. Enough of those and you get a night inside with a concierge."

"Concierge?"

A nod and a huge smile. "Just like it sounds. They are there to provide you whatever you ask for."

"What if I just want to get the hell out of here? Can they help me with that?"

"I guess I never thought of it that way. I was just grateful to get some tail." Lou got lost in thought. "I can only tell you it's like staying a night in the finest hotel with a lot of amenities. After spending time here the break from the intensity in there makes it Shangri-La."

"All this happens where?"

Instead of answering Lou stood. "Come with me, I'll show you. Anyway it's getting close to the time when the masochist makes his run."

They walked away from the center to an edge on the right side of the tunnel. A few other people congregated in the area, waiting. The door to the tunnel stood closed.

"This is the entranceway to it all. The tunnel giveth and taketh away. Like one big rectum, shitting the men in black on us, but also a gateway inside."

"What's inside?"

"You just want all the information, don't you? Somethings you have to experience yourself. I been here just about as long as anyone, and I can tell you if you asked three guys what their night on the inside was like you'd get three very different answers. That's the true secret of this place." He leaned up against the fence and pointed to the outside.

Frank looked over there and first thing that struck him was a haziness on the other side of the fence. When on the outside looking in, the clarity was crystal. But it's as if the other way around wasn't cosmically worth it, so outside the fence was out of focus. Just a blur until movement caught his eye and he saw a man scaling the fence.

His pale-yellow jumpsuit didn't look horrible. The guy himself didn't have the poorly fed appearance of so many of the other guys. He slowly crested the fence, carefully put a leg over the side, and started his descent. A group of guys waited for him at the bottom. An ethnic mix of expectant, upturned faces, each one lit up with anticipation.

Lou provided commentary.

"This guy comes everyday like clockwork. He times it when the sun hits the top of the fence just right. We think he believes the light will shine in our eyes and give him an advantage."

The man hit the ground and crouched in a fight stance. Frank stifled a laugh. The disconnect between the posturing of his scrawny and pathetic physique and the intensity on his face was pure comedy gold. Lou pointed out the four men surrounding the attacker.

"These guys bet each day who's going to be the target. The rule is they can't say anything to lure him; if they do, they're disqualified."

On the beach this yellow guy would get sand kicked in his face. Here, he was the aggressor. Squaring off in turn with each of his opponents he bowed slightly. It was an endearing act of delusional grandiosity given the odds stacked against him. Then he put a scowl on his face and lunged at the Black guy.

"Oh, he went for the brother," Lou yelled, taking on the persona of John Madden calling a Cowboys--Redskins game. "And what a dive that was, right at the legs. But he missed, Scraggins easily dodging that assault. Back on his feet now, circling, bobbing and weaving. And he throws a haymaker! What a punch! Unfortunately, it didn't hit its mark and—OOHHH!— Scraggins lands a right cross smack on our hero's jaw and down goes Frazier! Down goes Frazier!"

The weakling lie lay on the ground, out cold.

Frank looked over at the door to the tunnel expecting it to open any second.

When it didn't, he looked to Lou for explanation. He just indicated to watch the guys surrounding the fallen aggressor.

The four looked like they could be his best friends. Convivial with each other, already

retelling the grand story of this incident, they gently sat him up against the fence. Slapping his face they brought him to.

"Did I get close?" he said.

"Neh, but you done good today," Scraggins said. He took a package out of his pocket and tucked it inside the loose yellow jumpsuit.

Lou spoke quietly to Frank,: "Some meat from last night and a pinch's worth of mash for the effort. By the way, he went for Scraggins cause of the limp. Everyone thinks the limp means weakness, but Scraggins is one of the toughest bastards here."

The four guys stood up scrawny man.

"You ready?" Scraggins said.

The weakling mustered a brave face and went back up the fence.

"He'll nurse his wounds tonight and make another try tomorrow," Lou said, walking away from the fence. "That guy is like Old Faithful."

Scraggins walked passed Lou and made a gesture meant just for him.

Frank saw it but kept silent. Instead he asked Lou, :

"So why don't the men in black come for the loser?"

Lou shrugged. "I'm guessing it's because it's not a real attempt, not a real threat. Each day he does the same thing. It's just another diversion for us, you know, to break up the monotony.

"Speaking of which, I heard they got a guy to take on Betsy tonight. So that's something to look forward to."

He stretched his arms high over his head. "I'm going to go back to bad."

"You just got up."

"Not much else to do here. See ya." Lou walked off.

Frank crouched down against the fence and observed. Most of the activity from the morning died down, guys heading to their tents to sleep. A couple walked the fence's inside perimeter. Frank's position was about twenty meters from the tunnel's door. Had he not been focused on it he would have missed the door opening just enough for Chucho to slip out and reclose it. Frank tailed him very loosely to confirm the location of his tent then he retreated back to his spot near the fence where he could observe and think.

CHAPTER 26

Rather than sleep (and in no small part owing to recent tent memories), Frank opted to stay active during the day. He tracked the "sun's" movement across the ceiling, did a good amount of stretching and massaging of his aching muscles. Rubbing the bruises hurt like hell, but he knew it would lead to faster healing. He did a few laps around the inside perimeter, studied the various areas of the pod. Little action around the fire, just a few embers still burning.

When the sun descended to the level of the other side of the fence, some things kicked into gear. Those guys in lime, laden with materials, came to the center. Frank watched them put together a makeshift boxing ring, posts at each corner and rope connecting them. Guys emerged from their tents and collected in groups, making an informal perimeter around the boxing ring.

Frank saw a familiar face gladhanding the crowd. He walked up.

"Well, if it isn't the main man of the cloth."

Pastor, in his same cream outfit, kufi on his head, smiled and said,: "You seemed to do okay for yourself. Nice to see you, Frank."

They shook hands.

"I'm happy to see you, too, but admittedly a little puzzled; who did you subdue in order to be here?" Frank said, though he knew better.

"I already told you, I have license to roam the pods, to do the good I can do."

"License from who, I wonder," Frank said but turned toward the ring. "And now you're here for the fight."

"Lots of people to hear the word of God. So, you find what you was looking for in here?"

"What do you know about what I'm looking for, preacher?"

"Pastor, not preacher."

Frank shrugged. "What's the difference."

"Guys like you think you got it all understood. Man, I've been around, you know. I seen it all. You the frustrated type who looks the world over for something that existed all the time here." And he pointed in the direction of Frank's sternum careful not to come too close.

"You're just the wise old Buddha, that it? Wonder what you did to land here."

Pastor shrugged with an all-knowing look that irritated Frank and moved on to others.

When the sun went below the domed ceiling's horizon, anticipation built. Frank looked around but didn't see Lou anywhere. Some of the Black guys loitered around the ring without Scraggins who should have been in the front with his crew.

Chucho stepped between the ropes and into the ring. He held up his hands.

"Amigos, we have a great match for you tonight. One of the desperados has challenged our own Betsy."

The assembled rabble booed.

"And Betsy has accepted the challenge to defend our honor."

The requisite cheers, though the enthusiasm felt contrived to Frank.

Betsy entered the ring. He didn't wear boxing shorts, though, but the same jumpsuit. The only difference were two vintage looking gloves. He made the requisite nod to the crowd.

"And now," Chucho continued, "let me introduce you to our challenger. I'm told he just arrived a couple of days ago and is still fresh."

Scattered shouts from the crowd expressed appreciation.

Frank took all this in but kept scanning the area for Lou.

The crowd jeered and Frank turned back to the ring as a dazed-looking white guy ducked between the ropes. True to Chucho's word he wore a bright yellow jumpsuit, snug on his pudgy frame. Chucho led the confused bastard to the corner. A guy was assigned to challenger's corner, and he put a pair of vintage gloves on the challenger's hands, like a teacher putting mittens on a kindergartener.

Chucho stepped to the center of the ring and motioned both men to draw near. Betsy complied, but the challenger had to be pushed by the guy in his corner. Speaking in a thundering voice, Chucho addressed the combatants and the throng crowding the ring.

"Okay, now I want a clean fight. No hitting below the belt—until after, of course."

He retreated to catcalls and whistles.

Frank couldn't take his eyes off of the poor schmuck facing Betsy. He couldn't decide if the cruelty lay in the knowledge he was overmatched and headed for a beating, the impending rape, or the ignorance of both. It heartened Frank to know it still bothered him. After his experience in Iraq, he often wondered if sheer brutality could engender pathos as it once had.

Somebody near the ring hit metal to simulate a bell, and Betsy advanced on his challenger. The sight of Betsy bearing down on him, dazed or otherwise, galvanized the poor guy to flee to the edge and try to try bounding over the rope. No matter where he went, though, several crimson jumpsuits blocked his way and forced him to capitulate to whatever fate lay with the Black Goliath.

For his part, Betsy looked to be savoring the anticipation. The knockout was a foregone conclusion; this was sexual foreplay. Frank slowly backed away from the spectacle, keeping his eyes on the bout while also scanning for Lou. Confident no one noticed him slipping away, he began an earnest hunt for his tent mate and, he assumed, Scraggins.

Ooohs and aaahs reached him from the chorus of spectators. Intermittent glances only afforded him a view of Betsy's head towering above and an occasional gloved hand cocked back and released towards his opponent's head.

A few seconds of scanning behind tents. Frank swore at himself.

"I gotta do this more smartly." He ran to the edge of the pod, climbed the fence to its top. Better. Aside from some blind spots he could see much of the west side of the pod. No sign.

He sprinted to the other side as Betsy landed the knockout blow and the challenger went down like a sack of dirt. An unconscious sack, at that.

Frank monkeyed up the east fence and finally spotted Lou crouched with Scraggins in a little nook at the nexus of the fence and tunnel. Before he climbed down, he had an unobstructed view of the ring and the savagery on full display. Both men were stripped of their jumpsuits—; one removed, the other ripped off. One man prone, one cheek resting on the sandy ground, the eyes mercifully closed.

Betsy lay on top and was thrusting with frightful force. With each push Betsy grunted and the crowd cheered him on.

"Boom. Boom. Boom."

Like a stage performer, Betsy drew strength from the crowd and played up to their exhortations.

He's going to kill that poor bastard, Frank thought. Sickened and done with the sight, he jumped down from the fence and made his way towards where he'd spotted Scraggins and Lou.

The crowd yelled out in unison at what must have been Betsy signaling his own climax and the show's conclusion. Formations broke and Frank blended in with the scattering crimson. He nonchalantly made his way to the tunnel. Lou, feigning a similar blasé attitude, walked with his hands in his pockets whistling a tune.

Frank angled his stride and fell in step with him.

"You gonna tell me what you got planned with the brothers?"

"What the hell you talking about? I was just enjoying the spectacle and anticipating dinner. Whenever Betsy has a fight, we get franks and beans."

"That's very funny, Lou," Frank said. "But I'm more interested in whatever play you got in mind."

Lou stopped Frank and stood opposite him. "You're new here, so I'll cut you some slack. But you better learn quickly this place has eyes, ears, and both are super fucking sharp. If you want to talk to me about serious matters, wait for the night when we're in the tent." And he walked off, still whistling.

CHAPTER 27

Turns out, Lou wasn't joking. Really was hot dogs and baked beans. Frank had a couple of dogs but avoided the beans. Watching the men sitting around slurping up the brown beans all he could think about was the farting cowboy scene in Blazing Saddles. He hoped that was only artistic license.

He couldn't wait to be done for the night so he could retire to the tent. It wouldn't do to get there early;, he understood that. He also didn't need convincing that Lou's hesitation to speak too publicly wasn't paranoid exaggeration. This place had a mind of its own; he knew that firsthand.

It took longer for the pod to settle down after the excitement; people still milled about well into the night. Frank sought out Pastor. As he suspected, it was Pastor who tended to the poor bastard after everyone had cleared out. Pastor had said on a couple of occasions he'd been there to pray over the body as it passed to its heavenly (or hellish) reward. Not this time, though. The man had survived but would have a hell of a road back. Because he'd stood in with Betsy for the duration, the challenger would receive appropriate medical care. The guys in lime came and took the unconscious man into the tunnel.

"What kind of medical facilities do they have in there?" Frank had asked.

"I hope you never have to find out." Was all Pastor would reveal.

When enough time passed, Frank walked as nonchalantly as he could to his tent. Lou was already on his back, hands folded behind his neck.

Slipping in, Frank zipped up the door and settled down.

"Tell me what you're planning. I want in.." he said.

Lou didn't speak for a moment. Then,: "You're awfully impatient, aren't you." He propped himself up on one elbow. "Man, you just got here. You don't know anything about nothing. Why don't you just cool your jets and learn some stuff before you try to become a player."

"I was a sergeant in the Marines. You know what that means? Means I headed a rifle squad and did it for a long time. Fact I'm still alive after two tours in Iraq in that capacity tells you my qualifications. So instead of fucking around, why don't you let me in so I can help?."

A big sigh, then Lou sat up, hugged his knees.

"Look, there are things at stake here you don't yet understand. Captain of the pod is a big position, comes with lots of responsibilities, but a lot of perks, too. Chucho's been around a long time and has become lazy. It's time to replace him. Me and Scraggins were just discussing that point and who might take over."

"Why did you go with Scraggins when you had an alliance with Anderson. And you're white," Frank said.

"Nothing to do with race, if that's what you're getting at. See, Anderson and his merry band of neo-Nazis have done fine with Chucho. They're allies with the Ricans. So I gotta get with Scraggins to make an alliance. In here you can't go it alone. Too vulnerable."

"So what would your plan be?"

Lou hesitated. "I'm not going to talk about that with you. No offense."

"Okay. None taken. I'll just tell you if it's tactics you're struggling with, I'm the guy. I know about tactics in spades."

"Thanks, sergeant. I'll keep that in mind." He lay back down and turned his back towards Frank.

A few restless moments with Lou's snoring as company convinced Frank he wouldn't be able to sleep just then, and he exited the tent. He looked up trying to find the moon, as it were, and found a waxing gibbous. Whoever kept this place running took celestial accuracy quite seriously. It made for a darker night. Perfect. A leisurely stroll around the pod with the intention of ending at Chucho's tent. He staked a place nearer to the fence and sat, watched it from afar.

After a time of no activity he slowly stood, scanned the area satisfied with his night vision.

It seemed likely Chucho didn't spend the nights in his tent. Frank eased over to the entrance and crouched, quiet as a church mouse pissing on cotton. He looked left and right, saw nothing. Pulled the zipper down one tooth at a time ready for anything. At the bottom slipped both hands in and separated them, inserted his head.

Nothing. As he suspected. Didn't appear any different than the one he slept in apart from containing only one mat instead of two. He pulled his head out just as a hand gripped his shoulder and threw him backwards.

He looked up into a Rican face, but it wasn't Chucho. Took a moment then it came to Frank.

"Rodrigo."

"That's right, baby. What the hell you doing over here, huh? Looking for love in all the wrong places." The menace in Rodrigo's voice unmistakable.

Frank stood up, dusted himself off. "Just looking for Chucho, wasn't sure this was his tent."

Rodrigo, almost as tall, bodied up to Frank, centimeters from his face. "Wattchu need him for, anyhow? You got a problem? You come to me. I'm lieutenant."

Not flinching or giving an inch Frank replied, "It's none of your business what I wanted from Chucho. Just tell him I need to see him."

"You don't got the right respect, man. You know that? Maybe I teach you a little respect."

Frank looked deep into the other man's eyes. He saw balls and anger, but not cold resolve. Rage and impulsivity would only take a man so far. After the first wave, a man like Rodrigo could be easily overcome. But it wasn't worth it right now. Instead of continuing this pissing contest Frank held his hands up and backed up.

"Okay, man, you win. I don't need any trouble."

"That's the second time I make you my bitch." Rodrigo delighted in the turn of events. "Might be I got to break you with my dick next time. Might be. Might be."

Frank continued his retreat, eyes remained fixed on Rodrigo. Once he cleared enough space, he turned and walked away.

CHAPTER 28

A few hours of rest and Frank was up again. Lou snored impassively as Frank let himself out of the tent. Dawn was breaking along one side and the air had a nip to it.

He strolled around the perimeter and approached the first Black guy he saw.

"Hey, where can I find Scraggins?"

A wary look. "Why you need him?"

"Something that will be good for him; nothing bad, I promise."

A snort. "You promise. You don't know shit, do you?"

"Do you know where he is?"

Hands folded across his chest; the guy kept his mouth shut. Someone emerged from a tent walked up behind, put a hand on the guy's shoulder. "Don't worry, man, he okay."

Scraggins stepped up to Frank. "What you want, soldier boy?"

"For you to hear me out is all."

Breakfast consisted of the same oatmeal. Might have been the very same, who knows. The festival style dinner was the primary sustenance as far as Frank could see. He passed on the oatmeal. The protein-only diet left him hungry much of the day, but a different type of hunger. Not the ravenous, carb addict savagely looking for a fix. More of a background longing for food he could tolerate.

He sat on his perch by the fence observing both the fire pit and the exit from the tunnel. About the same time as yesterday Chucho emerged, looking well rested. Once he passed from sight, Frank made his way to the pit, spotted Lou eating his morning oats, and sat beside him.

Lou spoke into his bowl. "If you're serious, marine, follow me. But not so close, you dig?"

A subtle nod in response. Lou stood and walked off; a lime guy picked up his discarded bowl. Frank stretched to see where his tent mate walked and then stood himself. He kept a good twenty yards between them, almost losing him on a couple of turns. The spy game shit amused Frank. There weren't that many options for ambush. But the need for some measure of surprise, even if it was minimal, came at a high cost here.

Turns out Lou was in their tent. Frank ducked his head in to find Scraggins occupying his mat.

"Zip that mother up," he said.

Frank complied, then sat. It was a tight fit.

"Lou told me you offered your help. He didn't want you, but I thought any guy who could take out four guys in a flash"—he snapped his fingers—"was someone I could use."

"What do you have in mind?"

"Well, we have to end the Rican domination. Only way to do that is to cut off the head."

Someone rapped on the tent two times.

"What about Betsy?" Frank asked.

"Stay quiet, boy," Scraggins said through pursed lips.

They sat absolutely still for a long pause until another three raps and Scraggins relaxed.

"My crew is acting lookout and that mean someone unfriendly came close. You gotta be oh so careful, boy. Anyway, Betsy is hired muscle. He only in it for the boxing matches."

Lou picked up the thread. "There has to be violence for us to get fed, but it wasn't until Chucho took over we got the fights and fucks courtesy of Betsy. That ensures we eat when there hasn't been any blood shed for the day."

"Who decides these gruesome fucking rules?"

"Keep your voice down, boy. You don't need to raise it in order to be heard in this tight-ass tent.

"Those types of questions don't help nothing. You ain't never gonna find out so take our word for it. Things can only change with a different captain. So, you with us to get rid of Chucho?"

"What do you plan on doing?"

Lou spoke, "An all-out bull rush with overwhelming forces is how it's done. And we're close to having the numbers. Scraggins here has some of the neo-Nazis willing to go along with him if they think it will be successful."

"What about a single assassin?"

"Kill him? What the fuck you think we're talking about?" Scraggins asked, genuine anger on his face.

"You're not talking about killing him?"

"Hell, no. You take by force, but you can't murder. That's a no-no here. You do that you just bring the men in black on your ass."

"Okay," Frank said, irritated at being chastened about rules everyone seemed to know, but didn't share. "Well, how about small squads. One goes after Chucho to *subdue*"—he said it while glaring at

Scraggins—"him, another equalizes Betsy, and the third, a larger force, keeps others at bay."

Lou nodded. "Could work if well-coordinated. Problem is it is mighty difficult to get people on the same page. Not a lot of trust in this place."

"I think it could work," Scraggins said. "You put together the teams and let's get it set for tomorrow."

"That doesn't leave enough time to plan, rehearse, work out the kinks," Frank said.

"Sorry, boy, this ain't the shores of Tripoli. Time works funny here. The more that passes, the more people forget alliances and do for theyselves. Plans has to go from talking to walking in a minute." He snapped his fingers. "So, how you see it going?"

Frank got on his knees, sat on his heels like he'd done a thousand times in a dojo.

"We set a small perimeter six feet away from the tunnel. Three guys, arm's length apart. Two others keep tabs on Betsy. The last two jump Chucho when he comes out of the tunnel first thing in the morning when he is at his most relaxed. But who goes after him? You two already decide who wants to be captain?"

Both shook their heads in the affirmative.

"Who?" Frank asked.

Each one said their own name with a smug look.

"I been here longer. Should be me," Lou said.

A subtle shake of the Scraggins's head. "I don't see it as a reward for seniority; has to be the one with the most juice with the others. That's me, all day."

Lou turned to Frank. "What do you think? You'll go down with us if it should fail. You gotta an opinion?"

Frank looked at both in turn and spoke. "I think it should be Lou.

He's bigger, he's not handicapped, and he's not Black."

"Man, fuck you for all that," Scraggins said.

"Name me one Black leader worth anything?" Lou said.

"Besides Brother Obama?"

"You half white and half Nigerian?" Lou shot back.

"You ignorant cracka, the Obamas were Kenyan."

"I'm just sayin.'"

"I agree with Lou, the best military leaders were white. Stonewall Jackson, Patton, Schwarzkopf." Frank ticked them off on his fingers.

"Man, you ignorant." Scraggins shook his head. "You believe that you want to, but then why should I go along with you two crackers? What the hell's in it for me?"

"With the Ricans down a peg, you get more status. Plus," Lou hesitated, then continued, "I'll throw you a night inside every five days."

"Man, I don't know. I take down Chucho, I go inside every night. So, I think not." He stood and started making his way to the mouth of the tent.

Lou stood quickly, bent way over in the tight space, and made to block Scraggins's exit.

"Hold it." Frank put out a hand on each's chest to stop them. He could feel the tension transmitted from their bodies down both his arms.

"Heel, both of you, give me a second to come up with a compromise."

They didn't move but eyeballed each other from a span of inches.

"How about some sort of shared arrangement?"

Both shook their heads.

"That never works," Lou said.

"Alright, how about a night inside every fourth night?"

Scraggins made a face.

"Look, man," Frank said hastily, "If you're not *the* man, it means nobody is gunning for you. Don't you get it? Let Lou be the guy for everyone to see; this way you get some of the juice, but none of the downside."

"A night every other," Scraggins said.

"Gimme a break. That'd be like sharing. No way. Every fourth."

"Every third it is," Frank said.

"Fine," Scraggins said. "Just as long it means I can get the fuck out of this tight-ass tent and stretch out. My hip be killin'."

"Before you leave"—Frank turned to Lou—"every third work for you?"

Lou held an internal dialogue then finally nodded. "Yes."

"Okay, tomorrow morning, then. You both got your teams for Betsy and the perimeter?"

They both nodded.

"But if Betsy go off, ain't gonna be enough guys to keep him down," Scraggins said as he left.

Before Lou could leave Frank stopped him and asked, "Hey, what happens if a crimson attacks another crimson? I mean, you can't displace him, 'cause you don't need the spot, right?"

"We generally don't do that because it looks bad for the guy's crew. If we have a beef with someone, we go to the crew leader, and they hash it out. Usually it can be resolved."

"And it if can't?"

Lou shrugged.

"Thanks. You're a real help."

The tall man left. Frank worked out an impromptu plan in his head and got moving.

CHAPTER 29

He loitered by the Ricans for a few minutes checking them out. Chucho sat near his tent on a lawn chair. The tightest of his crew hovered nearby, including Rodrigo and two other guys, both bigger than Frank. One was muscular, the kind of bulk one gets from hours in a gym. The other had a pot belly, but the hard look of someone who earned his stripes in the field rather than by facing a mirror and lifting weights.

Frank willed his body to relax, breathed deeply into his abdomen. Prepared as he'd ever be, he made his move.

They only saw him at the last moment. He zeroed in on Rodrigo who wore a smug look until the very last moment; Frank threw a punch so fast it caught Rodrigo's jaw before he could mount a defense. He went down hard. Frank pounced, pressing his knee on Rodrigo's head while he faced the others. Their paralysis broke, they tackled Frank who offered n resistance.

Chucho stood ready to act but held back when he saw Frank's sudden passivity. Other inmates jogged over, drawn by the sudden activity, sensing a chance at violence, but Chucho held them off with one hand, his eyes fixed on Frank.

"Fuck off," Chucho said. "Nothing happenin' here." He glared the others away; his crew stayed where they were.

The muscular guy held Frank in a poorly held full Nelson. The other guy, the one with the pot belly, stood poised opposite Frank waiting on instructions from his boss. A subtle nod of the head and Potbelly smiled. He cocked his fist back and prepared to unload on Frank's exposed abdomen. When he threw the punch Frank went slack and easily slipped the grip of the muscle-bound guy who took Potbelly's fist right into his own gut.

Potbelly recovered quickly for a man of his size and grabbed at the front of Frank's jumpsuit as his comrade crumpled to the ground. He jabbed a couple of times at Frank's face, and it felt like being hit with concrete. Preparing another blow, he stopped at the sound of his boss's voice.

"*Basta,* Manolo."

Chucho crouched down and pulled Frank's head up by the hair, surprisingly gentle in the gesture. He looked a few moments into Frank's swelling eye, a puzzled look on his face.

"What is your game?" Chucho finally asked. "You have a plan, so tell me, what is it?"

Imperceptibly moving his lips, Frank spoke: "I needed to speak to you and you alone. But I can't be seen doing it. There's a plot against you."

It took only a few more seconds to give the particulars. Finished, Frank said, "Tell muscle-bound jerk to pick me up and have Potbelly hit me with some in the body."

"Potbelly? You mean Manolo." Chucho laughed. "Good nickname."

Frank put a light hand on Chucho's arm. "Make it look real enough, but not so much I can't function, you understand?"

Chucho nodded and exchanged some rapid words in Spanish to Manolo and his fallen muscle-bound comrade, still on the ground. Then in English, "Get up, Jose, you look like *coña*."

Petulant and holding his stomach, Jose stood and grabbed Frank's arms, and held them locked behind him. Manolo pulled his punches, but if that was him taking it easy, Frank resolved to never again be on the receiving end.

CHAPTER 30

I took a few minutes for Frank to get back to his tent. By then he'd already refunded anything he'd eaten and dry heaved a few times to boot. He wanted nothing more than sleep.

Lou did a double take when Frank entered the tent.

"You look like shit," he said.

Rather than respond, Frank eased himself into a lying position, his back to Lou.

"I heard you went after the Ricans," Lou said. "Not very smart if we're going to take down their captain."

"I settled a score, is all. That piece of shit Rodrigo has ridden me since the moment I arrived and was eyeballing me again. If I didn't act, I would have been acted on."

"Yeah, but now they're on guard."

Frank, with an involuntary grunt of pain, turned himself to face Lou.

"The opposite, man. The opposite. They have no reason to suspect anything now. It was clear my beef was with Rodrigo, and I didn't fight anyone else. You can see, can't you? I took a goddamned beating. You were the one who told me how it works; I was following your advice in this fucked-up place." He turned away from Lou. "I couldn't stand the way that guy eyeballed me. There was something more than menacing. That guy's a sexual predator."

"I guess he won't be fucking with you anymore," Lou said.

They were quiet for a while.

Then Lou spoke again: "You going to be up for tomorrow morning?"

"I'll be fine, don't worry."

He drifted off to sleep. His consciousness returned briefly, and he noted Lou's empty mat. Another time Lou stuck his head in the tent to tell him there was good food because of his knocking out Rodrigo. Frank waved him off and went back to sleep. When he awoke fully, it was already dark outside the tent and Lou was snoring next to him.

Getting to a sitting position hurt his face more than his gut. He stepped outside the tent and felt around his face, taking inventory. Just below his right eye throbbed like a mother. He closed the left eyelid and tested his right vision in all quadrants. Everything worked. Opening and closing his jaw was no problem. He moved on to his torso. Undoing his jumpsuit he pulled it down to his waist. In the moonlight he couldn't see well, but the bruising was obvious. Could have been a hell of a lot worse. Hunger gnawed a little, but he figured it best to give his stomach a break for now. A few body stretches limbered him up. Without much left to do, he decided to go back in and lie down until the sun came up. Wouldn't do to wander around now; could only get into more trouble. Anyway, he still wanted to go over his plan a couple more times in his head before game time.

Lou was in great spirits when he got up. Frank pretended to still be sleeping and then slowly turned to face him.

"I've been waiting for a chance at the title," Lou said.

"He won't be expecting anything. That's the best thing we got going for us."

"You just make sure the smokes keep Betsy away."

"They will," Frank said, standing up.

"You better be right. And you better be right Betsy will fall in line with a new regime. Because I don't need that kind of headache. And remember, soldier boy, act natural. These boys here are already paranoid enough."

They stepped out of the tent and walked with nonchalance towards the pit.

"Tell me something about yourself, Lou."

"What's there to tell?"

"How about your experience in the Army."

They approached the pit. Others milled around waiting on breakfast.

"Okay," Lou said, clicking his heels and standing straight. "I stood tall before the judge on my eighteenth birthday. He said, 'Son, you're a pain in this court's ass. You're a troublemaker. So, either I send you to prison, or you join up in this man's Army.' I chose the Army, but I probably should have just gone to prison. Things might have turned out differently." He shrugged. "No point in complaining about that now."

"What got you drummed out of the Army?"

Lou turned to Frank and grinned maliciously. "I knocked out a superior officer. That did the trick." He glared at Frank for a moment, then his eyes shifted to the sun that threatened to hit the top of the eastern fence.

"About that time, man. Good luck."

They separated. Just off the pit, about thirty paces away the entrance to the tunnel stood empty, door closed. Frank went left flank, joined by one of Scraggins's crew. Lou hovered right flank with another, but he gestured the man away—he wanted to be on his own, settling against the fence, his eyes darting around.

The Ricans stayed by the pit in their customary chairs and logs, waiting on their crew chief and captain. Manolo acted as first lieutenant in Chucho's absence. He had them loose; they joked around like on any other day. The only exception being Rodrigo who sulked a few steps away from the group.

Frank didn't have Scraggins in sight.

When the sun hit the top of the fence, Frank made eye contact with Manolo whose smile disappeared right away. Frank tugged on his left ear. Manolo walked away from the pit, heading directly away from the tunnel. Three of his guys followed behind, but not Rodrigo who continued to look petulant.

The door to the tunnel opened a crack; it's opening faced away from the fence. Frank, the lookout for the door's movement, tapped his chest twice like he was trying to clear some phlegm. Lou's eyes zeroed in, and he made his move to the door.

But it didn't open more than a crack. Lou slowed his roll, a puzzled look on his face.

At the last moment he froze and whirled his head around to see Manolo, flanked by his two guys, bearing down on him. Realization flooded his face, and he turned his head to Frank.

"You miserable piece of shit," Lou said, fixating only on Frank, and got into a fighting position ready to take on the world. When Frank and Scraggins walked passed the tunnel door, Frank gave a single rap on the door. Chucho emerged and fell in behind them.

Now Lou found himself surrounded by six.

Chucho stepped forward. "Take it off or we goan do it."

Understanding turned to despair and then rage. "No. You can't do this to me. It was a play, it failed, okay, but you gotta give me a different out."

"You want I should get Betsy and see what he say?"

"Fuck you, you spic piece of shit. And you, soldier boy, fuck you the most. Fucking race traitor. You take up with the nigger instead of me? You can go to fucking hell." And he lunged. He didn't get to Frank; Manolo's brick left fist landed in Lou's solar plexus and he went down, wheezing. The others worked quickly to strip him violently of his jumpsuit. Despite the obvious pain, Lou bounced up, surprising everyone. The feint worked, and Lou made to jump up the fence and over to the other side. Cursed by his long legs, Lou remained within reach even as his fingertips neared the top bar and the freedom of another day.

"Oh no, my *fanático* friend. You not goan get away that easy."

Manolo and Frank pulled hard, and Lou came back down to the ground where the others pinned him and waited for the men in black. Frank, standing at Lou's feet, locked eyes with him; he remained defiant despite being spread eagle with just his drawers for protection.

"This ain't right. This ain't a proper end for a man like myself."

"What kind of man is that, Lou? You don't stand for shit, but Lou, that's why you couldn't cut it in the Army," Frank said.

"I couldn't cut it because assholes like you tried to tell me what to do and you didn't know any better. If I did what they told me, I'd be blown to pieces in Afghanistan."

"At least you'd of died doing something worthwhile," Frank said leaning in.

Lou reared back and spit in Frank's face.

"You piece of shit." Frank gave a heel kick to Lou's abdomen. "Be grateful I left your nuts out of this." Just then the tunnel door reopened.

This time six men in black emerged, single file, sporting the same riot gear, right hands firmly on the shoulder of the man in front. They didn't have far to go. The crimson jumpsuits scattered as the single formation broke up elegantly forming a semicircle around the now fetal-positioned Lou; he lay there whimpering, the fight gone.

Frank watched as they carried him back into the tunnel. He tried to glimpse what it looked like inside, but the large, black-clad men blocked his view as the door closed behind them.

Chucho broke out in his full-face grin and clapped Frank on the back.

"You did good, *soldado*."

"I want that favor," Frank said.

"We'll talk more, tonight. It will be a good meal; I can tell you that." He gazed up at the sky. "She liked this little display; she'll reward us."

"Who's she? And where did they take Lou?"

"The secrets of Burning River are hers and hers alone," he said and walked away.

Scraggins walked up to Frank who hadn't moved. "You coming, man?"

Frank didn't answer, his gaze off in the distance.

"Hey, Marine, you there?" Scraggins snapped his fingers in front of Frank's eyes.

"Yea, yea. I'm here. I'll join you in a second."

Scraggins turned, then stopped and looked at Frank.

"How *come* you took my side instead of your boy Lou? I'm just curious."

"He wasn't my boy. Didn't matter what I did for him, he was always going to harbor anger over what I did to Chauncey—and him, for that matter. He wasn't ever going to stop coming after me. Plus, I gotta good sense of what you're like under pressure; I served with a lot of people like you in Iraq. They did you proud."

"People like me?" Scraggins said, eyebrows raised.

"Shit, man, you know what I mean. Don't get your panties in a bunch."

Another clap on the back, "I'm just giving you shit."

CHAPTER 31

Chucho stood when he saw Frank approaching the pit, pulled a lawn chair close to his own, tapped it. "*Aqui. Sienta te, por favor.* You earned it."

Dinner was in fact something special: lamb. The guys in lime scurried around like busy bees and put everything together to cook them. His eyes on the goings on, Chucho spoke: "You are unusual, *soldado.*"

Frank settled in the lawn chair. After so long of not sitting in something designed for the seated human, it was especially welcome.

"Why is that?"

"I know cons; you don't feel like one," Chucho said.

"Because I'm not."

The cooks rubbed spices on the skinned lambs and situated their carcasses on a spit.

After a moment Frank spoke again. "You give thought to my request?"

Chucho nodded. "I think you earn the night inside. So, my answer is yes. You go. One night in tent won't kill me." And he laughed.

A tingle ran down Frank's spine at the thought of getting inside. Sensing this, Chucho said:

"Look, I don't know what you expect to find inside, but I think you be disappointed." He cocked his head, then shook it. "You know what, maybe not? Who can say? *Claro*, not me. Anyway"—a hearty clap on Frank's shoulder—"this is a big night. We eliminate big risk in Lou, and we eat good. That is cause for celebration."

Every man who circulated the pit was a hearty fellow well met, the mood celebratory. They served the lamb skewered on sticks. The meat melted like butter in Frank's mouth, the taste every bit as delectable as promised by the aroma.

Afterwards another flask was passed around and Frank drank deeply.

Chucho was his usual gregarious self, eating, greeting, and filling the space with his vibrant and jovial voice.

"*Soldado*," he boomed, "Step up here and tell us a war story. *Venga, venga, venga.*"

"Neh. I'm good," Frank said.

Chucho spanned the area of the pit encouraging others to persuade Frank ,and they responded with cheers and exhortations. Finally enough momentum built, and Frank stood up, hands held in surrender.

"Alright, alright. I'll tell you all a story."

The pit quieted enough for the sounds of the crackling fire to be heard. Milking the moment, Frank was silent a moment, then began speaking:

"We had to do these patrols. You heard about them, right, about the IEDs, the improvised explosive devices, the skirmishes, the injuries. But I want to tell you about a different experience I had. Maybe I'm inspired by the great feast we had." A cheer went up. "Or maybe this has been on my mind.

"I'm in country on the road with my guys. That's five of us on a Humvee, traveling some of the backroads, out of the city. We were on a mission to pick up a local from a different town. I don't even remember who we picked up, but I remember well the trip. Out here in the sticks we're not as worried about IEDs because it's sparsely populated and wasn't part of the general fight. One of the few times we could enjoy a ride without the intense fear of a jackpot. Out there it's mostly arid land with occasional sheep farms and the lonely shepherd.

"And I mean lonely. We were humming along doing thirty or forty when my gunner gives me an elbow and points to a rise on the left. There I see what he's pointing to. In the distance on a hill with a lone tree a shepherd is tending to his flock. I ask for the binoculars and focus in on the shepherd. He's not studying the Quran or watering his flock. Instead he's got the poor sheep on its back, legs firmly grasped in his fists and he's humping that goddamned animal like it's Saturday Night in the whorehouse." A mixture of groans and catcalls rose up in the pit.

"I give my driver a nudge and tell him to slow down. I put down the binoculars and ask for the sniper rifle. I tested out pretty well during marksmanship, but this was a hell of a shot. On the move with a humping target." Frank pantomimed holding the rifle, looking through its scope. "I zero in on the guy and I can see he can't be more than a teenager; he's still rocking back and forth giving that sheep the all-star fuck of its life. I tell my driver, 'hold her steady, hold her steady' and just as we're passing by, I squeeze off a round. Nearly took that sheep-fucker's head clean off. His body broke free of the animal. It righted itself quickly and started limping its way back to the rest of the herd. I kept my focus on the sheep and squeezed off a second round. The bullet sounded loud to me, and its echo ricocheted off of the hill just as the sheep went down.

"My guys whooped it up. 'Great shot,' 'Best Marine shot of a moving target since Oswald,' and all that. The gunner looked puzzled. 'But, Sarge,' he says, 'Why'd you have to go after the sheep. I mean, it was the victim, it didn't do anything wrong.' And I says, 'Just think how hard it will be for the male sheep to live up to that teenage shepherd's marathon fucking—I mean, I did that lady sheep a favor. Now she won't feel a lifetime of sexual disappointment.'"

CHAPTER 32

Frank sat back down next to Chucho. The fire'd been allowed to settle to a ruby glow. They were far enough from it the heat wasn't too oppressive.

"Funny story." Chucho looked Frank over, nodding his head. "You something, man, you know that."

"Frank. Call me Frank."

"No problem. Frank. Short for Francis."

"It is."

"Your middle name Xavier?"

"Yes, again. You Catholic, too?"

"I'm from Latin America—course I'm Catholic." Just to be sure he made the sign of the cross and kissed his fingers. They both laughed.

"You a different, cat, Frank. I don't mind saying. I seen a few people roll through here and you gotta different vibe for sure."

"Somebody already told me everyone says they're innocent, but I'm not a criminal."

Chucho leaned forward and looked in Frank's eyes. He smiled and smacked Frank's thigh.

"I believe you, man, I believe you. Not that it makes much difference, though, right?"

"It actually helps that you say it." He waited a beat then said, "I suppose you're also innocent." Frank didn't mean it to be condescending or snide and he waited for Chucho's response. To his relief, the grand laugh lines reappeared.

"Fuck no, man, I guilty as hell. But not like you think." The lines vanished and he leaned in again. "I grew in Porto Rico. My father, he was a cop. Yea, a police officer, big shot in neighborhood. I used to go around with him on his beat, him so proud to bring his boy with him. I remember, he went to all the shops, and they give little gifts to me, make me feel real important right next to him. He was a big man, too. Big belly. You know, in Latin country, big belly mean you got a lot, and you can afford to get fat. So I look up to my father. But I take after my grandfather, his father. He was criminal like me." A hearty laugh.

"I pulled a lot of shit in Porto Rico. Break mother's heart. My father kept me out of a lot of trouble, but I did some time in prison, and he die when I was inside. Broke Mama's heart. She move here to Cleveland, be closer to my sister who move here. When I got out, I promise to come here to take care of her."

Chucho stood and punctuated his next statements with a beat to his chest with each one:

"I promise to Mama, I come here, I straighten up, I do right by you and Papa's memory." He sat back down. "You know, I wasn't a pup when I got outta prison. I already thirty-eight and knew better. So when I made those promises, I mean them. And then I come to Cleveland, and I look for job and is hard. My English is okay, but not great. My record back home don't help.

"An amigo of mine comes up a few months later. Miguel. We did some jobs together, did some time together. I thought he was brother.

Do anything for him. He come to me, he say, 'Chucho, I got a can't-miss job. Easy money.' I know better, now, right, I know there is no easy money, that shit always come back on your head. Too easy, look out, here comes trouble, right? But I don't got money, and my life is a little more complicated, so I say, okay, I do this job with you."

He stopped his monologue, and Chucho's face took on a new look Frank hadn't seen. The Greek tragedy mask. Deadly serious and conveying intense gravity, he continued.

"We hit a drug dealer. He wasn't supposed to be at home, or that's what Miguel say. But he at home and he fire at us. Miguel fire back; I don't have a gun, I hiding behind a wall. We take off. The drug dealer die from gunshot. I get picked up, Miguel still on the loose. What you think that mean?"

Frank shrugged.

"Means, he gave me up. My brother,"—he smacked his chest surprisingly hard—"a piece of shit, *chivato*. You know how that hurts?!"

He glared with such intensity, Frank felt a chill despite their proximity to the fire.

Just as fast as he'd ratcheted up the intensity, he went back to the fun-loving Chucho.

"But that is past. I deserve to be here. I mean, I don't shoot drug dealer, but I went with Miguel, like a stupid kid instead of grown man I was. I let myself down, I let Mama down, and I let Papa down."

They sat silently. It was Chucho who spoke first.

"I know you want to get inside. You did for me; I honor our agreement. I know you did for yourself, but still, in here a favor is a favor." He stood and extended his arm. "*Vaya con Dios*, Francis Xavier."

Frank got up shakily. Chucho grabbed Frank and righted him. "Too much *bebida*, I think. But they straighten that out for you." And he laughed.

"What do I do?" It came out in a whisper.

Chucho gave him a gentle nudge in the direction of the tunnel. "Just go and open the door, step through. The rest take care of itself."

"Isn't the door locked?"

"It will open for you, trust me. Burning River see verbal deal like written, *entiendes*? You see. Just go, I see you in the morning."

With Chucho's encouragement, Frank took some wobbly steps towards the tunnel. As he closed in on it, his breath quickened, his pace slowed. The entrance grew larger in his vision, the anticipation welling inside almost threatening to burst him open.

He put a light hand on the doorknob, almost expecting a shock, but it was just a knob. Warm to the touch. Gentle twisting pressure and it gave easily, the door offering a satisfying and welcoming click. He opened it enough to slip in, and it softly closed behind him.

CHAPTER 33

H is eyes slowly adjusted to the dim light. A foyer of sorts, square area with a maroon rug on the ground in front of another door. That one had an opaque diamond window. He made to step forward onto the rug when a soft metallic voice rang out.

"Please take off your shoes."

Self-conscious of his filthy clodhoppers, he hesitated.

"It's okay. Don't be ashamed. I'm here to help."

Slowly he stepped out of his shoes.

"Now move forward to the mat."

The softness of the rug felt ravishing.

Consumed with the tactile sensation, he missed the door opening. A petite woman peeked around the door. She wore a silk robe and had flaming red hair (like Laurie though hers had darkened with each of the two children) pulled back in a plait.

"Please come in and stand right over here." The feminine timbres of her voice startled him, like he'd been caught doing something shameful. He complied with the timid steps of a toddler. The first thing to hit him was her perfume, an exotic scent, something he remembered from a trip to Thailand. He felt renewed shame in the extreme contrast with his own unwashed, ripe body odor.

As if on cue, she spoke: "We'll take care of you, don't worry."

Another woman came over, and the two silently peeled his jumpsuit off of him. They pulled down his briefs unceremoniously. He self-consciously covered his genitals, but the women went undisturbed through their ministrations. The redhead took him by his hand, peeling it away from his groin. The other woman bagged up his clothes and exited stage left.

He followed the redhead down a carpeted hallway to a door. She opened it and gestured for him to go in first. It was a large tiled room with a shower on one side. To the left of the shower was a small room equipped with a lone toilet. He almost wept.

"Do you need to use the facilities?"

He didn't, but wished he did. "I'm okay." They were his first words, and they came out stronger than he expected. She stepped forward and turned the water on. The spigot delivered a stream similar to an Amazon rain.

"Step in the shower, please."

The water felt hot at first, but he got used to it quickly. Dirt ran off of him in rivulets. He held his face up to the stream, luxuriating in the heavy downpour. Through the sheet of water he watched her remove her robe and daintily set it on a chair to the side. Then she removed her flip-flops. She had an athletic build with small breasts. Near the chair she picked up a shower caddy with shampoo and soap and stepped into the shower with him.

Frank spun quickly away to hide his growing erection.

"There's no reason to be ashamed. Relax. I'm here to help."

He heard her squeeze one of the bottles then he felt warm hands massaging the soap into his back. Eyes closed, water running down his face, he let his arms hang slack. She ran her hands over every surface of his torso, his arms, down his legs and back up again, slowing the progress as she neared the erection he couldn't stop. Pressing her body against his he felt her breasts against his back. Desire welled up in him, and he turned, prepared to embrace her, the red hair, the petite body. She kept hold of his penis as he turned.

They stood close, his breathing heavy; he looked deep into her eyes, a light shade of green, almost yellow. He shut his eyes for a moment and saw Laurie's luminous blue eyes. He opened them again, and it jarred him from the intense lust he felt. Anger welled up in him, and he grabbed this woman's arms in a fierce embrace, freezing her stroking actions.

"Stop. Please."

She didn't look offended or even scared. The erection receded.

"I'm here to help. Why don't you let me shampoo your hair."

He felt weak in the knees, overheated from the sexual stimulation, the hot water, and the residual effects of intoxication. Wordlessly she reached behind him and dialed the water cooler. Rejuvenated, he stood straighter, bent his head down. She applied shampoo and worked it into a lather. The scalp massage felt amazing. She turned the water warmer and rinsed his head off. That completed, she shut the water off. He stood dripping on the tile floor as she grabbed a towel from a hook and dried him off then tied the towel around his waist.

She grabbed her own robe and put in on. There wasn't a hint of regret or anger in her actions. He held the towel cinched in one hand and accepted her hand in his other to be led out of the shower. Back down the hallway.

A distant part of his mind registered the need to explore, to seek, to find something tangible. But his consciousness seemed overtaken by a cleansing, both spiritual and physical. The plushness of the carpet, the softness of her hand led him to total surrender in the moment.

Another door to a room with a plush bed, clean white sheets. She held them open, inviting him to lie down. He made to get in with the towel, but she gently kept hold of it letting it slip off as he crawled into the bed, the sheets blessedly cool.

Frank lowered his head to the pillow, closed his eyes. He felt her slip into bed beside him. A distant part of him noted the feel of skin against his own, and he put an arm around her and slipped off into a blissful sleep.

At some point of the night, he registered a deep longing and felt her near. He turned to her, saw her eyes open and inviting. Wordlessly he kissed, embraced her. She turned him on his back and mounted him. It wasn't happening to him; he observed the action as if outside himself. She remained stationary letting him increase his thrusts until he climaxed soundlessly, his face contorted. He sat up, hugged her tight, tight, then slipped back on the pillow and fell back asleep.

CHAPTER 34

Consciousness returned in gentle waves. His eyes gradually opened to fiery red hair splayed on his chest. He'd not moved the entire night. The room shined brighter now than it did last night. Watching her draw deep breaths he synchronized his respirations to hers.

"I don't want to go back."

She didn't move, but indicated she'd heard with a gentle hmm.

He played his hands over her back gently running his nails all around.

"That's nice, Francis," she said.

"How do you—" he began then stopped himself. "I don't even know your name."

Lifting her head she offered a smile. "I know a lot of things about you, Francis."

"Only my mother and my wife call me that."

"But your mother is gone, and your wife has left you." Her eyes looked greener in this light. The look on her face and her use of his full name unnerved him.

"I don't like how you know so much."

She sat up, back to him, grabbed at her robe. When she stood up, he became aroused at the shape of her from behind. She had a perfect little ass. He suppressed that and refocused on his original goal for getting inside.

"How do I get out of this place?"

"Where would you go?"

"What the hell do you mean?" he said. "I don't belong here. You got me trapped in this bizarre fucking world against my will. And no amount of beauty and good treatment can change that."

"I don't know why you're getting so upset. Didn't I show you tenderness, love?"

Said so much like an automaton.

"What the hell kind of place is this?" He stood up abruptly, became acutely aware of his nudity and pulled the sheets to cover up. "Where are my clothes?"

On cue the door opened and the other woman from last night laid his neatly washed and folded briefs and jumpsuit on the edge of the bed and retreated out the door. He grabbed at his clothing. They were still warm when he put them on, buttoned up.

"Francis, why are you agitated? We made love. Why should you be angry?"

"Because," he said as he dressed, "this whole place is one big ruse. And I can't understand it. I just want to go home."

"Where would you go? Your wife has expelled you from your home—you are jobless. But here you could make a life."

He froze in mid-buttoning of his jumpsuit. There was no guile in her face; it was an open expression of genuine curiosity. She walked over and looked up at him. Put her hands on his cheeks. He let her for a moment then his eyes flashed with anger, and he grabbed her hands roughly and pulled her arms apart. To his dismay she showed no surprise or concern for her own well-being.

He spoke not to her, but the room.

"I am going to split your little whore in half if you don't tell me what the FUCK IS GOING ON HERE?!"

The door opened and two men in black, without flak jackets, but with the helmets and vizors, took a step towards him, then stopped. He spun her around, stepped back, held her by the throat.

"Don't take another fucking step, or I'll snap her neck."

It unnerved him to see his threat having no impact on the two men. Whatever orders they took, from whomever issued them, had zero to do with his threat to harm the hostage. They operated independently of his actions or verbiage. And he knew it.

"Frank," a voice said. He knew the others heard it, so it didn't come from inside his head, but he didn't see either the speaker or any device.

"Are you in charge?" he said, looking around the room, hand still around the woman's throat. The men remained in repose by the door.

"I am." The timbre of the voice suggested a more mature woman. One who was used to being in charge and would not rattle easily. She continued, "And I want you to know this isn't necessary. You're not going to harm this woman, and I'm not going to be moved by threats. I am interested in you. That is why I relayed the message delicately delivered by the pretty young thing you're manhandling. So, let her go. These men are not going to do anything to you after you relinquish what you believe is a bargaining chip. Let her go and we'll speak."

He released his grip and she walked between the men and exited. Like nothing had happened. Not even a glance back at him. He realized, their bodies close together through his aggression, her pulse hadn't quickened, and she hadn't perspired despite the bodily harm his threats suggested.

True to the disembodied voice's promise, the men in black stood at ease, made no moves towards him.

"Okay," Frank said. "Tell me what the hell is going on."

"I'm afraid I'm not going to be able to satisfy your need for information. I can only say it is my wish you remain here with us."

"What the hell does that mean? By what right do you hold me here?"

A deep-throated, Kathleen-Turneresque chuckle. "Ah, Frank. You're the kind of man I seek."

"Who the fuck are you?!" Despite his agitation the men didn't flinch—didn't move an inch.

"You can call me Warden. That's good enough for now."

He looked around, not sure where to focus his gaze. "But that's not good enough. I want to go home."

"Home? And where is that, pray tell? Because you certainly aren't returning to your life with Laurie."

"How the hell do you know what I will or won't be doing? Besides, my liberty isn't dependent on my relationship with my wife."

"C'mon, Frank. Let's face facts—ex-wife."

He waved that off. "Not yet. Again, don't matter who or what I do, you still can't hold me here against my will."

"Can't I? But I digress. I'm not looking to hold you against your will. I seek out men like you."

Frank rubbed his temples. "You got me real confused."

"You've had enough for now. Your life here could be very different, and I'm glad you were treated to real tenderness."

He balled up his fists and flew into a rage. "Let me the fuck out of here." He made to split between the two men in black. They quickly sprang into action and subdued him with greater gentleness than he afforded them. He squirmed and fought to free himself, but they were far stronger yet didn't seem to be making much effort.

"Are you done yet?" the voice asked.

Tired, out of breath, and dispirited, he ceased his struggle.

"There is no home, Frank. I'm sorry to have to tell you. Laurie found the cameras you installed in the house. She was furious enough to consider going to the police. In the end, she didn't because of the children. But she's done. Done, Frank, do you understand? It's over."

He hung his head. "You don't know what you're talking about."

"Just keep an open mind, will you, Frank? You have skills we can use, and, in turn, we can provide you what you need."

Some unspoken signal went to the men in black, and they gently escorted Frank out of the room and down the hall. He barely registered the movement and just like that he was back outside the tunnel. His downtrodden eyes followed the path to the pit and fell upon Chucho, in a squat like he was playing dice, with that broad grin on his face.

CHAPTER 35

"How did you enjoy your night, Francis Xavier? Was it a revelation?" He laughed heartily. "I see you get cleaned up. My first night inside, *Dios mios*, I'll never forget."

Frank's confusion at what he'd experienced receded, and anger came in its stead.

"I'm no better off now than I was."

"*Mierda*. You smell better and you got laid, right?"

In lieu of answering he started down the path. Chucho followed behind.

"I get it, amigo. You're not the kind who kiss and tell. I respect the shit out of that. But me, I kiss, fuck, eat pussy, and talk much." More laughter.

They sat in the lawn chairs. Frank slouched in his own, down in the mouth. Chucho looked him over, gave him a couple of light smacks to the thigh.

"What the fuck, Frank? I give you great gift and you come back like you buried your mother. You need to lighten' up."

"I need to get out of here. It boggles my mind how you all just take this without a fight."

Chucho grew angry. "What you mean, no fight? What you think, you only one who want to leave? Man, you stuck in you head. You think I no want to leave? Shiiiittttt, I fought every day when I first come. How you think I get to be *capitan*?" He stood up straight, chest out. "But no matter how much I fight, it don't change that I here. You still don't get it. There's nothing to fight. This ain't no regular place, man, you should know by now. You gotta accept that."

Rodrigo walked up to the two looking like he was going to pull up a seat. Chucho waved him off.

"Not now, Rigo, come back later."

Frank watched Rodrigo slink off, a sulky look on his face.

"He's not going to like that." Frank said.

"I don't care." He turned to Frank, real concern on his face. "You need to get happy; there's going to be a nice meal tonight. Betsy been gettin' horny so we bring some *tonto* from outside to fight him. Going to be fun."

"I got two kids. How the hell do I just accept not being able to see them."

"Boys?"

"One of each."

"I gotta son," Chucho said proudly. "I mean, I got three girls, too, but I always wanted a boy. Funny, happened last and with some random chica I met in a bar. Oh, was my wife pissed.

"Yea, I play around, but never had another kid. I ran away from home and met this young thing in a bar in San Juan. I thought she just some puta but turn out she got real spirit. She get pregnant and tell me, 'I don't want nothing from you, but you be a father to our son.' When I realize it's mine, I was very proud. My first son. I thought I couldn't have sons, 'cause I had three girls and maybe I wasn't meant to pass on my father name. But it happened. My wife never like it."

"All your kids in Puerto Rico?"

"Sí."

"And you're in Cleveland?" Frank said.

"Well, I was. I don't know where the fuck I am now, but yea, I came to Cleveland. I tol' you, I had to take care of my mama." He paused a moment then said, "I din't think I be here long," and burst out in genuine laughter.

"What's your son's name?" Frank asked after a beat.

"Jesus, like mine."

"I thought your name was Chucho?"

"Is fun name, not real name."

"Nickname."

"Sí. But Jesus is my name. My son, we call him Chuy, also nickname."

"How do you feel not seeing him?"

The laugh lines vanished. "I don't want to talk about it."

"That's what I feel, too. I can't stand the idea of not being there for them. My last tour, we already had my daughter and then I found out my wife was pregnant while overseas. She sent me pictures of her progress, and then my son was born while I was still in country. It was a different tour, man, knowing I had kids waiting for me." He stared off into the distance. "Made me more cautious."

Chucho leaned in close. "I like you, Frank. I can see right away, you different. Don't give up on me, man. We'll figure something out." He smacked Frank's knee and stood.

"I gotta go see about Rodrigo," Chucho said.

Frank also stood. "Wait. You say there's gonna be another fight tonight?"

CHAPTER 36

The sucker, or *tonto,* as Chucho put it, chosen to fight Betsy turned out to be a twenty-something lumbering block of a man. He stood well over six feet and no less than three hundred pounds; he had a pear-shaped body and perpetually slapped cheeks. If his look of confusion and fear could be turned into electricity, it would power a small city.

Frank stood and watched as they led him on the path to the ad hoc ring being erected.

"Deliverance is here!" someone shouted. "Squeal like a pig, boy!"

"Oh, Jesus," Frank said to himself.

"He's going to need prayers, that's for sure."

Frank turned to Pastor who'd sidled up.

"I notice you're never late to the festivities. Heard about the fight, huh, decided to get in on the feast," Frank said watching them parade the would-be sheep to slaughter.

"I'm sure you wasn't always so cynical. I imagine war had something to do with that."

"You'd be wrong, preacher; my contempt for religion comes from my father."

"That so."

"Yes. If Jesus is God incarnate, then my father was hypocrisy the same way."

"He no longer with us?"

Frank shrugged. "I don't know. He's alive as far as I know. I wrote him off a long fucking time ago."

"And he taught you not to like religion?"

The lime guys finished putting together the ring. A cheer went up from the right where Betsy emerged from a tent, stretching his neck.

"I don't like this shit. This ain't right. Man, look at that kid. He looks like someone stuffed a giant with marshmallows. He'll get destroyed." Frank turned angrily towards Pastor. "How can you let this shit go on?"

"What do you suggest I do?"

"I don't know. Something. You know this place better'n I do."

"Way I hear it, you're getting to know it pretty well, too. Look at your clean clothes, man. You don't look like the same guy as before. No longer hungry. That's what this place does to you eventually."

"Man, you are so full of shit. On the other side of the fence you tell me I'm going to waste away. Now you tell me I'm too soft. Make up your fucking mind."

"Does taking your anger out on me solve any of your problems?" Pastor asked without rancor.

The tone of placidity bothered Frank more than if Pastor had shown anger. He scoffed. "You people are all the fucking same. Talk up the Son of God in the safety of your sermons but fade away when there's real courage required. Well, I'm not going to watch this."

He walked away. Another voice called after him.

"Ain't you going to stay for the fight?"

Rodrigo stood, hands on hips, sneering at Frank.

"Sodomy doesn't excite me like it does you."

"Whatchu mean by that?"

Frank walked up to Rodrigo, face to face. A crowd formed around them.

"It means, you get off watching a man fucking another man, faggot, and I don't."

Rodrigo shoved hard, "Who you calling faggot, you fuckin' *maricón*."

Before they could mix it up, Manolo grabbed Rodrigo and pulled him back. Chucho put a hand on Frank's chest. "Hey, man, you gotta calm down." He turned to the others. "*Soldado* here is just a little raw; he okay, though. He be okay." Back to Frank and sotto voce, "Come on, man, take it easy."

He didn't like being handled by Chucho but allowed it. Frank walked over to the lummox waiting on his fight with Betsy. The man-child sat on the ground contemplating a pair of boxing gloves laid out in front of him. He had a shock of blond curly hair and a pudgy, pinched face.

A newbie, his banana suit looked pristine.

"What's your name?"

No answer.

Frank crouched down and snapped his fingers. "Hey. You there?"

The guy slowly turned and regarded Frank.

"Tell me your name."

After a moment. "Seth."

"Okay, Seth, good."

Frank put his hand on Seth's shoulder and attempted a reassuring smile. It shocked him when Seth grabbed at his chest, drawing fists of Frank's jumpsuit and pulling like a drowning man; his face contorted in abject fear. "Where am I? What is this place?"

Seth's speech bore the unmistakable slowness of a dull intellect. Gently removing Seth's hands Frank got on his knees in front of the big kid.

"Where were you before you got here?"

"I live with my mom and dad in Mayfield Heights."

"That's the east side, right?"

Seth's eyes turned, his pupils widening. Frank followed his glare to Betsy, getting in the ring.

"Focus on me, Seth. You ever do any boxing? Seth! Look at me, you ever do any fighting?"

A pathetic head shake.

"Alright, buddy. Nothing to it. Just gotta make sure you keep your guard up and move around the ring."

Frank didn't think there was a less nimble individual on Earth.

Chucho stepped into the ring, full MC mode etched on his face.

He began his loud spiel for the spectators. Frank hastily put the gloves on Seth's puffy hands. His hands were soft and milky white, like they'd never seen a hard day's labor.

"What do you do for a living, Seth?"

"Huh?"

"How do you have money?"

"My Dad gives me an allowance."

Frank turned the gloves over and tied them. "What do you buy with the money?"

"Mostly baseball and Pokémon cards."

"Okay, buddy, stand up with me." They both stood as Chucho announced Betsy to the cheers of the crowd.

"And in the challenger corner we have…" Chucho looked expectantly at Seth.

Frank gently pushed Seth aft and stepped forward. He bellowed,

"This guy ain't fighting!"

Chucho walked over to Frank, concern on his face. "What are you talking about? He has to."

"I won't let it happen."

"Frank, c'mon. You know how it works. If he's 'sposed to fight, he got to. Nothing we can do."

"The place needs a fight. It don't matter who's involved, right?"

"I spose," Chucho said, his brow furrowed. "What are you…?"

Frank yelled theatrically, "How would you like to see me fight Betsy?!"

The assembled crowd went from hushed surprise to a great cheer.

"No, Frank. You can't." Chucho looked genuinely concerned.

"I'm touched, Chucho, I really am," Frank said softly as he ducked under the top rope and got in the ring, then loudly, "I will fight Betsy on one condition."

He let the suspense build for a moment. "I will fight Betsy only if we aren't allowed to wear gloves."

"Jesucristo, Frank, that's even worse."

The crowd loved it. Betsy didn't look like he cared one way or the other. He untied his gloves and pulled them off with his teeth.

Chucho stepped in close to Frank. "This is a bad choice, man. I lose either way, you unnerstan'? I don't like it."

"Too late. It's done. Burning River needs its tribute. Looks like it's going to be little ol' Frank." He retreated to his corner.

The crowd grew as word spread of the new challenger. Wagers were shouted across the ring. Scraggins came over to stand next to Frank outside the ropes.

"Man, you one crazy motherfucker. But I respect your balls so I'ma stand witchu."

"That's real nice. Got any advice?"

"Yea. Watch your six." Then he laughed uproariously and clapped Frank's back.

Frank did some rudimentary stretching while his mind rifled through all the lessons he'd accrued his whole fighting life about facing a larger, implacable opponent. Betsy just stood in the corner waiting. The jumpsuit didn't camouflage his huge chest and arms. Frank thought his own waist probably equaled one of Betsy's thighs. With gloves padding his fists he'd have no chance, but bareknuckle, if he could score some shots, he just might fell this mighty oak.

They squared off at the center of the ring then retreated to their corners; the makeshift bell dinged anemically, and Betsy lumbered forward, arms raised.

CHAPTER 37

Some in the crowd shouted encouragement to Frank, though he knew it probably meant they had him falling in round two.

He moved lightly on the balls of his feet circling the larger man. Betsy eyed him dispassionately, like a man ordering a steak knowing it's coming even if it takes time to cook.

"Come on, big man, let's see what you got."

Rope-a-dope was not an option, Frank decided. A couple of shots from Betsy could land him in a coma. He kept his distance, then launched a reconnaissance left cross, retreated immediately. The shot landed square on Betsy's jaw but did little to change his demeanor. Hard to say if the shot surprised Betsy or if he simply didn't believe anyone could hit him hard enough to matter.

Either way, Frank continued to mix it up with different punches; Betsy turned in a tight circle absorbing the blows with no inflicted damage.

The shouts and jeers from the crowd intensified.

"C'mon, quit dancing with him, Betsy, and get to the main course."

"Let's see that ass, Frank. Keep dancing, you bitch."

Frank focused on Betsy whose heavy-lidded eyes never showed any response.

"What do you say, big man. You ready to give in yet?" Frank said between breaths. "I heard you got a little dick for a Black man." And threw another cross, this one missing the mark. Off balance, he braced for a blow that didn't come. Instead Betsy shoved him; it didn't look like much, but it put Frank on the ground. He scrambled quickly up but needn't have; Betsy didn't make a move towards him.

After a couple of more feints, the bell rang.

The crowd booed.

"No more of this foreplay bullshit!" someone shouted.

Frank went to his corner; Scraggins held a flask of water for him.

"Why you think Betsy isn't attacking?" Frank asked.

"Cats don't eat the mice right away. They like to play with they food first."

Frank spit some water out. "Thanks, man, you're a real help."

"Look"—Scraggins pulled Frank in close—"just because Betsy likes to box don't mean the rules say you gotta box. You dig? The rules are there are no rules. You built like one of those American Ninja dudes. Play to your strengths. Endurance, quickness that's your ticket. Now go out there and survive another round."

The bell dinged again. This time Betsy moved more quickly to Frank. He even threw in a bob and weave combination, a few rapid punches. Frank's insides went cold. No one that size should be able to muster so much velocity.

"I'ma enjoy ripping up yo asshole," Betsy said in a baritone voice.

"Ah, it speaks. I wasn't sure."

"Oh, you gonna beg for mercy 'fore it's over."

Betsy threw a couple of jabs. Frank decided if he was going to invite a haymaker, he needed to take a jab or two. He let the second land awkwardly on his own forehead, caused his vision to blur, then, blessedly, it returned. He stayed crouched over.

It drew a grin from Betsy. "Not as fast as you think."

Now or never. Frank wobbled a little. Betsy took the bait and swung for the fences with his right hand. Frank easily evaded the right, leaned in, and delivered a swift leg kick to Betsy's abdomen, the sharp tibia landing squarely in the solar plexus. He gave it extra oomph and it at least registered something on Betsy's face but did little else.

"Oh, it's like that, is it." And he bull-rushed with such suddenness Frank had no time to evade. This must be what it's like to fall down in Pamplona.

Letting his bulk completely fall on Frank, Betsy simultaneously rocketed Frank's torso with rapid body blows. Gasping for breath, struggling to shield his ribs, Frank saw one opportunity—he kneed Betsy in the groin while jabbing with his thumbs at the big man's eyes. Betsy reared up enough for Frank to squeeze out and roll to safety. He felt like tenderized beef but didn't think any ribs were broken.

Betsy stood up, rubbed at his eyes. Then he cursorily checked his testicles.

"Should'na done that."

The big man moved in again, throwing jabs. Frank parried and weaved. Betsy didn't vary his attacks; he just intensified them.

Frank feinted up, then went to the ground and tried a foot sweep. It was an effective move, well executed with enough power to take down another man of equal or maybe a little greater size. Unfortunately, on Betsy, it caused him to buckle, but not fall. Gravity already pulling him down, Betsy simply opted to drive his knee down almost catching Frank right in the throat.

Frank rolled away and jumped back up. Betsy pushed off the ground and resumed his stance. The crowd erupted.

Before he could make another move the bell rang and the spectators booed lustily.

Back in his corner, Scraggins handed over the flask.

"Man, I thought you was a goner there when he jumped on top of you."

Preserving all his energy he opted to roll his eyes rather than speak.

"Why don't you try that police choke move you done before? That worked."

Frank had considered it but gave it up because it meant getting in too close. The second bell came way too soon, and he dragged himself away from the corner to a waiting Betsy who looked nearly as fresh as when they started.

CHAPTER 38

"You don't look so good, boy. You best keep some energy so you can squirm on the ground. Don't be disappointin' me." Betsy actually grinned. He had a mouth full of perfectly white and straight teeth.

They circled each other. Frank thought he detected a little wear in Betsy's tread, but that could have been wishful thinking.

"Holy shit, I'd've thought all your teeth would be knocked out, but look at you. You got a whole set."

"Mama told me to brush and floss or I'd lose 'em. I took her advice."

"What'd she tell you about being a violent, homicidal ass pirate?"

Betsy lunged; instead of taking a head shot, Frank went right and kicked him low, at the knee joint. Not a kill shot, just a swift leg jab, but it packed a lot of heat. Betsy limped a little, shook it off.

"Good, you keep that up, boy, its must going to make it more sweet."

"Tell me more about your mama. Did she work or was she a cock-sucker like you?"

He didn't lunge, but Frank detected more malice behind those hooded lids. They continued their slow dance.

"Hey," Frank added, "Did she knock out her johns and give you free rein on their asses? Is that how you got started?"

A haymaker this time. Moving to his left, Frank felt the wind of it blow by his face as he just managed to avoid it. He gave a mule kick to the other knee joint. This one landed better, and a crack sounded out, loud enough to be heard by the spectators who oohed appreciatively.

Now visibly limping, Betsy flashed rage and moved in suddenly, caught Frank off guard. Rather than try to get away, Frank moved closer to Betsy and threw compact, rabbit punches into his ribs. The larger man pulled Frank in tight and squeezed for all his worth, cutting off Frank's breathing. Betsy groaned with the effort and just as Frank saw spots, he lifted both hands above his head and clapped both Betsy's ears with as much force he could muster. The grip eased enough to allow Frank to slip out and catch his breath; he knew he had to act fast. He jabbed at Betsy's throat, then his eyes. The big man gasped and closed his eyes in pain.

Frank got behind Betsy and kicked his knee again causing it to buckle. A rapid succession of shots to the legs brought the big man to one knee. Frank turned to face Betsy and executed a front heel kick to the solar plexus; it drove Betsy onto the ground. Frank pounced on the supine Betsy and rained haymakers and elbows on his head, MMA style. Despite all this, for a moment it looked like Betsy might rally; he kicked up, ejecting Frank with enough power to throw him. But he seemed to spend his last energy on the release, because when he got up, he wobbled and stood unsteady on his feet, looking dazed and still struggling to breath and open his eyes.

"Now Frank, take him out!" Scraggins yelled.

Frank willed his body to pull in oxygen, Betsy's bear hug echoing in his chest cavity. He stood about four feet from Betsy who continued to seesaw just in front of the rope. Taking a running start, he side kicked

Betsy square in the chest expelling the large man from the ring.

The crowd dispersed in that area to give Betsy space or because they feared he was still functional. A few cheers, but most stood in stunned silence.

Frank walked over the felled rope and knelt on top of the fallen man, one knee on the ground, the other pressing down on Betsy's cheek. Shallow breaths, blood running down his nose, but conscious, one eye squinting open. No fear in that eye, but perhaps some realization.

Adding pressure to his knee. "You give up?"

Betsy didn't answer.

Frank moved his whole body weight forward, pressing Betsy's face into the soft ground. The big man sputtered, tried to fight, but his strength was sapped by probable internal bleeding.

Chucho stepped forward.

"Don't kill him, Frank, we need him."

Frank, his face filled with rage, leaned in close to Betsy. "You fucking yield right now or I'll beat you to half to death and have this whole fucking pod run a train on your ass. Before it's over they'll be able to drive a Mack truck up there."

A sigh, one eye closed, Betsy nodded subtly. "I give up," he said almost inaudibly.

"Louder!"

"I give up!"

Frank let his knee up slowly and backed away. Betsy rolled onto his back and closed his eyes. The look on his face said he wasn't going to pull a Lou and hold a grudge.

Frank walked up to Chucho whose face still registered shock.

"The fights are over. You understand? Over," Frank said.

"We need something to get fed. That's the rules."

"I'll figure that out. In the meantime, you and me are going to share the captaincy. Are you okay with that?"

In lieu of answering, Chucho put out a hand. They shook on it.

"And I get the first night inside," Frank added.

"I guess you earn that," Chucho said.

"You work on Betsy, make sure he understands it wasn't personal and I still respect him. We're going to need him to keep the peace."

Chucho nodded. Frank turned and walked slowly towards the pit, adrenaline still coursing through his veins keeping him buoyed. Men in the crowd pushed past each other to pat his shoulder, desperate to share in the moment.

CHAPTER 39

A whole side of beef.

One hell of a meal.

Seth had to be figured out. Frank had gone back and talked with the kid and confirmed this kid was operating at an imbecilic level. He stood at the pit and loudly proclaimed Seth's inauguration into the pod and looked tensely at the tunnel's door. No men emerged, geared up to take him, so he figured the incantation sufficed.

That done, he lay down in his tent for a rest.

Chucho gently nudged him awake to come to dinner.

"I'm not hungry. Start without me."

"It don't work like that. You're guest of honor; you must be there."

He held out a hand, Frank grasped it and accepted the help up.

"Beside, maybe you tell another funny story."

Frank's entrance into the pit created a stir. Guys shouted out accolades. Chucho made an elaborate announcement, enjoining everyone to come and eat.

Betsy sat in a chair, stood gingerly when Frank made eye contact with him. Frank gave a little nod and Betsy retook his seat with a grimace.

Everyone crowded around the fire pit waiting on the butchering of the beef.

The lime jumpsuits handed out big hunks of meat. The grateful recipients took them and sat down. They ate them off the bone or with their hands. Frank collected a choice cut and made a big show of walking it over to Betsy.

Frank didn't each much. He accepted a piece from Chucho. Burnt on the outside, pink on the inside. He didn't enjoy it though; his thoughts were on next steps. He stood and raised his hands and silence fell.

"Brothers, I am grateful to be with you sharing in this great feast." He turned slowly to make eye contact with every man assembled there. "Let this be a new day for us. You watched me fight Betsy, but I don't have any animus for him. He is not responsible for the brutality displayed here. Were it not for his actions many of us would have gone hungry. So, no, I bear no ill will to Betsy, and I want you all to hear that loud and clear. In fact, you are all my brothers as of tonight. We are brother in arms fighting an invisible, but cruel enemy. I speak of the power that brought us here and keeps us trapped and fighting each other like animals. It is the true enemy."

He let that sit for a moment, continuing his scanning of the faces, seeing eager and receptive eyes hungrily looking back at him.

"Let us end the petty differences. No more dividing out by tribe. We are all together in this and only by working together can we get out of this place!"

He finished with a crescendo; the crimson jumpsuits leapt up with a cheer.

Frank retook his seat next to Chucho.

"That's a great speech. You really are the Podfather, now. I just don't know how we goan eat, but you say you gotta plan, so I believe you."

"Yeah. Phase two, tonight. In the meantime—" he called to Scraggins who limped over, a big grin on his face.

"Frank, you one fancy talkin' mother fucker."

"Scraggins, pull up a chair and sit."

Chucho got uncomfortable. "I don't know 'bout this. You don't understand the things that happened before you came."

"I'm sure you're right, man," Frank said. "But the divisions in this place is what leads to the confusion. Divide and conquer, it's the first rule of warfare. So we can't be split into groups anymore. Chucho, I'm asking you to make peace. No more beefs with anyone. Start with Scraggins here, then you two move on to Anderson and his boys. Rally them around the idea of moving against this place."

"Shit, Frank, you trying for racial harmony even the Reverend King couldn't bring about," Scraggins said. "Besides, you'd be better approaching Anderson, you being white and all."

"I don't have the time. I'm going in to get an audience with the management."

Chucho shook his head, a frown on his face. "No way that happens. No way. You got fantasy, baby."

"You leave it to me. In the meantime, make peace happen." He straightened out his jumpsuit as best he could. The crimson worked out well—the blood didn't show up as much. "Wish me luck."

"*Bueno suerte*, man. *Vaya con Dios*."

Frank walked to the tunnel; he wasn't surprised to find the door unlocked and ready to open to him.

CHAPTER 40

The door closed behind him with an unmistakable click of a lock. The foyer looked different. Or maybe his recollections from last night were hazy.

More spacious, brightly lit, no rug on the floor. And a single chair. Somebody had moved the door. Whereas before it stood just a few feet opposite the tunnel entrance, now it was to his left, nothing but a blank wall to his front. He knew enough to sit.

"What is it you want, Frank?" the anodyne voice rang out.

"You know. That's why you took away the whorehouse motif and replaced it with a waiting room. Am I going to wait for nothing, or will you meet with me?"

The silence lasted a couple of minutes; Frank found the quiet relaxing.

"The Warden eagerly awaits you."

A click sounded in the space, and a crack formed in the door opposite him.

He stood gingerly, his body aching from when Betsy pancaked him.

Through the door and down a long hallway. At the end stood another door. He pushed it open, but waited a moment before peeking in.

A plain empty chair in front of a plain empty desk. Something you might see in a hastily erected office for tax season where you could meet with a certified expert and file your W-2 for a reasonable fee.

"I'm sure the chair behind the desk isn't for me, so I'll just sit at this one." He pulled out the chair and sat. It had surprisingly good lumbar support.

He bobbed back and forth in the chair, warming up to the process. Like waiting on the principal only he didn't feel like he was in trouble. Mainly because he'd called for this meeting rather than being called to the office. It only mildly troubled him to be expected; the headiness of finally getting some answers filled him up, pushed everything else out.

The door opened behind him—he'd not realized it had closed after he entered—and he turned as a figure passed him. He found it hard to process what he saw.

A woman. She wore the shit out of a pencil skirt suit. He could see maturity in her, but she also looked much younger than she probably was. A stunning figure and a strikingly beautiful face smiling at him benevolently. He felt like he should stand like you did when a superior officer of high rank walked in. Instead, he did a little rise out of his chair and sat back down.

"That's very cute, Frank. I appreciate that." She extended a hand. Her hand was soft, but firm. The kind of shake he insisted his son model after him. A limp handshake broadcast weakness to the world. Warden sat down and looked at him expectantly. "I'm the Warden. I appreciate you coming to see me."

A part of his mind registered the inaccuracy of the statement, but his stomach, where he stored his anxiety, was in such a state of relaxation he didn't mind. In fact, he felt so at ease he smiled; it felt weird— he couldn't recall the last time he had occasion to grin like a child does when there is no purpose but to illustrate internal joy to the world.

They sat opposite each other in repose. Frank didn't feel the least bit awkward, or the driving need to break the silence. He had a lot of questions.

"I know you do. I don't know how many I'll be able to answer satisfactorily, but I can tell you things are looking up for you."

"What do you mean by that?"

"I've been watching you a long time. It's hard to find the right man for a job. Takes a lot of trial and error. You caught my eye with your highly developed sense of justice, and you've proven me right with your actions here."

"Where's here?" he said slowly, his brain and tongue fighting to properly enunciate. It irked him in a distant part of his consciousness, but, again, his overall sense of well-being displaced the agitation.

She waved the question off. "I don't want you to burden yourself with particulars. Better to accept the present as is and to work from there. I was impressed how you took control of the pod. It was precisely why I brought you here."

"You."

"Of course. But you knew that; it was why you wanted to talk to me. You see, I have plans for you. It begins with Burning River, but it is so much bigger than that."

His head swam. All the things he stored up, all the anger, indignation, and fury he sought to unleash on whoever was responsible for this—this injustice, this fucking disgrace of a miscarriage of justice— all that energy swirled out of reach. Frank shook his head to recalibrate.

Warden observed all this with a bemused smile. No concern, or even curiosity. As if she saw his anguish clearly and considered it light dinner theater.

Frank finally consolidated his emotions with a mind's-eye family portrait they'd done with their two small kids a couple of years ago. It did the trick; his anger rose up in a straight geyser from his core and spouted finally, "I don't give a shit about this place. I want to fucking go home!"

As quickly as it erupted, it dissipated, and he felt a strange shame for bringing negative energy into this serene space.

"Home? What do you have there? No family, no job. You weren't going to get the one you tried to interview for, I can assure you of that." Warden's face combined pity and compassion. It wasn't a mocking look, but a plaintive one. "You've burned many bridges since leaving the Marine Corps."

"What—what do you know?" It came out weakly.

"I know you've longed your whole life to live in a world with a consistent code of rules. Consistent in its application, consistent in its retribution for those who refused to comply. You see things a certain way, the right way, if I might, and you've struggled to create the world as you believe it should be. I'm the same way, Frank. We are of the same mind."

Her words burrowed straight into his soul. His mind rebelled, angry not to get answers, but his gut felt at peace.

"You see, I've created a place where such justice occurs. You've seen only a small part of it; I let you roam free to experiment just a taste. I have started to segregate the truly selfish, the irredeemably rotten from the rest of humanity."

"And what about Seth? Is that justice. He's half a retard. I can't see that guy being responsible for anything remotely serious enough to justify what Betsy would have done to him."

"Frank, everything isn't as it always seems. You operated on a battle-field, so you know full well sometimes you only have a piece of the puzzle, and it looks unjust until you take a step back and see the whole picture."

His will to fight ebbed, replaced by emotional fatigue. "So what would you have me do?"

"Just be you. Give expression to your instincts. They're good and I'm willing to ride them. Believe me, this is just the beginning. Work with me, Frank; I need someone with your clarity of vision combined with a mighty will to carry it out." She clapped her hands in delight. "Look how you tamed the Admissions Pod in so short a time. You exceeded even my most ambitious expectations."

He rubbed his temple struggling to coalesce his thoughts. "And if I want to leave? How about that? You let me go back to my life after some time, and then I'll give your offer some consideration."

"You'll start with Burning River—then together we'll branch out."

Frank leaned forward and smacked the desk. "You're not hearing me, godammit!"

Without any outward sign of being perturbed by the outburst, Warden simply sat back and smiled.

A queasiness came over Frank, and he had to sit back in his chair. He grew pale and sweaty.

"Listen, Frank, you think my offer over, heh? It's a great opportunity for you. I really believe you and I can do great things together."

He lacked the energy to respond; the slightest movement caused waves of nausea to crash over him. Warden continued to smile as she stood, tapped the desk like a judge banging a gavel, and walked out of the room. As soon as she exited, the nausea ceased as quickly as it had come.

Frank drew deep breaths, wiped his brow of the cold sweat formed there. He stood up, wobbled unsteadily, and fell back into the chair. He succeeded on his third try and staggered to the door only to find it locked.

"Wait!"

The room ate up his shout like his first cell had done. That memory brought back panic and a new wave of cold sweat. And then he understood once again.

"Alright, I give up. Please, just give me some time to think."

The Warden's voice rang out in the room. "Sure, Frank. You consider my proposal. Spend the night with us and mull it over."

He capitulated in his head. About to ask another question, the voice rang out again.

"Her name is Chantal, and she's waiting for you. Have a good night."

The door clicked open. Frank slowly exited the room and walked down the hall.

Chantal stood at an open door down two then left, a welcoming smile on her face.

"C'mon in, Frank. Let me take care of you."

He stepped in, shaking his head. "How can you be nice to me after what I did to you?"

"You're human. Mistakes happen, no big deal. Besides, I never felt in any real danger."

"How do you know?"

She began helping him out of his jumpsuit. With his question she stopped and looked at him. "Warden always takes care of us. If I'd been in danger, she would have asked me beforehand if I was okay with that. There's always a choice."

He played with her lapel, curious about what she had to say, but struggling to keep his mind off the body hinted at under the silk robe.

"Would you have agreed if there was danger?"

Without hesitation: "Yes."

"Why?" He reached inside her robe and cupped a breast playing softly with her nipple.

She reached for him. "You're marked for big things. I want to be a part of that."

He scooped her into his arms and gently laid her on the bed.

CHAPTER 41

Frank emerged from the tunnel in the morning; Scraggins and Chucho were there to greet him. They stood by the fence.

"Well, *jefe*, how did it go? You meet with anyone important?"

"How are things here?" Frank responded after a beat.

"The natives are restless, man," Scraggins said. "They don't do well when they not eating a steady diet of meat. They worry. You got a plan for that?"

"Working on it," Frank said.

"What about the management? You talk to someone?"

"More or less."

"Listen, Frank, I know how things go. Either they ask you to be part of management or you just another sucker."

The Aryan Brother Anderson walked up just then, and they halted the conversation.

"Well, if it isn't Mahatma Ghandi in the flesh. You gonna make us starve like Ghandi, or do you have something planned to get us fed?"

"We have something of a peace, man," Scraggins chimed in, "but it ain't gonna last if we starvin.'"

"The smoke has it right. You got some plan or what?"

"I'm working it out. How about giving us some space to discuss the particulars?" Frank said to Anderson.

The Aryan shook his head. "No fucking way *I'm* looking for a chair when the music stops. I'm going to be a part of this little meeting of the minds."

"Fine." Frank turned to the other two. "Let's stage an exhibition fight tonight. Find two guys who know how to fight, but not hurt each other and set them to it. Can you guys do that?"

Chucho looked skeptical. "It has to be real for one of them."

"Well, find a black guy and an Aryan. That should create enough heat," Frank said.

"Okay. Can't guarantee it, though," Scraggins said.

They split up. Anderson pouted for a minute, then drifted his own way.

Frank took a victory tour around the pod, something he'd not done last night. He familiarized himself with as many guys as he could.

He shook hands, offered words of encouragement. But the indeterminate nature of their situation weighed on him. How many days could he manage this? The concept of eternity hit him hard—if exodus from this undesirable place was not possible, what was his endgame? He pushed those thoughts from his mind. Forced himself to concentrate on the here and now. First had to see if they could manufacture their evening's fare without the previous brutality.

Midday they met again in the pit. Chucho and Scraggins came first, Anderson hovering nearby like an unwelcome guest who refuses to leave.

"So, what do you got?" Frank asked.

"We'll put on a show, right, Anderson?" Scraggins said. "I got a guy who's had a beef with one of Anderson's crew, been wanting to put a hurt on him for a long time."

"I don't see why I got to sacrifice one of my guys for the spooks," Anderson said.

"Who say it's a sacrifice? Maybe he win." Scraggins couldn't contain his mirth.

"C'mon, Frank, let me choose the guy, make it more fair." Anderson focused his attention on the new power center.

"Let me ask you this—do these guys have a legitimate beef?"

Both men nodded.

"Then you got to go with it, Anderson. We're not here for bloodshed. Once the winner has declared himself, we'll stop the fight. Everyone agree?" Frank didn't wait for an answer. "Great. Make it so."

Chucho pulled up a chair next to Frank. "You unnerstan' how this place work, no? People come in every day. If you don't find a way to thin the herd, it goan get very crowded, very fast, *entiendes?*"

"I'm working on it."

"Now that we got some time, just you and me, tell me who you meet with?"

Frank let a little tension build. "Warden."

"*De verdad?*" Chucho whistled through his teeth. "I ain't never met with the Warden." He sat silently, his usual laugh lines congregated above his eyes, his brow working overtime.

"When was the last time someone met with Warden?"

"I be here long time. Was three guys Captain before me. None ever met with Warden. We heard there was Warden, but we never see."

"She's taken an interest in me."

"She? *Dios mio,* what she look like?" Chucho's grin was back.

"Foxy older lady. Like Jennifer Aniston," he said.

They sat silently for a moment. Chucho shook his head and muttered, "*Una mujer como* Jennifer Lopez. Not bad".

"No, not Lopez—Aniston." Seeing disappointment on Chucho's face, he added, "You know what, like Jennifer Lopez, too."

"Well, Frank, you gotta problem. 'Cause you know who we are. We criminals, bad men. Is only a matter of time 'fore shit break out. You not going to be able to keep control without letting animals blow steam."

They rebuilt the ring for the afternoon fight. The crowd assembled around the edges. Scraggins walked his guy over, helped him between the ropes into his corner. Anderson came from the other side and inserted one of his crew, a wiry kid with tattoos up his neck and one wrapping around his left eye invoking any reader to copulate themselves.

It looked like a mismatch. The black guy could have been a middleweight; his opponent not much more than a lightweight.

They touched gloves as the ding sounded.

Frank stood next to Chucho watching. Betsy pouted on a lawn chair several feet away.

"You know, it doesn't have the same heat as your fight," Chucho said. "That was the best fight we ever seen."

"I'll bet," Frank said and looked down at his swollen knuckles.

The two guys circled each other, testing with lazy jabs, flat combinations.

"C'mon, you guys. Let's see some fire!" Chucho yelled, clapped his hands. "Hey, Anderson, I hear your guy likes black *bicho* in his *culo!*"

"What the hell does that mean, huh? Is that an insult? Cuz I don't speak Spic!" Anderson shouted back, his eyes on his boy in the ring.

"It means, he's a maricón. Let's see some passion!"

Softly to Frank he said, "I try, man. You can't say I didn't."

There were few punches landed in the first round. By the third much of the crowd had lost interest. Only those with a betting interest hung around.

The skinny guy fought with spirit, but his eyes broadcast fear; seemed like the Black guy was only playing around. In the fourth he landed a wicked right cross, and the Aryan hit the ground with enough certainty that no count was needed.

For a minute the crowd held its breath; so used to a consummation of buggery, they were unsure what would happen next. Chucho entered the ring, looked down at the defeated man with contempt, and raised the winner's arm to a smattering of applause.

He retook his place next to Frank.

"Now we wait to see dinner."

They didn't wait long. After dismantling the ring, the workers platooned out of the tunnel carrying sticks in each hand. It lacked the grandeur of previous culinary displays, but it took someone identifying the bill of fare for Frank to receive the Warden's message.

"Looks like fucking roadkill!"

In fact, that's what it was. Squirrels, woodchucks, and parts of what might have been deer cobbled together for dinner. And there wasn't enough for everyone. Guys began jostling for position to get the better or at least most visibly appetizing cuts of meat. One of the less fortunate fellows grew enraged with the gopher passed to him, and he shoved the lime server hard into the fire.

Frank jumped in to pull the guy free and rolled him around on the ground until he smothered the flames. With parts of his lime jumpsuit burned away the guy looked like a roasted pepper.

Little fights broke out in pockets. Frank stood in the middle ready to quell things when Chucho pulled him back.

"Better to let them blow off steam. I'm telling you, *soldado*, they must be allowed to be aggressive, believe me. Much worse when it pent up. Remember, they don't got a sweet girl to go to each night." He grinned large and rubbed his hands together. "Which remind me, is my night tonight, right?"

"No, I'm sorry. Got to be me because I must have a word with the Warden."

"Oh, look who's such a *bichote;* you not goan share now?"

"C'mon, man, I'm the only one who has access to the Warden."

Chucho grabbed Frank's arm. "You have illusion, you know." He jabbed at his own head.

"Delusion, not illusion."

An angry wave of the hand. "Doesn't matter, you unnerstan' me. You think you goan change this place? Huh?" He made a sweeping gesture of the collection of hooligans actively rioting around them. "These are animals, man. They not goan change and the Warden, she a zookeeper, you unnerstan'? She like the place like it was." He stalked off angrily.

CHAPTER 42

The foyer grew since he last stood in its embrace. It sprouted a plush carpet, a loveseat, and even a Ficus. Two doors. The one on the right opened, and Chantal stood in the doorway smiling broadly.

"You are a hell of a sight for sore eyes, you know that?" Frank said.

"Then why are you just standing there. Come on in."

"I have some business with the Warden first, but I'll be quick. I promise."

He took the door to the left, down a hallway with only one door at the end, opened a crack. Knocking on the lintel he peeked inside. No desk. Two Eames chairs situated at an angle. The Warden sat expectantly in one, wearing a sharkskin pants suit, one leg crossed over the other. With a pleasant expression on her face, she said, "Come, Frank."

Taking a seat opposite the Warden, he made sure his knees didn't knock hers. He felt self-conscious of his jumpsuit, out of place in this room. A sense of euphoria washed over him once again, and he struggled to remember why he came.

"You had a bone to pick with me, no?"

"The dinner."

She picked at the crease in her pants. "You haven't been here long, but I think you understand the nature of the place. This is a house of justice and, by extension, of retribution. You might feel a certain way about the nature of your incarceration, but I can assure you, the others are a different story. Justice must be served."

"Whose justice? Who gets to decide?"

Warden frowned like a parent might do to child who asks a silly question. "Isn't it clear who's deciding? Do I need to spell it out for you."

"How do you expect me to maintain order if I can't deliver on my promises?"

She nodded her head. "Perhaps you need to better understand the paradigm; it will lead you to make promises with a better chance of fruition."

He shifted uncomfortably in his chair, the warmth in his midsection fading.

Warden leaned in and spoke in a silky whisper.

"Those emotions you're experiencing. The ups, the downs. I can make them come, and I can make them go. You get that, no?"

For a moment he felt confused, but then the spreading of the pleasant heat returned to his abdomen, his anxiety dissipated, and realization hit.

"Who are you?" Fear gripped him.

"That isn't material right now. What is, though, is your acceptance of certain basic tenets of your mission. Justice must occur. It cannot be skirted, nor can it be defined away by your own sensibilities. You must rely on mine and mine alone. And there will be no comfort or rejoicing until someone is served their retribution. Only then will the food return as before."

She paused, lowered her head, and looked at him through her eyebrows.

"Do you understand?"

He nodded gently.

"Good." The bright smile returned. "So, tomorrow it is time for Anthony Scraggins to get his due reward."

"Shit."

"Yes, you have developed some fondness for Mr. Scraggins, haven't you."

"I have."

"That is understandable. He is a man of action. I like him, too. Unfortunately, he is also a stone-cold killer. You see, he went into a convenience store on an impulse to rob. He pointed a gun at the aging store owner, Hamid, who busied himself emptying the register. In one of those most unfortunate twists of fate, Hamid's wife, Fatima, finished balancing the books in the office and went to tell her husband some good news about their finances. She saw the hold up and for a moment the three of them, owner, wife, and Mr. Scraggins, stood frozen in time, all of the possibilities of their futures laid out and hinging on their actions over the next millisecond. Fatima panicked and bolted back up the aisle to the office believing the shelving would provide her cover.

"With coolness of resolve Mr. Scraggins fired off his large caliber handgun six times along her route. Unseen by him, obscured as his vision was by the shelves laden with products, one of the bullets from his pistol struck Fatima in the right shoulder and hurled her into the refrigerator with enough force to break the glass door. Also unseen by Mr. Scraggins, a teenage girl looking for the perfect soft drink sat huddled on the ground, shaking in fear when she heard the robbery underway. She, too, believed the Doritos would provide refuge. One of the six bullets tore through a bag of Cool Ranch and took off the top of her head.

"Mr. Scraggins turned back to Hamid's terrified face, loose bills gripped tightly in his sweaty hands, and with nary a hesitation pulled the trigger and ended a second life. He reached over, grabbed scattered money, a honeybun and limped out of the store munching on the pastry.

"Fatima came to in a few seconds and called 911. Her husband and the teenage girl were pronounced dead on the scene. All told Mr. Scraggins profited $88 and a honeybun from that particular impulse."

They sat silently. Frank couldn't take his eyes from Warden's. Her irises were a peculiar color, changing from grey to blue at different angles. She held his gaze without self-consciousness or sign of emotion on her unblemished face. No lines, no wrinkles, yet it held a sagacity usually earned with a lifetime of performing various expressions.

"What is it that needs to happen?" Frank finally asked.

"He must be stripped of his status on the pod and left for my messengers to collect."

"You call them messengers?"

"I'm aware they are colloquially referred to as the 'men in black.' They are my special emissaries and must be allowed to carry out Mr. Scraggins's punishment. You may decide how he is stripped of his jumpsuit, but it must happen tomorrow before the sun reaches the top of the sky; otherwise, I will visit his penalty on all your heads."

She deftly stood up, barely using her arms, like a much younger woman.

"Go be with Chantal. Enjoy your night and be refreshed for tomorrow." She extended a hand. "You should know, Frank, I very much enjoy your company."

He stood puzzled by that remark for a moment after she'd already left, then followed her out. The hallway stood empty. At its end, Chantal waited.

In the afterglow he held her. Sex had provided a brief reprieve, but now the thoughts tumbled through his mind like shoes in a dryer.

"I can see how conflicted you are," Chantal said softly. "Don't be. The Warden knows the way forward. She's always right."

He lifted himself up a little to look her in the eye. "You sound like a cult member."

"Maybe. But that doesn't make it not so. Believe me, Frank. If she tells you something needs to happen, it does."

"How do you know what she said?"

Chantal sat up, crossed one leg over the other like a yogi. "All of us who live inside have made our own deals with the Warden. It's why we get to do what we do."

"Including the men in black?"

She nodded. "Them, too. We each were brought here for a reason. For some the retribution is the only reason; for others, like me, it's a compromise for things we've done."

He massaged her calf. "What could you have done?"

"I don't want to say; I'm too ashamed. But I made my deal with the Warden, and I live with it daily."

"Well, I didn't make any deal. I don't belong here." He swallowed the last thought—and I won't be here for long.

"You still think you're going home?" she said, pity on her face. "Frank, your wife is pressing charges against you. She intends on cutting you out of her life entirely. You will not see your children again. Don't you understand? There is no life waiting for you on the outside."

Anger flared up. He stood up abruptly, threw on his clothes, his back to her. "Who the fuck are you to say those things?"

He glanced over his shoulder, hoping for a reaction, but noticed again how his anger didn't fluster her at all. She calmly untangled her legs and walked up behind him. Wrapping her arms around his mid-section and burying her head in his back she spoke: "You know it, too. Your wife threw you out of the house. Don't you remember the terrible feeling, the desperate pit in your stomach?"

He turned abruptly, grabbed her arms. "How do you know about that?"

"After accepting this position Warden gave me all the information I would need."

"Jesus, who the hell is this bitch?"

Chantal didn't answer. She wore resolve on her face, and it made clear—no amount of physical violence could dissuade her from her silence. And he believed her; let go of her arms.

"This Warden doesn't know everything."

He turned to leave. Hand on the doorknob she spoke up.

"Don't go, Frank. Come back to bed with me, and we can discuss. But don't leave like a child in a huff. It doesn't suit a man of your position." She got back in bed, pulled the blankets over her while folding out a welcoming spot for him.

It took a lot of pride swallowing to make the short walk back to bed. He didn't remove his clothes, just lay on top of the blanket.

"She wants me to do something I don't want to do."

"I know, honey." Chantal patted her lap, and he relented, put his head there. "She doesn't ask for the easy, but for the just. Plus—"

She stopped so abruptly he lifted his head to make sure she wasn't dead. She smiled down at him pleasantly.

"Plus what?"

She caressed his head. "It is so much easier if you just let go and submit your will to hers. You end up realizing she was right all along, and the fight wasn't worth it."

"Sounds like the path of least resistance."

"It's the smart play."

He didn't have a response. In the silence she began humming, and his tension melted away. Frank stood up and disrobed, returned to her ministrations.

After a few minutes he said, "Maybe you're right."

"Of course I am, honey."

CHAPTER 43

Frank exited the tunnel early next morning with the resolve that eluded him while inside. Perhaps a toxin in the air inside, like an aerosolized euphoric or stimulant. His iron resolutions went out of focus almost as fast as they coalesced when he was near the Warden. But out here, where the rule of the jungle reigned, he knew what he had to do.

He walked quickly to the pit, scanning the area. Spotted Scraggins, surrounded by his crew, eating from a bowl.

"Come with me, please." He didn't even check to see if Scraggins followed.

Chucho still lay in his single-man tent. He lifted his head and smiled when Frank poked his own in.

"You gotta let me have tonight. My back is killin' me."

"We got bigger fish to fry."

Scraggins stood outside. "I ain't trying to squeeze in there, man."

"What is it, Frank?" Chucho said, standing and exiting the tent.

"We got a big problem. I met with Warden last night and she made some demands."

"Okay, okay, shush, shush, shush." Chucho put both hands on Frank. "We shouldn't talk here."

"But this is important; we don't have much time."

"*Ay, calla te* for a minute, will you? *Jesucristo*." He led Frank away from the tent and strolled like he had no place to be. He moved towards the western part of the fence, the farthest from the tunnel. Scraggins lagged behind.

They came to a piece of the fence, looked like all others. Chucho looked around, then subtly nudged his hip against a piece close to a pole. It clicked open offering a small exit to the outside.

"After you, *Capitan*." He held the fence open for Frank, and Scraggins squeezed himself through after them and closed it back up.

Returning to the area outside the fence flooded Frank with emotion. The area, hazy when scanning it from the inside, came into focus once again and with it high doses of despair. Bedraggled figures lying around, the smell of decay and detritus. He spotted Pastor going about his rounds. They made eye contact but didn't speak.

Chucho led them to a darkened nook.

"I guess that's how the good pastor flits in and out," Frank said, his eyes still following Pastor around.

"He one of the people who know about the hole. Now you do, but I know you keep it quiet," Chucho said. He got into a crouch like he was going to shoot dice; they followed suit.

"Speak, Frank."

"Warden put the hit on Scraggins here."

"Shiiiiiiiiiiiiitttt. Well, it was only a matter of time." Scraggins stood, paced around.

"I sorry," Chucho said.

"No. I don't accept it. I don't accept the whole premise of this fucking place."

"Don't matter what you accept, Frank; it is what it is." Scraggins returned to the crouch.

"No place to go; no escape," Chucho said. "When it's you time, thass it."

They stayed huddled for a moment. "I'm not just sitting back and letting her pick us off one at a time until there's no one left. Has anyone fought?"

"What you mean?"

"I mean, has anyone ever rose up against the Warden?"

The two men laughed. "You got some illusions, Frank, I told you," Chucho said.

"Delusions. And why are you laughing, man?" He looked at Scraggins. "It's your time that's up. I figure you'd be game for anything."

"I don't want to die or whatever happens when the men in black come for you, but what you think we can do against them?"

"They're men just like us. Has anyone ever challenged them?"

Both were quiet. Chucho, fumbling around with stray pieces of cement on the ground, spoke: "I heard about someone who fought off like three guys before they got him, but in the end, they got him because in the end everyone gets got."

"How do they subdue their target apart from numbers?" Frank asked. "Do they carry weapons?

"I've seen a baton here and there, but that's it. What would you have us do?" Chucho said, a look of amusement on his face.

"What we didn't do when Lou got his."

They went their separate ways once they re-entered the pod through the trick fence. Each had their assignment, and they went off to spread the word to their crews. There was debate about who should know what, and they decided to keep the operation small. Frank knew coordination would be shoddy; there wasn't enough time to set things up properly. But they could overcome their deficiencies with numbers and ferocity.

He looked up. Now that he paid attention, he watched the sun climb perceptibly towards the domed zenith far faster than the real thing. Meant they didn't have much time.

Guys milled around the pit; some knew the deal while others could be relied upon with predictability to jump in whenever action erupted.

With a nod from Frank, Scraggins started his thing.

He pulled down the top half of his jumpsuit and began pounding his chest with one fist.

"Hey, Anderson," Scraggins yelled out, "It's time you paid for your shit." He barreled over and slugged the big Aryan in the face.

Anderson was caught off guard but rallied quickly. He charged Scraggins, grabbing him around the midsection and driving into the ground. The Aryan boys flew to his aid as did Scraggins's crew to his. There were some good shots, but a lot of shucking and dodging; no one's heart was in this fight. A crowd formed around the few combatants.

Anderson disentangled himself and scrambled to his feet. "What the hell, man, what the hell?!"

Standing and breathing heavy, Scraggins looked over at Frank who pointed up where the sun looked down on them all from the crest of its climb to the other side.

Scraggins went back into a fighter's pose. "Let's go, cracka, show me some of your Gerry Cooney."

"Why you coming at me like that, Scraggs—we have no beef?!"

"Give me your best shot you pale-faced, small dick, motherfucker!" Scraggins lunged at Anderson who swung wildly and landed a blow on the side of his would-be nemesis's head.

Down went Scraggins, an Oscar-worthy performance from Frank's perspective. Anderson stood over him.

"We had a peace, man. Why'd you go and do that?"

Before he could answer the tunnel door flew open spitting out a line of four men in black. "Four!" Frank yelled. "Get the door!"

The black-clad figures didn't break their stride; one hand on the shoulder of the man in front wending their way to Scraggins. Behind them, three guys, including the portly Seth, went to the tunnel door and jammed a large block of wood between the door and the ground, then laid their bodies against it to ensure it stayed shut.

The men in black went straight for their target oblivious to the triplet formations shadowing their movements. Once the men in black reached Scraggins, they stopped and surrounded him leaving openings in their ranks.

"Down low, now!" Frank called.

From their blindside one crimson jumpsuit dove at the legs of each black clad man. In synchrony exceeding even his best hope, they chopped legs out bringing the predators to their knees. The leader reached into his vest for something.

"Topside, now!" Frank yelled and dove at the torso of the lead guy, his legs already immobilized by crimsons smothering the feet. All four men in black were brought down to the ground; every available crimson vied for a position atop a messenger. It looked like a pile of football players after a fumble. Only there was no referee to pull bodies off.

Frank wriggled free of a pile and looked at what he confiscated from his quarry.

A taser.

He tested it, watched as the blue electricity shot between the prongs.

A loud banging sounded out through the pod and everyone's eyes turned towards the door from the tunnel. The door shook in its housing with the repeated blows, but it held. The wood and the extra bodies made sure no one else came through.

The lead messenger squirmed beneath four guys, his helmet turned askew.

Frank went down into a crouch and ripped the helmet off revealing a young guy, struggling to catch his breath. Jamming the taser into his neck, he said, "Quit fucking moving."

The guy became still, but there was fire in his eyes. "Get these pieces of shit off of me and I'll make sure the retribution is quick and relatively painless."

Frank stood back up. "Hear what this arrogant bastard said! He wants the pieces of shit off of him in exchange for mercy! I got mercy for him right here!"

He dropped down and drove the taser into his neck and pressed the button.

All four guys atop jumped off as the messenger flopped in pain with the tasing.

"Frank, watch that shit!" Chucho yelled as one of his guys, dazed and grimacing, rolled away.

Ignoring him, Frank continued to address the leader who now bore only an expression of pain as he curled up like an infant, saliva hanging from his mouth.

"We've had enough of your shit."

The leader didn't open his eyes, but he whispered something.

Frank bent down low. "Say it again, shithead; I didn't catch it the first time."

"She's-not-going-to-like-this."

"You need another shot of this, huh, motherfucker?!" Frank stood and kicked the leader in the midsection, the flak jacket taking a lot of the energy out of the blow. This enraged Frank more who kicked wildly at every exposed part of the leader's body until Chucho and Scraggins pulled him off.

All four men in black were lying prone, several knees on them to keep it that way.

"What do we do now?" Scraggins asked.

"Now we tie them up," Frank said.

Someone ran and brought lengths of ripped up tent for the job. Once complete, they took the other helmets off. Each man wore the same expression—shock at the turn of events.

The leader recovered enough to speak normally. "Frank, don't do this. It will not end well for anyone. Let us go, leave us to our job and maybe the punishment won't be as harsh."

"You should be worried about yourselves right about now. I'm pretty sure Warden's not going to reward us with any protein, so we might just have to cook up your ripe bodies." He winked salaciously at the leader and raised a hand in the air to get quiet from the crowd around him. "We're sending a message to the Warden—'You don't fuck with us from now on without some pain!'"

A guttural cheer went up. Frank exhorted the crowd to increased decibels as he circled around their captives. The fervor crescendoed, euphoria mixed in with adrenaline.

Despite the cheers a voice boomed from above and drowned out all else.

"I hear you loud and clear."

Everyone's attention went skyward. For a suspended moment they all looked at a blue sky awash in hope and the potential of each new day; then everything went pitch black.

CHAPTER 44

Back in the desert, with enough cloud cover you could barely see the hand in front of your face. Those were the blackest nights. He couldn't imagine being out there without night goggles. He'd read histories of desert warfare when he knew he was shipping out to Iraq; older Middle Eastern conflicts where the combatants would tacitly agree to a pause at night, each acknowledging both the need to regroup and the inherent difficulties to such conditions.

Experiencing those zero dark hundred nights when the darkness pressed down on everything helped him understand the rationale: battling your enemy was hard enough without adding those inner childhood demons of what prowls in the shadows. Those nights were instructive, to be sure, but they didn't prepare Frank for this level of darkness.

CHAPTER 45

Fear gripped him. Terror originating in the deepest, most ancient parts of the central nervous system. It existed in the brain of every animal and evolved to its highest form in homo sapiens. Alarm system at DEFCON 1, constant. Pupils dilated to the extreme, unable to accommodate to draw even a single particle of light.

This wasn't normal darkness. It was the complete eradication of illumination of any kind. His very movement felt impeded, like walking in water, though he knew, or rather his mind insisted, that couldn't be the case. He'd been just a moment before on terra firma, and now he couldn't get his bearings. He sensed danger constantly lurking just out of reach of his grasping hands.

And the nausea. Like he experienced in the Warden's presence or that fucked up elevator. His middle ear struggled to accommodate the lack of visual input, the absence of anchoring sight. He got on all fours and forced himself to listen to his surroundings. Nothing. No movement, no cries for help, not even the sound of his own breathing. The darkness swallowed all like an Earthbound black hole inhaling all light, matter, and sound.

Then, quite suddenly, he felt a cover come over his head and hands, many of them, grabbing at him, lifting, and carrying. The nausea grew more intense, cold sweat popping up all over his face and neck. And then unconsciousness.

CHAPTER 46

A gentle hand slapped at his face. It was still dark, but a muted blackness with light poking through in the characteristic way it does when wearing a hood. His hands were tied behind his back and his shoulders ached.

He felt sticky, like he'd run in his clothes and didn't change out of them. Hands gripped him under the armpits, carried him and laid him down on his knees. His hands were freed, then the hood ripped off.

It took a moment for his eyes to acclimate. He was in the Warden's office. He'd remembered the light being dim, but now the walls shone brightly. He looked around, Chucho right next to him, also on his knees.

"Maybe not such a good idea after all," Chucho said and made a brave attempt at a smile.

"No. Not a good idea." The Warden stepped from behind and produced a chair to sit in front of them. She clasped her hands together and leaned forward to be closer to their eye level.

"You two were going to be my A team. You were going to organize and manage Burning River. Instead you decided it preferable to spit in my eye. Ah, such a waste." She stood, began a slow pace of the room.

Frank's first stab at talking produced a croak. He cleared his throat and tried again.

"Warden, you want to blame someone, you put the onus on me. This was my idea and my doing."

She stopped and regarded him sadly.

"How gallant of you, Frank. Truly. But hollow. You both accepted the role of Captain of the pod, meaning you both take responsibility for what happened."

The face, modeling sadness, pity, morphed almost imperceptibly into one of anger; not superficial, but a visceral expression of rage writ large by her facial muscles. Frank's insides went cold.

"You attacked my messengers doing their appointed duties. You understood the role they had to play, and you put them in danger. Such a gross violation of ethics."

Warden turned away and continued her pacing, hands behind her back. His voice and courage, fed by self-righteous anger, returned.

"Ethics?! What the hell are you talking about? You keep us here against our will, no due process, no ability to plead our own case."

"Your case?" she said. "You feel unjustly imprisoned, is that it? What about Ramadi? Huh, Frank?" She sat back down in the chair, eyes piercing Frank's while her voice resumed its usual huskiness. "See, I know how you've buried the memory of Adbul Aziz and his daughter Amira. Not to mention the poor, innocent Fadi, his only crime being beguiled by Amira's charm. You didn't hesitate to carry out your precious notion of justice then."

Frank's face blanched. "How do you —?"

Warden laughed lightly, then turned to Chucho.

"I am being accused of not allowing a man to plead his own case. So, Jesus Wilfredo Fuerza Fernandez, Sr., would you like to plead your case?"

"I don't have nothing to plead, ma'am. I belong here." He said it not as a confession or even a rouse to garner a reverse psychological edge. He declared it as it was, plainly and without inflection.

It angered Frank. "What the fuck, Chucho—why do you say that?"

A simple shrug. "I guess finally I speak what is *verdad*, no bullshit. It feel good."

"I don't care what Chucho says, I don't accept your fucking dominion over me."

"It doesn't really matter, now does it?" she said. "You know, I really am in awe of your spirit, Frank. Once again, you've impressed me with your ability to rally. Well, you're going to need that." She slapped her thighs, stood, and nodded to someone behind the two of them.

"Hands behind your back. Now, asshole."

Frank complied and felt his wrists bound with a zip tie. Then rough hands again grabbed him under the arms and lifted. He shook free of their grips.

"I can walk myself."

"So you can, Frank." Warden came within inches of his face, spoke in a whisper (or it might have been in his head, her words reverberating in the center of his head). "It's Chucho's time. You understand what that means. And it must be you who carries out his retribution. No one else can do it. *No one else.* If you choose not to, all will die. Only you can stop the deluge. Good luck, Frank. I truly hope you return here."

His eyes widened with each word.

"No. You can't make me——"

Strong hands pushed him out of the room and marched him down the hall. Men in black in front, behind, and all around. Even if he'd wanted to fight it would be a debacle. The hallways were narrow, twisting, and who the fuck knew where they led in this funhouse? The messengers traipsed their captives around too many bends to count. With each step his fate drew closer. He'd been in battle; he'd been forced to think on his feet to save his life, and in all previous encounters his mind had churned things over and spit out a solution. Not always the best one, but a workable scenario.

And now he couldn't calm his thoughts enough to endeavor a plan. Frank turned around and caught a quick glimpse of Chucho. The Puertorriqeuño looked serene. Oh, shit, Frank thought, chastising himself for his pathetic inability to think of a way through.

CHAPTER 47

They walked him down a dead-end hallway. On the left stood two doors about three feet apart.

"End of the line, wise guys."

Both he and Chucho stood opposite a door.

"Whatever happens, Jesus, it's been good to get to know you," Frank said.

"*Vaya con Dios*, Frank."

Pushed up roughly against the door with several hands Frank had to turn his face to breathe. In one movement the door opened, they cut his wrist ties, and pushed him through the door.

He spun around quickly, but the door was already closed. No knob, no hinges, just a blank wall. He futilely banged his fists on it, then turned around. He stood on a small platform, an edge, maybe three by three feet. Too dim to make out any details. He inched forward carefully and looked down. Blackness, unnatural density.

Frank turned again prepared to try another approach. Just then a whirring sound started up and the little platform he stood on began a slow retraction into the wall.

"That just fucking great!" He yelled as he backed up as much as he could. Then, rather than wait for the floor to literally drop out from under him, he jumped.

Feet hit a bottom quickly, a tweak to his ankles, unprepared as they were to hit any surface, and he slid down at a steep angle in the darkness. If being suspended in black animation weren't enough, now Frank hurtled towards oblivion without any guideposts whatsoever. Hands and feet felt around and identified a tube. He screamed, part bravado, part sheer fucking terror.

A break in the darkness appeared like a pinpoint in the distance; it grew at the alarming rate of his sliding body. He used his hands and feet to slow him down as much as he could, but he jettisoned to the mouth of the tube and it spat him out, rolling ass over teakettle until he finally came to a stop on the former.

Laughter erupted in him from deep inside, appreciation for the demented ride not ending with him decapitated or impaled through his ass on a sharpened stick.

"What the fuck you laughing at, ol' man?"

Frank shielded his eyes from the brightness, took in his surroundings. Looked like a culvert in the LA river. He'd spent three years in his youth hanging out around there, breaking shit, and causing what really amounted to little trouble. Concrete embankments on either side and a trickle of water running through a center depression. Skateboarder's paradise.

A swift kick to his hindquarters brought his eyes back to the person in front of him. A black boy in an orange jumpsuit. Maybe thirteen, fourteen, but with a chip on his shoulder the size of a boulder.

"The fuck you doin' here, man?!"

He aimed another kick, but Frank grabbed his ankle.

"Hey, cut that out."

Other youths, about the same age, came to their comrade's aid, switchblades clicking open.

"Relax, boys. Don't do anything stupid."

Frank stood up. One of the ballsier kids stepped forward, knife brandished. Frank grabbed the knife hand and brutally twisted until the boy dropped it with a clank and cried out in pain.

A bunch of boys sat on the top of the embankment looking down, heckling.

"What you doing here?!"

"Get the fuck out,ol' man!"

And so on and so forth. Frank ignored them in favor of walking the territory. His ankles were sore as hell, but he ignored the pain.

His association to the culvert of his youth belied the cramped dimensions of this place. He stepped over the stream, then bent down to feel the water—cold, more so than the ambient temperature. A fence ran with the little brook, bisecting the culvert. It wasn't very tall, but razor wiring at the top discouraged any crossing. Chucho stood on the other side among his own baby bangers.

Frank walked to the chain link, felt the chilly water running over his feet. Chucho joined him from the other side.

"One hell of a ride, huh, Frank? So what happen now?"

"I'm not sure." But that wasn't exactly true—Frank suspected, just didn't know specifics.

More heckles rained down on them from both sides.

"Maybe we supposed to tame these *jovenes*." Gripping the chain links, grinning at Frank. "Teach them be better men."

"I think so. We have to protect them from themselves. Keep them safe."

They both looked down at the same time. The rising cold water raced over their ankles to get to the other side. Frank looked at the far opening in the culvert, its mouth completely obscured by the onrush. The sound of the water rose in pitch until its surge crowded out all other noise.

"Shit." The water rose at a rate disproportionate to the amount coming in. As panic registered in Chucho's eyes it already had reached their knees.

"Go!" Frank said, the sound lost in the water's roar. Chucho turned, already moving as one does when water prevents ease of passage. Frank scaled the fence for a better look at the areas atop the embankments and saw what the kids guarded: small patches of land at the corners with evidence of habitation, tents and such. He let go, fell back in the water and gasped. The level, up to his testicles, gave him an intimate appraisal of the water's frigidity.

He pushed his way to the embankment and began to crawl up. Little rocks and debris rained down on him from above. The baby bangers in their orange jumped and yelled on the top's edge, knives out, hurling things at him. The water continued its ferocious rise, now midway up the embankment, nipping at his shoes. Frank turned to check on Chucho's progress.

Chucho already stood on top, back against the wall flanked on either side by threatening figures. A wiry white kid stepped forward from the group and tried to push Chucho down the embankment. On the edge and almost off balance, Chucho grabbed the kid's arm and used the momentum to both regain his perch and hurl the kid into the rising water.

The kid flailed about in the water, obviously not a swimmer. Frank, recalling Warden's warning about any losses besides Chucho's, cursed and dove in, the coldness gripping him threatening to incapacitate. Emerging at the water's surface, he attempted to freestyle over to the kid, but the roiling pushed him farther away. He dove back under and found the going easier. He reached the fence, now submerged a couple of feet below him, and gave himself ample space to clear the razor. The water churned making it difficult to see. Below him, on the other side of the fence, he spotted the orange blur of the white kid sinking. As he made to cross over to the boy, a current forced him back, and he felt the razor wire cut into his jumpsuit and snag on his thigh. Pulling himself free with a cringe, his lungs screaming at him to surface, he grabbed desperately for the collar of the sinking kid and pulled them both up, his legs pumping furiously.

They emerged, the kid sputtering.

"Cough that shit up," Frank said and pulled the boy to the embankment. He hoisted the boy by the waist allowing him to grab the edge.

"Can you haul yourself up?" Frank had to yell in the kid's ear. A weak attempt and a shake of the head as a response. Frank kicked himself out of the water, grabbed the edge and pulled himself out. Then he yoinked the kid onto the ledge. Catching his breath, head between his knees, he examined his thigh—some nasty slices into the skin, but superficial.

The water's level continued its relentless rise. The ledge they stood on sloped gently up to the patch of land with tents. These might be kids, but they wouldn't go easy. They yelled and gesticulated wildly, their intensity impressive.

Chucho stood along the same wall, his eyes darting back and forth between the water and the orange rabble. A no brainer, he made to push his way through the kids, who stood like a soccer team blocking a penalty kick. Frank stepped forward and held him back.

"Don't hurt them!" he yelled.

"I ain't dying for 'em, neither!"

The water made its way to the ledge, gushed over, and crept up the slope.

"Now or never, Frank, no choice!" He pushed away from Frank's grip and launched himself at the group. They thrust their blades about like the gang novitiates they were. Chucho disarmed them easily and cast the youths aside. He picked up one of the knives and held it loosely in his hand.

His push through their soft front flank left Chucho now surrounded by orange. Not yet adults, their numbers and sheer panic intensified their ferocity, and they threatened to overwhelm Chucho.

Frank jumped into the fray, standing back-to-back with Chucho. The orange rabble jumped and yelled like macaques on monkey island. He used long kicks to disarm a few close to him. He grabbed one and swung him around and sent him pinwheeling into the crowd knocking down a few of them like bowling pins.

That kept them at bay for a moment. He turned to yell in Chucho's ear. "Listen to me—the water won't stop until you're dead!"

Chucho got out of his defensive crouch and stared at Frank. "Warden marked me?"

Frank nodded.

"I shoulda known." Chucho regarded the water a moment, looked at the baby bangers and their childish mimicry of adult antisocial behavior. His face became sad for a moment, then he stood up and retained the calm Frank saw before. He dropped his knife. "So, come on, do it."

"We'll find another way."

"There is no other way! Don't you get it? She in control."

The pressing throng forced Frank to face them once again, to kick his way to some perimeter space. But the two of them had to move up the slope now to escape the creeping water. They faced the crowd of baby bangers at a bottleneck. Behind them the water continued its assault on dry; in front of them, a line of orange jumpsuits blocking their way. A clever kid passed mats to the front and now they appeared like a Greek phalanx, shields in front of them.

Frank slouched, realization settling in. He picked up one of the knives, gripped it loosely. "Give us space," he said in a normal voice, and its message carried easily. Baby bangers spread out backwards forming a circle and the water leveled off anticipating their need.

Chucho smiled.

"What the hell you smiling about?" Frank said, the two of them slowly circling each other.

"Always wanted a shot at the title."

"I don't want to hurt you."

"No choice. *Así es como es. Ademas*, why you think you goan win? I tell you, I am master of the *cuchillo*."

CHAPTER 48

The good Lord endows some of his creations with special gifts. Francis Xavier Wills wasn't a genius, a chess grandmaster, or a Mozart. What he was, though, was an exceptional judge of a battle situation. He could estimate his chances with cold analysis and know how to proceed. This led to the rare retreat, but more frequently victory. Sizing up Chucho in this moment proved no different. Frank would take some slashes—no one walks away from a knife fight unscathed—but he could subdue Chucho with a few basic moves, and it left him feeling lonely again, like when he first arrived.

CHAPTER 49

A twinkle in his eye, a grimace on his face, and Chucho lunged with the blade in his right hand. In slo-mo Frank stepped back, parried the thrust to his right just enough for it to slice through his jumpsuit and cut his lat. Frank turned his hips tightly, thrusting his left elbow and planting the flat of his forearm in Chucho's ear while simultaneously hooking underneath Chucho's extended arm. Frank yanked hard. The momentum of his blow sent Chucho to his left, the grip on his arm prevented Chucho's body from following momentum and caused a grade-four dislocation of the shoulder. Frank let go.

Chucho rolled over, his torso at an abnormal angle, his face ashen. Sputtering, no words forming, he looked at Frank, mouth opening and closing like a fish out of water. Then a plaintive look in his eyes that didn't need translation.

Frank gripped the knife tightly in his right hand and stood for a suspended moment. With stunning alacrity he went to his left knee, torqued his hips, and swung the knife. His aim proved true as the blade entered under Chucho's jawline and penetrated through to his brainstem. It killed him instantly.

Frank removed the knife, and a great numbness filled his soul. A familiar sensation, one he'd prayed would never return. Still crouched he looked over to his left—the baby bangers stood frozen, each staring at him with a combination of fear and awe. Some had telltale urine signs down the front of their suits.

Behind him he could hear water moving. Finally, standing slowly, he confirmed the water receding rapidly. The price had been paid, all debts cancelled, and the flood mandate lifted. Just like that. And all he had to do was damage his soul possibly beyond repair.

He had no doubt the sadistic bitch would have let the water drown all of them, even the youngsters who knew no better and deserved a chance to grow up and get smarter. But saving them at Chucho's expense didn't assuage.

In his right hand, the knife gleamed at him, its blade bloodied, but still ready for action. Anger blossomed in his gut, spread everywhere equally, and pushed out the numbness. He glanced at the crowd of orange, and they stepped back in unison. At the edge he surveyed the water and estimated he still had about four feet of rapidly receding water remaining. Without a thought, he jumped.

CHAPTER 50

For a terrifying moment during the plunge, the receding water made the drop farther than his eyes first informed him, and he feared landing on concrete without sufficient water to slow his deceleration. He splashed in and hit the ground hard, but without further injury. Knife grasped like a lifeline, he waded, then brought his knees up high and made better time. At the culvert's intake he'd espied a door he knew was meant for him.

His shoes sloshed on the concrete, the running water now returned to its central and meek stream, mocking him with a 'what me, flood?' vibe. At the door he looked back. The baby bangers slowly descended, eyeing him wearily. They kept their distance. He turned the knob and went through.

A moment's pause to acclimate to the dim light. Only one way to go, a slope upwards. He took it without hesitation. She'd want to see me, he knew, and at least gloat. He knew her now well enough to predict this scenario. She'll be glib, but without the decency of showing true smugness, rubbing my nose in it. No, she'll couch it in sympathetic tones and continue my rehabilitation. But I am broken now; have reached a point of no return and can no longer be redeemed.

Up and around many twists and curves. The only sound his own measured breathing. Mustn't lose this focus, this determination. Her presence has a way of clouding judgment, jumbling thoughts until they can no longer coalesce into action. He gripped the knife tighter.

There, on the left at the end of the hall. The only door he'd seen the entire time. This was it. No men in black anywhere, no one at all in fact. She didn't fear him. He turned the knob, opened the door, stood in the doorway. There she was, sitting on the edge of the desk, her arms folded, that same bland smile on her face. A face without judgment, open to his contrition, welcoming of his penitence, his submission.

"Welcome back, Frank. I am truly glad you made it. Have a seat."

She stood, pointed out the chair in front of the desk and turned her back to take her own seat behind it.

Like a cobra, he pounced, wrapped his left arm around her neck and jabbed the knife into her mid-back, all the way up to its hilt, bruising his own knuckles with the force of his thrust.

CHAPTER 51

Frank let go and his knees buckled. The hyperintensity that propelled him on this last mission now spent, he had no reserve energy. He fell backwards onto the ground, his eyes still fixed on the Warden's body, slumped prone over the desk. Time moved impossibly slow. He imagined the men in black swarming to the office as he sat in his heap, but he couldn't move. No amount of impending danger could move him at this moment.

Then the Warden stirred. Her right hand reached around and felt the knife.

"Do you feel better now, Frank?" She slowly righted herself, knifed back still facing him. The hand feeling for the knife grabbed the handle and pulled it slowly out. He noted with a distant puzzlement the absence of any blood on the blade.

Warden tossed the knife onto the desk with a clatter and resumed her seat on the edge.

"You're pathetic, you know that? Not just you, but all mankind. You, even as a representative of what I imagined could be a laudable version, are all too predictable."

"Who are you?" He finally managed.

"I really believed in you, Frank. You know, it's funny, but in a way I still do. Your resourcefulness, determination, and self-righteousness are all attributes I prize. But you are like every other inveterate human who has ever come before you. There's an arrogance in your species that is mind boggling.

"Who am I? Who are you? Do you know who you are? More importantly, what you've received without any awareness or sense of purpose? You are the fortunate outcome of the Master of the House's desire to create something with the capacity to make choices. The ability to have free will. To test yourself against a world with endless possibilities."

She smacked the table and thundered on. "I have always envied you. Do you know how lucky you are to have all the world as a stage to play out your strengths, to test your faithfulness to justice? I have for eons desired such a thing but could only watch from afar.

"You, who arrive on the scene at the last second of the last hour of the last day and have the gall to want to expound on the universe. To peer into the cosmos and question why? To demand your brain puzzle out the mysteries from the microscopic to the grandest celestial forces? But you have absolutely no perspective. That brain of yours is just so much organic mush. How could you ever expect it to conceive of forces it cannot ever hope to fathom?"

Frank sat up. "Are you Satan?"

She threw her head back and laughed. "He is not the only angel in the firmament, you should know. But how he would delight in the reputation he's laid for himself? No, I am not Satan. You can call me Gabriel."

"What do you want with me?"

"Just what I've already told you, Frank. I've recruited you to work for me. I offered you a way to redeem yourself and do justice a good turn. It was, I have to say, a generous offer. But you can't shed the arrogance of your perspective; you believe in yourself too much and your own sense of right and wrong."

"My sense of justice is arrogant, huh," Frank said. "I'd say I have a fairly good perspective of your sense of justice. Sending me to kill Chucho, protecting a gaggle of pubescent thugs." Frank sat up straighter. "Not to mention what you were intending for Betsy to do to Seth. He's a half-wit, not guilty of anything, but taking the fall for his father."

Warden stood, circled the table, and sat down in the chair behind the desk, wheeled it to face him still seated on the floor. Her face took on a look of consternation.

"I don't expect you to understand the big picture," she continued. "In fact, how could you? You are a gnat on an elephant's rump. If I asked you to describe your surroundings, you would wax poetic on the endless expanse of gray fields and the occasional brown boulder to fall from the sky. What would you understand about generational justice, millennial justice? Huh? Perspective, Frank, perspective is the key. You must learn to trust in something. Might as well trust in me; I'm in front of you offering a glimpse into the cosmic abyss."

"And God. Shouldn't I trust in him?"

"Between you and me there is a chasm your mind can't possibly traverse. At this moment I am cradling your fragile psyche in my hands. You know this because you've felt what it's like when I release my gentleness even for a moment.

"You cannot contemplate how simple it is for me to see your thoughts. Not even like reading an open book. It's like a book's meaning being injected into my consciousness as each thought forms. You are beyond vulnerable. Not unlike how a butcher might gaze upon a bovine passively grazing all the while unaware of its destiny for the blade and Sunday family dinner. That's what separates the two of us.

"I won't try to impress upon you the order of magnitude existing between me and the Master of the House. No, far better for you to see me as an intermediary on your behalf."

Warden's face returned to its impassive blankness.

"Well, Frank, I think we're done for now."

The door opened and two men in black walked in. She stood.

"What's going to happen to me now?" he whispered.

"You're going to cool out in a different pod. When you return, we'll see where your head is, so to speak."

One man on each arm began walking him out. "For how long?"

"As long as it takes. Don't worry, I'll still be here. I can hang around here for an eon and still return in time for celestial dinner."

They helped walk him out on his rubbery legs.

CHAPTER 52

Expecting the ninth ring of hell, he was relieved to see the amenities where the messengers dropped him off.

A perfect circle with a diameter no bigger than a baseball's infield. On the perimeter, partitions sectioned off areas for individual mats. Not exactly the privacy of a tent, but not terrible. Several people lying down, some milling about. In the center some picnic style table. And a small hut in which the toilet assumably made its home.

They left him sitting on the ground, still in a daze from the Warden's revelations. His mind turned over the words she'd said, trying to recall and make sense of everything he'd heard. Still immersed in those thoughts, he didn't register someone squatting next to him. He became aware of a buzzing in the background. Like the hum of fluorescents, but, like everywhere else, there were no light fixtures to be seen.

"Hey, how you doing? You need some help?"

Frank looked up. A young guy, purple jumpsuit, in his twenties, unkempt, but with a pleasant face. His hair pointing in all directions of the compass.

"I'm okay." He waved the kid off.

"I know what's happening here." The kid looked around furtively, leaned in conspiratorially and whispered. "I am one of the initiated."

Frank perked up. "Did the Warden reveal herself to you, too?"

A knowing, important nod.

Frank got on his knees, leaned into this kid like a thirsty man. "What did you think? Can it be real?"

Another nod. "Oh, it's real."

"So what do we do?"

The kid looked around again, elaborate glances to his left and right, then he unzipped his jumpsuit, pulled out his cock and began stroking.

Frank jumped back. "What the hell?!"

"The only way to ward off the ministrations of the devil is through the spiritual power of semen." He looked up to the sky and continued his penile ministrations with a rapturous look on his face.

"C'mon, Daniel, you know there's no masturbation in the center and not during the day."

Another guy gently pulled Frank away from this particular jacker who meekly replaced his tool in his jumpsuit and sulked off.

"Thank you —"

"Rico. Name's Rico."

"What the hell was that?" Frank said, allowing himself to be led away.

"Don't be bothered by Daniel. He means no harm. What's your name, by the way?"

"Frank." He didn't take Rico's extended hand, gun shy given recent happenstance.

Rico smiled warmly, didn't take any offense at the hanging handshake. "Well, Frank, welcome to our little pod. Let me show you our humble accommodations."

He looked to be about Frank's age, balding, but clean shaven, his jumpsuit clean.

"So, you can see we have arranged our sleeping to be on the edges. We meet in the center for meals and over there is the bathroom."

"Is there a shower?"

"Sure is. Pretty good pressure, too." Rico stopped and looked Frank over. "Say, were you in the service?"

"I was. Marines. How did you guess?"

"You have the look of a Marine. I was also in the service." He re-offered his hand to Frank who took it this time. "I was a Navy Seal."

"Wow, man, that's impressive," Frank said, involuntarily wiping his hand on his jumpsuit. "Which unit were you in, cause I knew a lot of those guys."

Rico grew quiet. "I don't like to talk too much about it; you under-stand, right?"

"Sure. I know how that goes."

Two guys ran past just then, playing some sort of aggressive tag. They ran, stopped, pushed each other savagely, then continued their running. They did two of these laps then one stopped abruptly at a partition between mats. He pulled out his pecker and urinated over the floor in great crisscrossing motions. Even though he wasn't close to the offender, Frank stepped back, horrified.

"Hey, man, the fucking bathroom's right there."

The pisser didn't looked perturbed. He just zipped his jumpsuit back up, hustled to catch up to his nemesis. Frank, entranced by both the spectacle and the lack of alarm on anyone else's part, followed their progress two more laps when the other halted to perform his territo-rial counterpiss.

"That's how they tell who's winning." Rico nodded in approval. "Was how we did things in Delta Force."

The two guys continued running laps, periodically shoving each other.

"I thought you were a Seal?" Frank said.

"Special Forces." Rico crouched down, ear cocked as if listening for something and looked up at Frank expectantly. "You hear that?" He sprang up and stalked the pod.

"Don't think you can come up on me from behind! I see and hear everything!"

Nobody reacted to Rico's tirade. While Frank's attention was elsewhere, Daniel sidled up to him. "Get the fuck away!" Frank yelled and pushed him away. Daniel said nothing and slunk off.

Rico continued his stomping around, yelling at the prone figures who didn't budge from their repose. The two guys kept up their laps (though they'd slowed to a lazy jog) and shoving (those, too, lacked much intensity) periodically urinating on the floor, the walls.

Layered over this cacophony the sound of fluorescents rose and fell. Frank covered his ears, but this did nothing.

Daniel was back close to Frank, leaned in and whispered huskily, his eyes wide and fixed, "You must listen to me. I am a prophet of God." As his hand moved to his zipper, Frank pushed him away harder this time and escaped to the bathroom.

He leaned against the sink, head down, breathing heavily. Opposite, on the wall, a flawless mirror gleamed and glistened. His bearded visage looked back at him. It was the first time he'd seen himself in he couldn't remember how long. Bags under his eyes, a weariness in his very skin, he almost didn't recognize the image. Anger welled up and he punched the mirror hard enough to shatter it, but no harm came its way. Frank's knuckles, though, barked angrily at his sudden outburst.

Two stalls equipped with toilets were situated behind him. No doors. And the areas around each metal receptacle were marred with generations of filth. He walked over to the shower stall and found it rank, as well. The drain oozed and radiated a sewer smell, rust stains abound among other indeterminate discolorations. In fact, the only spotless aspects to the bathroom were the two mirrors over the sinks.

A shout rose outside. Frank shook his head. "What the hell now?"

He walked outside and his heart lifted. A cart stood in the center, the kind you might see a vendor pushing around a city, peddling greasy fast food. Frank drew close and inhaled deeply through his nose. Hope springs eternal. It smelled tantalizingly good. His mouth watered and he bodied up to maybe ten or twelve guys, hovering around the cart. He stood on his toes and spotted what looked like southern fried chicken, honey biscuits, potato salad, and coleslaw. His favorite meal.

"It's my turn to serve."

"You served yesterday, douchebag, it's my turn."

"There's never enough after you put your grubby hands in."

"Look who's talking, fat ass."

Jostling turned to pushing, pushing to shoving. Hips bounced off the cart, and the disturbance threatened its precious contents. Frank panicked and yelled above the fray.

"Hey, hey, relax, we can do this."

To his amazement the hubbub died down and all eyes were on him.

"Okay, why don't we form a line, and everybody takes one of each and moves on. Then, if there are leftovers, we can split them fairly."

To nobody's amazement pushing resumed as everyone jockeyed for position at the front of the line. However, because the cart had two sides and two ends, no one quite knew where to establish themselves, so a demented game of musical chairs erupted without music or chairs.

Frank felt like a crowd controller in a mosh pit. He held onto a collar here, an arm there, but the thrashing proved too great. Then, suddenly, the jostling ceased as if every inmate was frozen by an external force. They held these positions for a hanging second then launched into a hodgepodge of fighting. Kicks, pulls, punches all flew and someone, hard to say which cretin, reached into the food tins and deployed their contents as ammunition.

A fistful of potato salad hit Frank on the face, temporarily blinding him with redskin and mayonnaise. Pulling the food from his face he took some blows to the torso and groin. He had no choice but to extricate himself. Stumbling to the bathroom he put the faucet on; a meager dribble came out and he cursed.

He turned to the shower, groping and fumbling for the knob and turning it full blast once he found it. The water came out and he dunked his head in. For a moment he felt relief and then the temperature reached near boiling, and he jumped back with a shriek.

"Fuck! Fuck! Fuck!" He bounced up and down with fury, lumbering around, eyes closed until the stall cut off his movement with a slam against his forehead and nose. He collapsed to the ground, the steam building around him. After a time the heat grew unbearable; he collected himself as best he could, rubbed his eyes sufficiently to squint through them and navigated out of the bathroom.

By now the fighting had died down and he could see why. The cart lay on its side, its precious contents already spilled out and pored over by hungry hands and mouths. Looked like a horde of locusts had passed over the food debris and consumed anything edible. He was too exhausted to mourn the satiety that might have been. As he stood there darkness fell on the pod unnaturally quick; suddenly feeling extremely exposed, Frank scanned the area looking for refuge.

All the stalls were populated by inmates sedated with full bellies, some already snoring loudly. Frank finally found a vacancy, and he quickly went over to it. Exhausted, he crashed on the mat, his various injuries be damned; he could already feel blisters forming on his forehead.

CHAPTER 53

After a minute he understood why this stall stood vacant.

Daniel's voice rang out through the thin partition.

"In the beginning God created the heaven and the earth." Daniel shouted at breakneck pace, the words tumbling out in machine gun pace. "And the earth was without form, and void; and darkness was upon the face of the deep. And the Spirit of God moved upon the face of the waters."

Frank turned away, covered his ears, but that didn't help. The droning voice continued, rushing through the King James Bible. It was a feverish, brilliant display of speed talking any auctioneer would envy.

At the end of each day of creation Daniel with end with a flourish: "And God saw that it was good!"

The night went on like this. Frank tossing and turning, never entering a full sleep, listening to Daniel's ramblings as he skipped his way through the Bible. At some point Frank gave up the ghost of sleep and simply sat up. His head throbbed, the skin felt raw and on fire. Thoughts raced.

There was a hint of light at the edges where the walls faded into domed ceiling when Daniel reached Acts and the story of Paul.

"And immediately there fell from his eyes as it had been scales: and he received sight forthwith, and arose, and was baptized."

That sentence bounced around in Frank's head. He remembered a pastor of some sort thundering from a lectern about Paul's revelation and how we all carry our delusions like blinders.

Now, in his exhausted state, stripped of all psychic energy, Frank *lived* that experience rather than felt it. He lay on his mat in a twilight between sleep and consciousness as scenes played out before him, memories flooding his mind's eye like a highlight reel of his worst behavior.

The living room of their shitty apartment, mousetraps laid out along each wall. One of their many stopovers, before he reluctantly agreed to return to Cleveland where her parents could help them. A lousy rental with promises to Laurie of a house to come once they got settled. Their fights, like that of so many couples, caused by financial strain. His wife, truly a patient woman, losing her shit with him. It was always worst for him when she grew angry.

"It can't be just bad luck. This is has happened too many times."

"How can you take their side?" Frank pleaded. "They were cutting corners and putting people in jeopardy."

"How many jobs have you lost now, huh? Seven, eight? I can't even keep count. And each time you find a reason to blame someone else."

Frank biting his lower lip hard, fighting back retorts, and losing that battle each time. "So you're saying, you're just like them? Better to give in to mediocrity, do a half-ass job, but bring home the bacon? I thought you understood me; you're just like everyone else."

"Frank!" Laurie yelling, tears in her eyes, "you don't always have to be the one who points out the faults of others. Nobody appointed you grand guardian of the world!"

And then calmly, always with a genuine love he couldn't ignore, she'd say a variation of "I need you to be here and to support us. I can't do it on my own."

The shame and guilt hitting like a tidal wave that couldn't be tolerated, always leading to a bile filled retort: "It was better when I was abroad; we didn't fight like this. Maybe it'd been better if I was KIA then at least you could have a picture, a flag, and some pride." He would pout, sometimes leave the apartment in a huff, but always return, contrite, but never to capitulate. Wash, rinse, repeat.

Now he replayed each incident and inserted a different understanding—what if he were the variable on which each crashing disappointment rested? Patterns emerged, cycles of happenstance—jobs begun with high hopes, two-three months of a honeymoon. Frank making tangible improvements to the organization. Real benefits to the company and commensurate delight with his contributions. Then, a consistent moment when these recommendations were now seen as intrusive and overly critical. Frank, feeling rejected and unappreciated, turning these company insights (once so valued) into condemnations of a derelict management.

A queasy sensation overtook Frank, on the mat hovering in subconsciousness, as he recognized this pattern repeatedly. When viewed outside of himself, it became clear where the problem lay.

He now took it further, examining personal relationships and recognizing similar disturbing tendencies. Great beginnings devolving into accusations of betrayal and callousness. Women desperately attempting to convince him otherwise and him viewing those ministrations as further evidence of their inherent mendacity. And round and round that went. Finally meeting Laurie, taking the plunge. But even that he destroyed. Come to think of it: how did Laurie tolerate him for so long?

CHAPTER 54

Frank's eyes snapped open to the morning light and an eerie quiet on the pod. He'd simply slumped over at some point and leaned unnaturally against the partition. He sat up straight, his head throbbing. Silence save his pulse keeping time in his ear.

No Daniel speed reading the Bible, no Heckle and Jeckle racing around and pissing all over the place, and no background hum of fluorescent lights. He leaned over and peered into the next stall. Daniel slept soundly.

The night's revelations hung over him, draped him in weariness and confusion.

Eyes closed, he lay back down and did some tentative stretches. He heard footsteps coming his way. Immediately back on guard, he sat up and saw a familiar sight.

Pastor gestured to the unoccupied half of the mat. Frank nodded a welcome.

They sat opposite one another.

"Strange, yet not so strange, to see you."

"I figured you could use a friend."

Pastor held out his fists palm down and invited Frank to choose one or the other. Frank tapped the right one. It opened to a yellow earplug. Pastor opened the other fist to display its partner.

Frank smiled wanly and accepted the gift.

"You look precisely like a sane man who spent a night in an insane asylum," Pastor said.

Despite his best efforts, his absolute fucking determination, Frank Wills began crying. And once it started, he couldn't stop it. Pastor got on one knee and placed a hand on Frank's bowed head as he shook and wept. After a time the sobs subsided enough for Frank to regain control. He made no effort to wipe the tears, just looked up at the older man with gratitude.

"Too much has happened. Too much." And then another spate of sobs rocked him, but this time more briefly and easier to control.

Pastor said, "I know about Chucho."

Frank's face contorted with anger. Before he could speak, Pastor cut him off.

"There's a system of justice at work here you do not understand. So don't try. I see you grabbing at anger like a drowning man for a life preserver, and I understand the temptation, but I tell you plainly, it won't do nothing but give you an ulcer. Stay with grief, let it wash over you and clean out the anger. That's what you need, son."

"Shit. I don't know how much more grief I can take," Frank said.

They heard some stirring in the stall next door. Pastor stood up and offered his hand. "Let's move away from here; we don't want Daniel to wake up just yet." Frank gratefully accepted. They walked to the center, sat down at a table. Pastor produced a protein bar and placed it in front of Frank. He grabbed it, glanced furtively around, then tore it open and inhaled it.

Fidgeting with the wrapper, eyes down, Frank said, "Am I supposed to believe I'm being held hostage by one of God's angels?

"She told you that?"

He nodded. "'You can call me Gabriel,' she said. I don't remember much from Sunday school, but I do recall the archangels."

"And what do you think?"

Frank smoothed out the wrapper, began trying to shape it into an airplane. "I'm not much of a believer. My father preached all sorts of shit to me, but was such a miserable hypocrite, I assumed all religions were a racket....until last night." Frank went silent, eyes still looking down on his paper aviation project.

Pastor kept quiet.

After a moment, Frank glanced up. "I came to some important realizations. It's as if someone removed a veil from my eyes, and I understand things more clearly." He teared up. "No matter how much I try, I can't go back to seeing things the way I did before. And I hate it." Frank crumbled up the wrapper and tossed it away.

"Revelation isn't good for man," Pastor said. "Better there is doubt so faith can grow. Makes free will that much more powerful. But if you had an epiphany, then you got to honor that. No choice now. Like Saul of Tarsus." A hard look in Pastor's eyes.

At the mention of Paul's name before his conversion, Frank broke down again. Arms folded on the table, head down, Frank sobbed.

Pastor let Frank have a moment after he'd finished. "Tell me what happened to you overseas."

Head still down. "Why?"

"I would like to tell you confession is good for the soul, and it is, but it's my own curiosity I want to satisfy."

"What happened was one of thousands of similar stories in a combat zone. Nothing special about it," Frank said.

"Maybe. But there's another piece to this. Warden don't bring people here unless she has some real leverage. When you have a better handle on that, it might help."

Frank lifted his head. He drew a deep cleansing breath, then spoke.

CHAPTER 55

I t is so fucking hot. No reprieve from the punishing sun during the day. Drinking water on an endless loop: down the gullet by the gallon, instantly sweat out of each pore into drenched fatigues.

Frank leads his squadron on foot in Ramadi. They are doing street patrols, combination of security and getting to know the locals. Maybe show a kinder, gentler side while looking for those still aching to kill the American invaders. One of his guys flanks him on the right. The others hang back several feet. The hot wind occasionally blows from the east, and he is hit by a powerful stench reminding him why the others lag.

"Dewey, what the fuck is wrong with you?"

"Sarge?"

"You smell like a backed-up sewer," Frank says. Was a time he gave this feedback in gentle packages, but the soft touch led nowhere with Dewey.

"Sorry, Sarge. I shower pretty frequently."

Frank stops and puts his hand on Dewey's chest. It's damp and Frank immediately regrets risking his hand.

"Yes, I know. But you've been wearing those same goddamned fatigues the past two months." The *khamsin* continues to blow, adds to the shimmering heat rising from the ground, the sun beating ceaselessly on their heads.

"What the fuck, Sarge!" Lawler shouts from behind. "You gotta warn us when you're stopping so we don't get too close to Dewey Stink." (He pronounces it 'Do He Stink.')

"That's enough of that shit!" Frank shouts to his rear. Then to Dewey, "Use the fucking laundry service like the rest of us."

"I don't want them stealing my shit."

"We talked about this, man. There's nothing to fucking steal. Don't you see? It's a uniform; if it's lost or stolen Uncle Sam will replace it, no muss, no fuss."

He's irritable even without the cursed heat which multiplies the annoyance by an order of magnitude.

"Alright, I've said enough for now, Dewey. Let's move."

Lawler draws a little closer.

"I told you we needed to burn Dewey's fatigues like we burned his chair."

They had actually done that to poor Dewey. After he'd ignored their pleas to do something about his stench, they'd sent him a message by burning the one place he could rest his smelly ass.

"You know I don't approve of that kind of behavior. No code reds in this man's corps." Frank says, a smile in his voice.

"Wasn't a code red, Sarge—was a code brown."

Everyone laughs.

They walk quietly for a few mikes. A sound from one of the domiciles. The buildings have the same look. Concrete with no discernible roofs. Kids grow up, have families of their own and fathers add floors to the buildings to accommodate. Multi-generational.

Shouting from a first-floor apartment. Frank puts up a fist and they halt, fingers closing on triggers. They tense up, but the sound is unlike the usual animus directed their way.

Ali steps forward, speaks softly.

"A father berating his daughter. Calling her a whore." They hear the unmistakable sounds of a scuffle, then breaking glass.

Frank leads them through the door and into the foyer. Out of the sun it is relatively cooler. They remove their sunglasses, follow him to a rear apartment. He knocks on the door.

"*Aftah albab.*" Frank says loudly, but gently. "American Marines."

Sudden silence, then the sound of steps approaching the door. Frank wipes his forehead futilely trying to prevent the sweat and sand from seeping into his eyes. He shuts them, tries to wipe again to no avail. He hears the door open and rapid, angry Arabic.

"Ali, ask him if everything's alright, tell him we're here to help, yada, yada, yada."

Frank steps back, pulls out a rag for his aching eyes.

His guys crowd around him in full gear, guns pointed down. Ali exchanges rapid words with the man who remains agitated.

"He says get away from here, this is none of your business."

From behind they can see a young girl. Difficult to tell with the burka, but in her teens perhaps. She's got pretty eyes, one adorned with redness and swelling. Frank looks at her through his burning eyes, and she averts her own, but not before he catches a glimpse of defiance.

His guys are antsy, standing in the hall, fidgeting and beginning the type of hijinks one expects from pre-pubescent siblings. They're pushing Dewey away.

"Finally, a little cooler air. Do we have to spoil it with his stink? Make him stand outside and keep watch."

Turning his back on the domestic scene, Frank snaps, "It's very difficult to deal with this situation if I have to discipline you children. Pipe down."

They continue their little pushes, jostles, finger pointing with 'he started it' rapscallion shrugs. He sighs deeply.

"Ask this gentleman if he would kindly let the two of us step in and close to the door to get a little privacy."

The man is resistant, but Ali pushes his way in, and Frank follows, a final warning look to his squad before closing the door. The air in the apartment is hotter, more stifling. They stand in a small living area, only a couple of seats and a table in the room. Windows closed, shades drawn. Behind them, a small kitchen. Father is wearing a traditional white *thawb*, exceptionally bright to Frank's sun and sand taxed eyes.

Squabbling continues between father and daughter, an undertone of guttural, angry sounds. In the corner, a twenty-something-year-old man sits. He looks like there are a thousand places he'd rather be.

Were it not for the two soldiers standing between them, the father would likely have resumed his pugilism. Frank speaks through Ali who interprets on the spot, returns responses to English rapidly and succinctly, their collaboration nearly seamless.

"I need you to calm down, sir." When the man has ceased his yelling—though his breathing is fast, his fists still clenched—Frank continues, "Is this your daughter?"

"Yes. And no," the man says. "She has shamed my family. Harlot!" he yells suddenly.

The daughter, no longer to be outdecibeled shouts back, "He raped me, Father, I am a victim here. Why can't you see that?"

"You must have brought it on yourself with your slutty ways," Father counters.

The young man hasn't spoken up. He doesn't look to be the raping type, but you never know, Frank thinks.

He leans into Ali. "Tell him to calm down and gently tell the girl to leave with us." With slow and calming gestures, he tries to extricate the girl. Up close her eyes shine deeply green, feline-like. In contrast to her dark skin, very attractive.

Ali speaks to the father, slow, soothing words, his body shielding the young girl.

This doesn't hit the mark. Father grows more agitated. Frank is sensing the edginess; he pulls Ali in close for a sidebar.

"What just happened, Ali, what the fuck just happened?"

"I tried to suggest maybe the girl was telling the truth. Pops here didn't appreciate it. He called me a pimp and suggested I was worse than his daughter ruining the family's honor."

Daughter spits out vitriol; Frank now recognizes the just used Arabic word for pimp.

The next instant happens both fast and painfully slow. Father's intense and glaring eyes fix on his daughter, he bullrushes both soldiers who stand in his way. Those eyes contain pure rage, and his intent couldn't be more explicit to Frank if he proclaimed it in the King's English. The men in fatigues step in to protect her. It takes their combined strength to hold him back. The girl shrieks. The sound galvanizes father, and he thrusts with even more forcefulness. They succeed in pushing him back; he pirouettes for the kitchen and returns seconds later with a big kitchen knife. Explosions fill the room and Father is thrust backwards into the kitchen, redness rapidly spreading like a tidal wave over his white chest.

Ali is still in position, gun pressed hard to shoulder, eyes locked on the sight. They stand this way, held in suspended animation until Frank breaks it, crouches down to press on Father's neck where, of course, no pulse can be found, what with the three bullets centered so beautifully around his sternum, his white *thawb* scoring contrast as well as any practice target. Frank stands back up ready to comfort Daughter, to soothe and prevent further hysteria, but she is calm. She stands over her father's body, steady as they come. Then she rears up and spits on his ruined corpse.

Frank, standing frozen, becomes aware of banging on the door. "You alright in there?! What the fuck is going on in there, Sarge?!"

"Lower your weapon, corporal." he says quietly, and Ali slowly complies. Frank's mind races with the implications of what's happened. Beyond their pay grades to sort out, he's trying to decide the next step. The thumping on the door continues.

Daughter is speaking rapidly with the man in the corner, his face drained of color. Ali's eyes glaze over. Frank snaps his fingers.

"Ali, what is she saying? Ali?!" His translator's daze breaks, and Ali focuses his attention on the Arabic.

Frank walks to the door, opens it just before a shoulder breaks it down. The remainder of his crew tumbles into the apartment like a Three Stooges routine.

Rapid fire Arabic behind them, high pitched then low rumble. Ali is arguing with the young girl, anger clearly etched on his face. The girl, though, isn't angry. No, her face remains composed, yet there is something else written there in her expression. It hits Frank like a sledgehammer: she's smug. He intuits what Ali translates:

"Sarge, I don't think she was raped at all. I don't think this poor schmuck here even knew what she was going to do. This whole charade was meant to get her out from under her father's thumb. Now she's telling us to get out of her house."

"Holy shit. What the fuck happened here?" Lawler stands over the bloodied body on the floor. "You zapped a civilian sheik."

"Keep quiet, Lawler."

Daughter's voice rises in pitch, and she's yelling and gesticulating.

Grabbing at the man's clothes, urging him to bolster her. Acting with authority as if she has the weapons, not the other way around.

"Who is this bitch, and why is she yelling so goddamned much?" Lawler says.

Ali is periodically translating bits and pieces, it involves reporting them to the Iraqi authorities, the American authorities, the newspapers, anyone she can. She keeps on shrieking at a piercing frequency, and Frank's mind races with implications, inquiries, reports. He's thinking of poor Ali and the craziness of the situation, and he is overcome by a rage that exceeds his mental capacity to rationalize and suddenly he pulls out his Beretta and puts successive bullets in the heads of the young woman and her would-be boyfriend, his wide eyes registering surprise evermore.

The reports from the sidearm echo around the room then leave them with only Frank's heavy breathing and the distant sounds of traffic from outside.

Lawler speaks first. "That shut her up."

The others stand and wait expectantly for Frank. His mind has cleared. As if the bullets discharged his roiling thoughts along with them on their journey through the brains of their target.

He turns to Lawler. "You still carrying some incendiary grenades, or did you use them up on Dewey?"

Silently Lawler produces one and offers it to Frank who signals two. Lawler gives over another.

"Now all of you, get out."

They comply, Dewey the last. He speaks, "Sarge, what about the others in this building? There looks to be at least three floors. We should evacuate."

"Good point. You let me handle it, okay," Frank reassures them. "Keep clear."

Looking skeptical, Dewey leaves but doesn't close the door. Frank waits until his guys exit the building. He looks around. Such a quick turn of events. All that training, repping, discipline and yet so many times it comes down to split seconds amid unpredictable situations. A domestic dispute becomes a mausoleum in a flash.

No choice. This couldn't be sorted out easily, and he wouldn't let a good soldier like Ali twist in the wind for the product of the fog of war. The time for wavering is gone, his resolve cements in his gut. A pull on one pin, then the second. A toss into the kitchen and a gentle underhand throw into the corner where the two other bodies lie sprawled near one another.

They stand outside in the heat, watch the building burn for minute before Frank calls it in. Possible insurgents, taking incoming fire, countermeasures deployed.

CHAPTER 56

During Frank's recitation the pod awakened behind them. The regular hijinks started up as if the pod itself ran on the crazy energy.

Pastor helped Frank stand and get over to a stall where they could seek refuge from flying cornflakes and cornbread.

Without looking up, Frank said, "You think less of me?"

"Neh. I know why you beat yourself up, son, but I understand why you did what you did. Morality ain't so easy in those circumstances. You made a choice. Maybe I would choose different, maybe I wouldn't. Who can say? But I can understand why Warden selected you. You're a man of action. Very few people can make such quick decisions, act like judge and jury in an instant and carry out the sentence."

One of the runners came to a stop right in front of them; Pastor shook his fist at the man.

"Pull out your pecker, and I will snatch it."

The man thought better of it, resumed his laps.

Pastor turned back to Frank. "She looking for someone from our world to help manage this place. She needs an inside man, and she's pegged you to be it."

"I just want to get the hell out of here."

"That's not in the cards right now. You need to decide, and you need to do it right quick. Spend enough time on this pod, and you'll have to adapt to crazy. Then'll come a time when you don't realize you crazy because you just doing what you need to get by in this crazy place and that will become your new normal. Long enough like that, Frank, and you won't be able to come back. You understand?"

Frank didn't answer. Pastor leaned in and looked intensely in Frank's eyes.

"It's her world, son. You cannot change it. All you can do is accept and decide your own fate." Pastor stood up, put a hand on Frank's shoulder. "I'm sorry to put more on you, but you gotta know."

Frank looked up, puzzled.

"When you and Chucho got picked up, was a vacuum of leadership. Can't have that nowhere. So Rodrigo stepped up, and he running things."

"Shit."

"Yea. And he don't like that you took a shine to Seth, so he giving the poor bastard a beating every day."

Frank stood up and needfully grabbed at Pastor's arm. "Can I go with you?"

He gently removed the arm. "I'm sorry, no. That's not possible. But when you're truly ready to return, she'll have someone fetch you to her. You can count on that." And he walked away.

Frank didn't follow—wasn't any point. He knew Pastor had it right.

CHAPTER 57

I t took three cycles for Frank to lose the anger. He stayed in his booth, lying on the mat. Having given up on getting any sustenance on this pod, he suffered intense hunger pangs the first day. Once they dissipated, his thoughts crystallized.

First to be slayed was his pride and anger; he'd intellectually conquered them quickly, but the emotional dregs continued their stinging pressure for a while. In between walks to the bathroom for drinks and less frequent micturition, he lay in repose and calmed his mind. Childish fantasies of going back in time, doing things differently, were the next to go. He embraced the options available to him; it helped his focus.

Resolution came as light dawned on the fourth day. A new mission.

He sat up in the would-be dawn, the pod in its brief sedate state, and clutched his knees to his chest. Acceptance, not just in his head, but in his entire being, filled him. He stood up and prepared to leave. Lightheaded, but feeling at peace, he saw the black-clad figure approach moments later.

CHAPTER 58

"Just one escort this time, huh?"

The guard, sans a helmet or nightstick, didn't acknowledge the question.

"Guess I'm not such a desperado anymore." There was no taunt in the comment, simply another confirmation to Frank that he was in a different mental place. He had no inclination to fight or flee. Acceptance continued to flow through him. This was one aspect to Burning River he liked: it read his moods and energy and respected them accordingly. His escort pointed to a door and retreated.

Warden wasn't in the office. On her desk stood three items: a peeled hard-boiled egg, a single package of Melba toast, and a bottle of coconut water. He reached over to collect them and sat down on the chair.

Munching on the snacks he felt at ease.

"After a fast it's best not to burden the stomach with too much right away."

Without turning to the voice behind him, he said, "Thank you. Very thoughtful."

Warden walked around him and took a seat behind the desk. She wore her usual impassive expression on her face as she let him finish his light repast.

"I'm glad you're back, Frank. I didn't like how things turned out, but there was no other way. You understand that now, I know."

He nodded. "I wasn't ready. And there was nothing you could do to reach me. I'm the kind of guy who needs to get there myself. Any pressure from the outside, no matter how right it is"—he nodded in her direction—"only makes me more stubborn."

"Very human, Frank. Don't be hard on yourself; you've made greater strides than even I could hope for."

"Thank you, Warden." He held up his bottle and empty wrapper, looking for a place to dispose of them, then leaned forward in his chair and deposited them on Warden's desk. He rubbed his hands together. "So what happens now?"

A look of disgust flashed across her face as she regarded his refuse, then she pushed the bottle and wrapper together to the edge and resumed her impassive look. "Now you get back in the game. I need you to get the admissions pod in order and then we organize the rest."

"You mind if I ask you a question?"

"Of course not."

"Why Cleveland?" Frank smirked.

"I have several beta sites; Cleveland is just one of them. I looked for out of the way places with small enough populations where I could see a difference." For the first time her face registered something akin to excitement. "I'm telling you, Frank, this could be big. You do a good job with Burning River like I know you can and then we move on to bigger things. Together we can recruit others and make a dent in the lawless chaos occurring all of over the Earth."

"You make a hell of a sales pitch. When do I start?"

She stood up. "No time like the present." Warden held a hand out indicating the door, but her eyes dropped to the discarded items on her desk in silent demand.

Frank bolted to his feet and saluted smartly. "I won't let you down, Ma'am."

He walked out and made his way down the long empty hall. Everything in his bearing brought back his earliest days of Marine command. The erectness of his spine, the cadence of his heel-to-toe walking, his straight sight line—they instilled in him a rightness to the mission. Those were great days filled with immense pride. Uniform pressed, ready to live a life of meaning and consequence. He never felt as fulfilled as he did during his time in command of a squad.

He exited the door and found himself in a familiar place. No one noticed him as he scanned the area. The morning was fresh, a few men milling about the pod. He walked to the center, passing people he knew. A ripple of excitement built as he moved about.

"Frank's back."

"Oh, shit, time's up for Rodrigo."

"Gonna be eatin' well tonight."

"You get 'em, Frank. We with you!"

He spotted Anderson and walked up to him.

The big Aryan offered a hand. "Fuckin' Lazarus, you are. Gotta say, happy to see you."

"Where's Seth?"

"Who?"

"The big kid, always looks like someone slapped his cheeks."

"The retard? Shit, man, I'm sorry. Rodrigo made an example of him right after you left. Beat him up so bad they had to cart him out of here."

Anderson kept speaking, but Frank didn't hear. He thought about Seth and his determined sense of responsibility to keep the boy safe.

The meaning that might have provided. He didn't even register the shouts coming from near the fire pit.

From a lawn chair, someone stood and yelled repeatedly for Frank's attention.

Anderson tugged on Frank's arm. "Hey, brother, snap out of it. Rodrigo's coming."

With unparalleled swagger, Rodrigo approached Frank, his entourage behind him exhorting him to action.

"I'm so glad to see you, Frank. I wanted so badly to thank you for getting rid of Chucho like you did. You make me king of this place." He held his arms wide to the delight of his crew.

Frank didn't respond.

Now Rodrigo stood inches away, the smile gone. "You should not have come back. I got no choice but to fuck you up."

"Why don't you put on a fight at noon?" Anderson stepped in between the two and spoke to Rodrigo. "It will be like the good old days."

"Neh, I ain't going to fight Frank alone. He cheats. But I ain't going to give him the pod, neither. I think I just have all my guys jump him."

"Wait!" Frank yelled. His sudden animation caused both Rodrigo and Anderson to jump back, both in exaggerated fighting poses. "Hold on," Frank said more softly, his eyes zeroed in on Rodrigo. "You've wanted a piece of me since I got here. Why don't you take your best shot.?

Rodrigo didn't act right away.

"Boy, you are a chicken shit." Frank taunted, walking a circle around Rodrigo and speaking loudly. "Need your *amigos* to give you courage. Isn't there a word in Spanish for someone like you? Isn't it *maricón*?"

Rodrigo charged.

Even in his weakened state Frank was clearly too much for the smaller man. Filled with rage, to be sure, but wild and inexperienced.

In three moves Frank had him pinned on the ground, begging for mercy.

It brought Frank no joy, no vindication. There was no sense of a completed circle or justice served. Even the act of stripping Rodrigo of his jumpsuit was as perfunctory as it came. Four men in black emerged from the tunnel and dethroned Rodrigo from his brief reign.

While the men in black retreated, the others on the pod already recast their attention to Frank. Celebrations, calls of return of greatness sounded out around the crowd. Someone began a rhythmic applause, and it caught on, the whole pod clapping. Frank held up his hands in triumph, then signaled for silence. Quiet descended. Someone wolf whistled and everyone laughed and celebrated more. Then they waited for Frank's benediction.

He stood, his hands still in the air, his head down. When he lifted his head, resolve filled his eyes. Slowly he moved his hands to his jumpsuit and unzipped it. Stepping out of it, he tossed it aside, made an elaborate bow and walked to the fence.

"What the fuck, Frank?"

"What are you doing, brother?"

He climbed the fence in his underwear and Crocs, careful not to snag anything on the top, kicked his leg over and jumped down, not to be seen by anyone on the inside again.

CHAPTER 59

His cell greeted him like an old friend. The door stood open as if it anticipated this move, but that he doubted. The idea to passively surrender his fate was impulsive; it'd only fully co-alesced in his mind when he had his knee on Rodrigo's head. He knew it was the right decision—the release of tension alone was worth it. He felt a sense of peace he'd not had since—well, he couldn't even remember a time of such contentment. No debts to be paid, no deeds to do. He would miss his children, but he realized when he sat with Warden that last time that going back wasn't ever in the cards, anyway. Didn't seem like Gabriel would let him leave once she'd got-ten her hooks in him.

It was warm in the cell. He was grateful for that, at least. He lay down on the mattress and slept for a long time.

When he awoke there were packages on the floor. That brought a wry smile to his face, and he tore into them finding a few items to re-charge. He recognized the Faustian bargain with the carbs and limited how much starch he ate. Having eaten a little, he set off from the cell to find some suitable clothes.

He stepped out into the hinterlands of the admission pod and held his hands up in blessing.

"The prodigal son returns."

No one stirred. The bedraggled congregation of the forlorn looked the same. A voice rang out.

"I heard it, but I didn't believe it until just now."

Frank smiled broadly at the older man approaching and bellowed. "The fine Reverend Pastor, I say to thee, bear witness—no man or angel has a claim on me any longer. I choose to be here and join you in your ministrations of those lost and dying."

"It's Pastor Roscoe, if you please." He hugged the near-naked man with genuine emotion; Frank returned the embrace equally, then collapsed into Pastor's arms.

"Whoa, whoa, son, I ain't a young man no more." He went to the ground as gently as he could, Frank's head ending up in his lap.

"I feared I would never leave the psycho pod. I'm very grateful to be here with you, again."

"While I'm grateful you still around, you now back at square one, Frank. What's going to happen to you, huh?"

A shrug. "I'll live on my own terms, doing things that make me proud of myself."

Pastor paused then nodded his head, the hint of a smile on his lips. "Well, shit, *I'm* proud of you, young man. You've proven to be stronger than I thought."

Frank suddenly remembered Seth and sat up. "Did they drop off Seth here, by any chance?"

Pastor shook his head sadly. "I know that boy meant something to you. When they come and get him after what Rodrigo done, they took him inside. Ain't seen him since. Sorry, son."

"Appreciate it." Frank slowly walked around searching and soon finding a grungy jumpsuit that might have once been yellow. Without hesitation he put it on.

The next day Frank came out and strolled among the human debris lying around, most of their faces burrowed in scraps of cloth to keep the light out. Halfway up the row he finally recognized someone. It was the guy they dubbed "Old Faithful" for his routine—though wholly inept—attempts to garner a spot on the pod. He looked more cachectic, like he was barely holding on. Crouching down, Frankly gently shook him awake.

"Hey, how you doing?"

The eyes opened slowly and looked up. There was little animation in those eyes, like bulbs with diminished lumens, barely registering internal life. But the hint of a smile played on his lips, and he reached up with a shaking hand to touch Frank.

"Yea, that's right. Me, Frank. Here, let me help you sit up."

It was like lifting dead weight.

"When's the last time you had real food?" Frank asked.

"Not since you left, I haven't been allowed to scale the fence," he said. "Rodrigo put the word out I would be killed if I came over again."

Frank reminded himself to ask Pastor for a stash of that jerky.

"Hey, man, I never got your name."

A weakly extended hand. "Ben."

"Pleased to me you. Just so you know, Rodrigo isn't in charge anymore so you can resume your daily pilgrimages to the inside."

Ben frowned and shook his head. "Neh, I'm done. I can't do it anymore."

"C'mon, you don't mean that. Gotta keep fighting." He put a reassuring hand on Ben's shoulder, felt the slack muscles. "Give me some time to find Pastor and get some protein in you. Then you'll feel like a new man."

A shrug was all Frank got in return. He stood and looked around, hoping to spot Pastor doing his rounds somewhere. Disappointed, he crouched back down only to find Ben slumped on the ground, his breathing rapid and shallow.

"Let me get you in a better position at least." Frank did his best to arrange Ben with as much comfort he could manage. "Alright, here we go, here we go. You gotta hold on, you hear me."

Like talking to a rag doll.

Each day began the same over the next few. A few bites to get a little energy then out on the pod to try and help anyone he could. Every time he stepped from the muted glow of the hallways to the artificial light, he scanned the area for Pastor. No luck. Before he'd shown up when Frank didn't want him and now that he needed him, nothing. As if he were purposefully avoiding Frank. And Ben grew weaker and weaker. Frank crouched next to him, trying to get him to eat little morsels without success. He felt like a doctor sans available treatments.

Ben's breathing was shallow and slowing..

Frank started to panic. "Oh, what the fuck." He got on his knees, feeling for a pulse, but he couldn't tell. His own heart beat hard and fast, and his stressed and malnourished mind couldn't register anything.

"Pastor, where the hell are you." His head darted around like a bird's, staccato movements, looking left, right. "Pastor!" he yelled. No one stirred. He looked back down at Ben, an ashen look now on his face that didn't require checking a pulse.

He sat back on his heels, hands on his knees, head down.

"Just the way you like it, right, Warden?" he said it to himself, yet he knew she could hear him. "I'm not coming back to you no matter what." The declaration felt necessary, a reinforcement as well as a resignation.

Frank stood slowly, put a rag over Ben's face and trudged his way back to his cell, head down. He parted with one more malediction.

"And fuck you, too, Pastor."

CHAPTER 60

Death row inmates will adjust their internal clocks to a sleep cycle of nearly eighteen of the twenty-four hours. With little else to do but wait, they set their brains to near hibernation.

Frank lay on his mattress in his boxers. He'd not gotten up for a couple of days, not even to pee, his shorts betraying evidence of the concentrated urine he produced. He'd not defecated in three days.

An apparition at the door. Out of focus and hazy. It coalesced in the dim light, and Pastor knelt by the bedside.

"Frank, you're not going to make it much longer. Here, take some of this jerky, eat."

A shake of the head, lips pressed together like a toddler in a highchair.

"Jesus, Frank, why you giving up like this?"

"Leave me alone. I'm not giving up; I'm accepting fate."

"Bullshit, son, you're capitulating. And I ain't gonna let it happen. Upsy daisy, now."

He pulled Frank into a sitting position. "Let's get your clothes on."

Pastor pulled one sleeve on Frank, then the other. Getting his legs in was more of a challenge, but Frank allowed it.

"Where were you when I needed you?"

The older man stopped, head bowed. "I'm sorry." It seemed like he had more to say, but he didn't. He grabbed the crocs and placed one on each foot.

"You're coming with me."

"I don't want to go back out there anymore. I'm done."

"We not going out there, Frank. Eat a little of this—you're going to need some strength."

"Where we going?"

Pastor pulled Frank to his feet and steadied him.

"Outta here," he said and gently pulled him to the cell door.

CHAPTER 61

Down the familiar hallway, Pastor dragging Frank along by the waist.

"What do you mean out?" A little stronger after eating some jerky.

"I'm sending you out of Burning River. I want you go to home."

A harsh bark of laughter. "You lost your mind, old man?"

They came to the T and Frank immediately noticed a difference. To the left, the tunnel to despair central. That much the same. But to the right, the light was brighter, that same nourishing energy he remembered from when he'd just arrived. He turned towards it and let go of Pastor's shoulder, standing on his own.

"The light," he said.

"Yea, Frank, we going to the elevator."

Frank took the turn and after a few steps he stopped, breathed deeply. Hope seemed to fill his lungs while at the same time memories of that accursed elevator intruded.

"I don't like where it takes me."

Pastor put a hand on his back. "You with me. The elevator will take us where you need to go."

"And where is that?"

"We'll talk about it when we get closer."

Silently they went down the hall; the doors opened to their approach, light spilling out of them.

"I guess you have the magic touch," Frank said.

"Like I told you already."

After a moment's hesitation, Frank stepped inside. Now it looked like an ordinary elevator minus the buttons. Lit up it was like a defanged tiger.

The doors closed and the car descended at a leisurely pace.

Pastor looked intently in Frank's eyes. He held something in his hand, concealed in his fist.

"Frank, you gotta do exactly as I tell you. Once you go on your way, I won't be able to help you, so please listen up. You're going to go through that pod with the ladies in it. You remember, right? They the ones with the drug problem. They gonna react to you being on their pod, make like they gonna attack you. That's when you gotta give them this."

He held up a small Ziploc bag. Frank took it and held it up the light. A white powder, faintly crystalline in its appearance.

"Where did you get this?"

"A man gave it to me before he died. He knew he wouldn't make it, so he gave it to me; We was real close."

"What is this? Meth?"

"Don't make no difference what it is. You see it as a ticket through. Because through the pod is where you gotta go. You must hand it to one of the women and get something in return. That's important, Frank; it has to be an exchange for something. Then, once you're through don't stop to talk to anybody. You'll pass a notorious serial killer who will want help but keep walking." He made to push Frank out, then grabbed his shirt. "Oh, and remember the plight of a rich man entering the kingdom of heaven."

"What the hell does that mean?"

A shrug.

The elevator came to an easy stop, the doors opened.

"This is your stop, Frank." He gripped both shoulders warmly. "Good luck to you. You're a good man and I wish you well."

Frank stammered, had trouble getting words out. "What? I can't do what you're saying. You have a golden ticket and you're giving it to me? Why don't you take it and get the fuck out of here yourself?"

Pastor looked nervously at the open elevator doors. "I don't have much time to explain. You have to trust me."

Frank stood frozen in place. Pastor looked away, sighed, then locked eyes with Frank.

"Listen to me. I'm where I belong. I was a pastor on the outside, yea, but I was a broken man. I liked the position I had, the role of confidante to many who trusted me. I was weak and I took advantage of many married women. Lonely women if you know what I mean. I enjoyed too many forbidden fruits."

"A husband come after you?" Frank asked.

Pastor shook his head, and there remained some pride in his face. "I treated those women like queens, and they didn't say a word. In a way that's why I'm still here, I never received any comeuppance for my deeds. I gotta lot of penance to do yet. But you don't belong here, and I can't watch you wither and die. So go."

"She's never going to let me leave, man. Don't you understand?!" Frank cried out.

Pastor steadied Frank's shoulders. "She can't control certain things, Frank. She can't control gravity and free will. Those remain in the purview of our Earthbound world. Remember that."

Pastor gave a sharp shove and Frank stumbled out of the elevator. The doors closed, Frank only catching a glimpse of the older man serenely waving goodbye. He stood stunned for a minute; how long had Pastor been holding onto this bag? he wondered, holding it up to the light. It all could fit in a roll of quarters. Fear broke his paralysis; he squeezed the bag, and moved with purpose away from the elevator, towards the T.

CHAPTER 62

One hand on the door to steady himself, deep breathing in preparation for the plunge. He remembered well the palpable need oozing from the zombie-like women clawing at him the last time. Like they were programmed to wait for just such a prize he held. He tried to conjure up pictures of his kids, but it was hard. He filled himself with the intense love he felt for them as much as he could, then yanked the door open.

Nothing had changed.

He might have just left a second ago. Women shuffled around the pod, their fronts sporting dual circles of wetness around their nipples. And the wail. The rise and fall, but ever- constant sound of crying babies.

He strode forward into the fray, heading to the center of the pod to a chorus of pleas.

"You got what I need?!"

"You holding!?"

"Whatchu got for me?!"

Frank pincered the Ziploc bag, displaying it high.

"I've got the good shit here!" he shouted. It was barely out of his mouth when something hit him on the back of his head while hands swatted the plastic bag and sent it flying through the air.

He landed on his knees, prostrate before a swarm of addicts. In their impaired state they didn't realize Frank didn't have the bag. They clawed at him, and he felt crude shanks cutting through his jumpsuit, lacerating his skin. In between crouching and protecting his face, he took quick peeks through the many legs and spotted the bag ten feet away. Crawling through this cauldron, he pounced on the bag then executed aggressive rolls until he found sufficient room to stand.

It was quite a sight. A circle of women standing over the space he just vacated, desperately pawing and kicking. At first, he thought maybe somebody else had come in or maybe the bag wasn't in his hand but was still at the bottom of that pile. He had to hold the bag inches from his face, feel it repeatedly to convince himself that, in fact, they were like a pack of zombies unable to integrate new information.

A few women sat on the sides, uninterested in the scrum or too out of it to realize the stakes. He calmly walked over to one holding a tangerine, his eyes darting back and forth from the lone woman to the rabble. The group of women continued in their relentless tussle with a now-absent dealer.

Frank eased himself down the wall into a sitting position right next to her. She paid him no attention. Rocking to and fro, holding the tangerine, eyes glazed over.

He leaned in and spoke as loud as he could to be heard over the crying. "Hey, I got something for you."

No response.

Using his body as a shield he positioned himself between the bag and the mob behind and almost thrust the Ziploc up the woman's nose before her eyes lit up and she came alive. She made to grab the bag.

"Give me the fruit, then you can have it."

She thrust it into his chest; he held out the bag and she performed a light-speed snatch and tuck-away. In a flash she headed away from him casting furtive glances over her shoulder every few steps. The rabble was none the wiser; they continued their fruitless assault.

Movement caught Frank's attention. A crack of light on the far side of the pod. He made sure no one was watching, and power walked his way over there. He almost cried when the door pushed easily open, and he stepped through and closed it behind him. Immediately the wailing sounds of crying ceased. Frank took a moment to breathe deeply. His clothes were in tatters, and he felt too many cuts to take inventory.

He stood in a dimly lit narrow hallway, the ceiling just clearing the top of his head. It was so difficult to determine what lay ahead apart from the faint hint of sound. Walking onward, claustrophobia settled in. With each step darkness descended until he was forced to play blind man, hands held in front. The tips of his fingers hit a wall and he began desperately feeling around until he appreciated a dogleg to the right. After a few more steps another wall, this time a dogleg to the left. Sound grew in his ear, a rushing; the unmistakable signature of moving water.

"Motherfuckers. I've had it with water."

A few more steps and a room materialized on his right, just enough light to make out some details. At the same time, he felt freezing water moving under then over his feet. He stopped short.

"Christ. When do I get to leave this fucking place?"

Frank stood over a room like a big funnel, opening below him to his right; water streamed in from all sides. The plank-like ledge he occupied went clockwise around the pool. In its center stood a smallish, waterlogged man.

"Hey, can you help me?" He extended a hand up.

Frank ignored him and moved rapidly, but with each step the water level rose and the center, where the man begged, filled up rapidly.

"Don't let me drown in here! C'mon, just give me a hand up."

Another step.

"Stop! Don't let me die!"

Frank trudged forward against the rising tide, the water threatening to drag him into the pit to drown alongside this poor bastard. Pressing upwards on the ceiling stabilized him, and he made progress. He snatched a glance down just as the man succumbed to the water's vortex, like being flushed down a giant toilet. Frank double timed it to the end and just as he got to a dog leg left, he glanced back and saw the water abate unnaturally fast, the man re-emerging, sputtering and gasping for air.

The serial killer destined to drown on an endless loop.

Back in a hallway, nearly pitch black again. With his hands on the ceiling, Frank inched forward. His extended arms drew in with the diminishing proportions until he felt his head scraping the ceiling. Squinting, he thought he could make out a pinpoint of light, but it seemed so far away. A few more steps and he was crouching down, the air thinner, his breathing becoming shallower and more rapid. His eyes told him he would run out of space. When he got to his knees, the panic in his brain went on full tilt and he tried to turn around, but there wasn't room. He glanced between his legs backwards, like a dog and saw a mirror image of what lay ahead. The same pinpoint in the horizon.

Like being back in the coffin tunnel at the entrance of the arson pod. Only this time he didn't think there was a way out. Pastor had been wrong. Frank would die right here, suffocated by Gabriel's demented idea of retributive justice. This felt like something she would do. It wouldn't have an impact if he didn't have hope. Dangling the possibility of reprieve, even though he thought he'd expiated it from his psyche, she was exacting every last ounce of vengeance she could. This made sense. He lay down like an animal who knows it is going to die.

He closed his eyes and paid attention to his breathing, the sound loud in his ears.

The last moments with Pastor played out in his mind's eye. The man's deep baritone intoning the parting wisdom, "Don't forget how the rich man gets into heaven."

Rich man in heaven? Rich man didn't get into heaven, right? The acquisition of money for money's sake so frowned upon in the New Testament making it tough, making it an impossibility, would be like…a camel passing through the eye of a needle.

His head snapped up, eyes open and focused on that pinpoint of light. A camel through the eye of the needle. Frank's eyes were deceiving him, his brain trying to incorporate data for which it had no frame of reference. He shut his eyes and pressed forward despite the alarm bells coming to him tactilely, the tunnel shrinking, pressing on him until he was crawling on his belly forced to move like a snake, pulling his toes forward and then pushing with all his might, wriggling through an ever-tightening aperture, pressure on his chest, breathing difficult, the compression on his skull even as his rational mind argued the incompatibility of the space exerting force on both his head and chest equally eyes squeezed shut then…

…a pop and a surge forward with no tactile input whatsoever falling through darkness, falling, his stomach in his throat, the air ripped from his lungs and then frozen water, his balls rocketing into his stomach, every cell crying out crying out shrieking you cannot survive this and then finally instinct at last taking over kicking his legs furiously, clawing his way to the surface, emerging into Cleveland's December frigid air.

CHAPTER 63

"C'mon you bastard, don't give up on me."

Dave Logan sat astride the pulseless man's abdomen, cranking on his chest.

"One, two....where are you fucking assholes?!"

He looked out the back of his truck for the flashing lights; listened briefly for the sirens as he felt again for the pulse. Thought maybe there was something thready, but he couldn't tell as his own hands had begun shaking. He'd turned off the heaters thinking the cold might protect Frank and, despite the wetsuit, or maybe because of it for fuck's sake, he was colder than shit.

"Christ, why does it have to be so fuckin' frigid in this town?" He laughed maniacally.

A sound behind him grew and he held compressions.

"Ah, the sweet sound of rescue." He spoke to the bluing face inches from his own. "I ain't letting you go, you fuck. You're coming back to us. Ain't never lost one who I saw arrest and not starting today."

Dave continued on listening for the squeak of the brakes, the pulsing red lighting him and Frank up like a disco strobe. A tap to his right and he stopped compressions.

"What up, Dave. I got ya. Move off so I can attach the AED."

Dave sat heavy in the tight space available. He pulled a blanket around his shoulders and shuddered mightily. Through violently chattering teeth Dave said, "Jimmy, never been happier to see you. I came upon this fuckin' guy in the water. In the fucking water."

"A suicide?" Jimmy asked as he pulled out the pads to attach to the chest and turn the machine on.

Dave shrugged. They both turned their attention to the monitor.

The AED indicated a V-fib, then rang out in its anodyne voice, "Shock advised; stay clear; charging." Dave held his breath as the medic pushed the button and Frank's torso jolted. Each of the men's attention went to the rhythm: still V-fib.

"Hit it again." They waited again for the AED to fire up.

"Shock advised. Stay clear. Charging."

Another convulsive jump from Frank and again they waited.

Normal sinus rhythm.

"Alright, motherfucker!" Dave shouted.

"Christ, Logan, you'll break my eardrums."

They continued bagging Frank and transferred him to their rig. Just before leaving, Jimmy said, "You gonna be alright? You look like shit."

"I'll be fine, buddy. You just take care of him. Where you going?"

"Metro."

"Top notch. Godspeed."

The rig turned around, put on its lights and sirens, and sped away. Dave got back into his truck and cranked the heat as high as it would go and just sat for a few moments thawing before he drove off. Another memorable December day on Lake Erie.

CHAPTER 64

The opening crack of consciousness came without pain. All-encompassing comfort. It seemed like he rested on a cloud, the mattress extravagant. Surrounded by warmth and gentle hands on him ministering to his needs.

Light filled his eyelids with reds, oranges, and yellows. He became aware of a steady beeping, hustle and bustle, and from a distance the sound of a television. It was still a struggle to open his eyes, so he just rested, enjoying the various sensations.

"Looks like someone is stirring. Could you let Dr. Portnoy know her patient is waking up."

A soft and warm hand patting his arm.

"Mr. Wills, can you open your eyes and look at me."

I don't want to. Still down in the depths, but with comfort. As if someone turned down all the dials of trepidation, anticipation, and fear.

Another voice. "What's going on?"

"Hey, Dr. Portnoy. He's starting to wake up. Moving all his extremities nicely, squinting against the light."

Rougher hands on his face, then a blinding light in one eye, then the other.

"Pupils are reactive. Stop the Ativan drip; that'll help."

"Yes, Doctor."

"Well, maybe we'll get some answers. Call me when he's alert."

"Will do."

The sounds receded...then returned. Increased awareness came with it. Hearing sound to his right, he turned his head and opened his eyes.

A nurse had her back to him, taking care of his roommate. She looked to be young.

Mouth dry he attempted to speak but couldn't produce sound. The second attempt did the trick.

"Ma'am."

She turned and smiled at him.

"Well, look who's rejoined the world." She stepped towards his bed, put her hands on her hips. "How are you feeling?"

"Okay, I guess. Where am I?"

"Metro. I'll let Dr. Portnoy know you're up."

"How long was I out?"

"Only a couple of days. Glad you're back with us."

Frank made to sit up. She put a gentle hand on his shoulder and without a sound grabbed the handheld from the side of his bed and pushed a button to raise the head of the bed.

"Thank you, ma'am."

"Everyone's dying to know how you came to be in the lake in December. I'm going to get the doctor now."

A couple minutes later the doctor came in, nurse just behind her. He sat up straighter. She folded up her white coat, pulled a chair right next to his bed and sat.

"Well, good morning to you, Mr. Wills. My name is Dr. Portnoy and I'm going to do some basic tests to see how you're doing."

She pulled out an instrument with a rubber hammer at one end and a sharp point at the other.

Frank smiled. "I hope that's not going anywhere delicate."

Portnoy looked at it. "Looks fierce, but you'll be fine. I understand you're a Marine."

He nodded. She pulled his sheet down below his feet and went about lightly tapping different places on his body with the hammer.

"Tell me, Frank (okay I call you Frank?), what's your last memory before being hospitalized?"

It was difficult to remember; he watched her exams, the satisfied look on her face after each brief check of his reflexes and muscle strength. "Uh, I don't really know."

"I wouldn't stress yourself over it right now. I don't find any abnormalities on exam, and the MRI of your head was normal. That's all good news. So, I encourage you to get up, eat, and do what you feel capable of. But listen to your body and make sure not to push yourself too much." She seemed to think about it more then said, "You know what, I'm going to have a physical therapist come by just to be on the safe side. You probably won't need much, but I'd feel more comfortable."

Frank found the handheld that controlled the head of the bed, returned it to a lying position and re-closed his eyes.

CHAPTER 65

Back in the tunnel, its bore shrinking with each step.

The path he is walking on is dreadfully narrow, less than shoulder width; forces him to walk a tightrope. On his right the rushing of water.

"Hey man, you gotta get me outta here. You owe me, *cabron*, after what I did for you."

Frank looks down at the big toilet bowl to his right. The serial killer is in there, panicking as the water rises above his knees. Frank's mind races: I'm fucking back in here? I got through, didn't I? Didn't I escape? Jesus, how did I do it. I can't fucking remember.

He hits his head to jar the memory. Screwing his eyes to see past into what lay ahead, but he can't make out any details. All he can see is blackness. The screams intensify as the water level rises, and he can feel some of the spray hitting him.

"Frank! You promise me, you help me get outta here. You gonna let me drown in here?!"

His legs feel rubbery, threatening to buckle and send him into the vortex. He chances a glance down and he's looking right into Chucho's lined face. No smiles, just pure panic, conveying the desperation only a drowning man can produce.

"I'm sorry, man," Frank cries out. "I didn't have a choice!"

Chucho rises up out of the water and grabs at Frank. Before he can sufficiently recoil, the hand grips his ankle with such force, he is helpless as he tumbles off the ledge into the frozen deep, dragged ever downward never to resurface again.

CHAPTER 66

Frank woke with a start, drenched in sweat. He leaned over to grab his water finding it just out of reach.

"Shit."

For moment he felt paralyzed sending a cold wave over his body. It broke and he again reached unsuccessfully for the water.

A soft knock came at the door and someone peaked his head him and saw the struggle.

"Here, let me." He said.

A middle-aged man who looked like he came from an L.L. Bean catalogue grabbed the water, and handed it over.

Frank sucked on the straw, gratitude in his eyes.

The man sat in the chair next to the bed and crossed his legs. "Mr. Wills, my name is Dr. Dale."

"You look like a backpacker."

Just a smile in return. "I'm a psychiatrist. You ever seen someone in mental health?"

Frank used the button to raise his head. "I did an exit interview when I left combat."

"Well, Dr. Portnoy asked me to come talk to you."

"The fact that I lost two months?"

The psychiatrist refolded his legs. "That among other things."

"Do shrinks deal with amnesia?"

"We sometimes see what are called fugue states. Periods of time where a person loses themselves sometimes traveling to distant locales. Trauma can lead to some unusual brain states, and I understand you saw heavy combat."

"How do you know that?" Frank asked, brows furrowed.

"Your wife."

"She's here?"

A shake of the head. "Dr. Portnoy spoke with her on the phone." Dale leaned forward, elbows on his legs, fingers interlaced. "She worried about you. Wondered if you were suicidal."

He let the last hang in the air.

"At no time, Doc. At no time."

"Good. So, I'm not going to ask you to delve into specific traumas; we don't have the kind of time needed to do that kind of work. I am curious, though, about your experiences in a general sense and how they might have impacted your psyche."

Frank contemplated for a moment, then, resolutely swung his legs over the side of the bed.

"Doc, could you do me a favor and close the door."

Dale stood, shut the door, and sat back down. He waited patiently.

"What if I told you I do remember what happened. And that what I remember will probably make you want to throw me in the puzzle factory and throw away the key."

"Crazy has a distinct look, Frank, and you don't have it. So lay it on me."

Frank started slowly, from his early morning bus ride that fateful morning, the conflicts that ensued and his unlikely incarceration. As he progressed his voice grew stronger, and he fell into a pattern of heartfelt recitation without embellishing or sparing his own violent actions. He described his time on the intake pod, his friendship with Chucho, and finally his interactions with the Warden—even detailing the identity she proclaimed. He finished with a vague recollection of how he came to escape because even he had only hazy memories of it despite the recent dream still echoing in his mind. When his story was complete, he felt spent, but better for having shared it. He looked up expectantly at Dr. Dale.

"I know what I just told you sounds supernatural or part of some elaborate dream, but it really happened. I know it did. Just as real as you and I sitting here."

"That you were somehow held captive in a subterranean jail underneath Lake Erie by the archangel Gabriel who'd gone rogue?"

"I know how it sounds," Frank said.

Dale quickly interjected, hands up. "I didn't mean it to sound incredulous. I was looking for clarification, but perhaps I worded it poorly. But I got the gist?"

"That about sums it up, yeah." Frank got back under the covers, chuckled. "Yeah, you'll have the boys in white coats in here just as soon as you leave. How could anyone believe such a story?"

"It's fairly elaborate, Frank. Even if were to be the product of a fevered mind, or even one in a brief psychosis, it's still pretty impressive. Let me ask you something—if this was just an elaborate dream, what are the residual emotions you're left with?"

"What do you mean?"

"How do you feel about yourself after this whole—let's just call it an event. What's your take home message?"

With eyes locked on the psychiatrist, Frank said, "I feel like I had an epiphany about myself, that I was holding myself prisoner, unable to get out of my own way and improve myself. Stuck in a loop that threatened to take from me everything. And now I feel like I'm out."

Dale sat back and folded his arms. "That sounds like a corrective emotional experience to me. What difference does it make if it was real or not?"

Frank didn't answer.

Dale continued, "I'm a little jealous, Frank, I don't mind saying. I can have someone in my office for years, and they'll never get to that kind of realization."

"I'm afraid," Frank said, "that the knowledge will fade, and I'll fall back into shitty old patterns."

"Always a risk. For now, be grateful that you've taken away this understanding and work each day to incorporate it into how you respond to life. How about you take my card and follow up with me. I'll help you as much as I can to make sense of this and ensure this leads to the kind of change you want."

"Thank you, Doc."

Dale stood, placed the card on the side table, smiled reassuringly, and left the room.

CHAPTER 67

"I really don't think it's necessary to get worked up every time I want to get out of bed."

Nurse Fiona doted on Frank like the good nurse she was. He kept trying to swat her hands, and she parried his thrusts expertly.

"I won't have you fall and mess up my stats."

"All I want to do is take a piss in the toilet. Is that too much to ask?"

"Sounds like a worthy fucking goal to me!"

A booming voice from the doorway drew both their attention. A tall man in a dark flight suit, red cross over his chest came lumbering in.

"Holy shit, man, you can't imagine how great it is to see you up like this."

Frank couldn't help but smile. The guy had an infectious joviality. "I don't mean to be rude, brother, but who the hell are you?"

"I'm the man who fished you out of Lake Erie and you were"—he held his arms wide—"this big if you were an inch. Name's Dave Logan." He held out his hand.

Frank stood, ignored Fiona's crooked eye, and extended his arms. "I think I owe you more than a handshake."

"Aw shit, bring it in."

Logan grabbed Frank in a bear hug, gave him a little squeeze and lift.

"Okay, okay, big man, don't kill me now," Frank said. He sat back down on the bed and Logan pulled the seat up to it.

"You gotta understand," Logan said, "It's rare for me to see someone in follow up. I do some trauma life flight, but a lot of organ donation work so this is a rare treat. I mean, I thought you were trying to leave your earthly shackles, I don't mind saying."

"Life flight. That explains the get up."

"Yeah. Just got off of a shift, heard you was up, and decided I had to say hello and get your story."

Frank didn't answer; his focus was over Logan's left shoulder to the open doorway where his wife stood apprehensively, worry all over her face.

Logan turned, saw the woman, and stood. "Oh, I'm sorry, I don't mean to be taking all your time."

Laurie took a couple of tentative steps.

"Hi, Laurie. This is Dave—he's the man who saved my life."

She offered a warm smile to Logan.

"Well, Frank, if I may call you that, I think I will take my leave. But you gotta promise me you'll tell me all about yourself over a beer."

"A pitcher."

"Done." He shook Frank's hand warmly and left the room.

Fiona didn't say anything, but pretended she had other work and flitted out of the room herself. It got dreadfully quiet.

CHAPTER 68

She looked very pretty, her dirty blond hair longer, blow dried in that Farrah way he always liked.

"I'm sorry I didn't come right away. I wasn't sure what I'd find."

"You got nothing to apologize for. Are the kids here?"

"No. I thought I'd see you first."

She walked up to him and without making eye contact she spoke. "Frank, I need to know. Were you trying to kill yourself?"

He reached out to gently take one of her hands in his. "I understand why you'd think that, but no. I wasn't. And I can't tell you exactly how and why I ended up there, but I promise I will one day. Is that okay?"

She finally looked at him, and this led to her breaking down in tears. He slowly pulled her into a hug, caressed her head. Laurie buried her head in his chest and sobbed.

"We'd thought we lost you," she said after she'd calmed down. "The kids were a mess."

"I'm so sorry. All I can tell you is it was out of my hands."

"The doctors are saying you might have gone crazy and traveled in a trance."

"I know. I talked with a psychiatrist."

"You did?" Laurie asked. She'd futilely tried to get him to see a therapist many times.

"I did. And I'm going to see him again." Frank said. They sat silently for a beat.

Laurie disengaged and looked him over. "You're dreadfully thin. Are you going to be okay?"

"I will." He took both of her hands. "Listen, Laurie, there's something I need you to hear." He paused a moment. "I haven't been the man I wanted to be since I came home from overseas. I blamed you for how things went and didn't take any responsibility for my own short-comings."

"Frank, you came back from combat. I understood that. I just didn't like you shutting me out."

"And you're right. I was to blame."

Laurie smiled weakly and stepped back.

"I appreciate your apology, but I hope you're not looking for us to go back to how it was. Because I'm not."

Normally the look on her face would set Frank off. He remembered well the internal script that went off when she had that mixture of disappointment and disgust written on her face like it was now. But he didn't feel the shock waves of shame and anger that normally followed. Instead, he nodded his head. "You're right. I will tell you that my goal is to be a better man. I'm going to do things differently. Regardless of whether you and I stay together, I will be treating you better. That's not a promise, it's a declaration."

"Okay, Frank. I can live with that."

He sat on the bed and gestured to the chair.

"Fill me in on all the goings on I missed."

She unshouldered her bag, took off her coat, and got comfortable.

.

CHAPTER 69

Winter kept her grip on Northeast Ohio well into April finally allowing spring to erupt one morning in May—followed by summer the very next day. On a glorious eighty-degree day in July, Frank found himself back at Lincoln Park in Tremont—the scene of his abduction ten months prior.

Today was different though; it was a Saturday and the Taste of Tremont festival. Every few steps led to tantalizing aromas as restaurants, food trucks, and peddlers hawked their edible wares. People flooded the park and streets. Some police on bikes mingled with the crowd; they blended nicely in their summer uniforms. A chill went up Frank's spine despite the heat when he thought back to that day. He looked over at JP and drew comfort.

"Are you going to come back and live with us?" John Paul asked.

Frank put an arm on his son's shoulder, gave him a half hug. Though only thirteen, he was already getting tall and lanky.

"We're taking it slow. Be patient."

John Paul sighed. "Alright. But I'll be happy when you're back. How's the job, by the way?"

"It's good," Frank said.

"Mom says it's a miracle—" JP stopped short.

"What is?"

They stopped to look at elaborate pastries. JP raised his eyebrows.

"Let's get some real food into us first, then we can come back for the doughnuts and stuff."

"Alright."

"But you were saying something Mom said..."

JP shrugged. "I don't want to get her in trouble."

"What you say to me stays with me, okay?"

They continued past burritos and tacos.

"Let's get this."

"You sure, bud?"

"I am."

Frank took out his wallet, gave JP the money who proceeded to order. They took their tacos over to a two-person table and sat. In between mouthfuls JP spoke.

"Mom says this is the longest you've held a job since you left the Corps."

Frank smiled despite the mild indignation at his wife's jab—"The Corps"—there was hope for this boy. "Mom is right. But I'm doing well. I've even gotten a couple of promotions."

"Have you met Jeff Bezos yet?"

"Not yet. I imagine it will be some time before he visits every fulfillment center he has, but I'll keep a weather eye."

They finished their food and stood up.

"Can we go back to the pastries?"

"Sure, bud."

They cut through the park, Frank enjoying the time with his son. The park was packed with people and the going was slow. A stir grew to their left by the gazebos. Despite himself, Frank looked and saw high school age kids getting rowdy. It was a mixed group, ethnically speaking, but it looked like some white toughs surrounding and taunting a couple of Black kids.

Lots of yelling, but nothing physical yet.

"Hey, I know those kids. They're complete assholes."

"Which ones?"

"The white kids. That's Tommy Genelli—he's a couple years ahead of me and a real asshole." JP stood up straighter. "C'mon, let's go over there and help. I would love to teach him a lesson."

"They're just jawing at each other. No reason to get worked up."

Just then some pushing and shoving commenced.

"C'mon, let's go," JP said and made to get in the mix.

Frank held him back by his t-shirt.

"What the hell?" JP said. "You've always told me it's not the bad guy who's the issue, but all the good guys who stand around and do nothing."

"Hold on." Frank scanned the area and spotted the two bicycle cops dismounted from their bikes, eating soft serve and talking up some young co-eds. He jogged over there.

"Hey, officers, I'm sorry to bother you, but I think a fight's going to break out over there."

He pointed out the area and both officers chucked their cones in the garbage, got on their bikes, and slalomed between pedestrians to get to the scene.

Frank walked slowly back to JP and pulled him away. The cops quickly dispersed the crowd.

They stood in silence, JP pouting.

Frank grabbed both of his shoulders and looked him in the eye. "Listen to me. There's a second lesson to what I've told you and it's just as important—you gotta look out for all people, that's true. But first and foremost, you gotta look after your own. Nothing is more important to me than you and your sister. If something had happened to me mixing in with those guys, I would have left you alone. And I can't do that. So, I went and got the professionals responsible for maintaining the peace. That's who's tasked with keeping us safe, and they did their job. You understand?"

"I guess."

"Alright then. How about those doughnuts?"

"I'm still hungry for real food."

"Great." Frank clapped his son on the back. "Let's go explore. In the meantime, if you're interested in protecting others, think about a career in law enforcement."

"I was thinking about the Army, maybe."

"Oh, a wise guy, huh?" He put JP in a friendly headlock, and they walked back into the throng in search of the best street food Tremont had to offer.

THE END

Milton Keynes UK
Ingram Content Group UK Ltd.
UKHW020645300424
441966UK00013B/208/J